Dark
Mermaids

Dark Mermaids

Anne Lauppe-Dunbar

SEREN

Seren is the book imprint of
Poetry Wales Press Ltd.
57 Nolton Street, Bridgend, Wales, CF31 3AE
www.serenbooks.com
facebook.com/SerenBooks
twitter@SerenBooks

ISBN: 978-178172-262-6
ebook: 978-1-78172-269-5
Kindle: 978-1-78172-276-3

A CIP record for this title is available from the British Library.

The publisher acknowledges the financial assistance of the Welsh Books
Council.

Printed by Bell & Bain Ltd, Glasgow.

Disclaimer

While the feats of the GDR athletes at the Olympics in the 1970s and 1980s
are well documented – as is the taking of performance-enhancing drugs by
sports people from all nations – this novel is a work of fiction. All characters
are fictional and any resemblance purely coincidental. Some of the locations,
Berlin, for example, exist. However specifics within place are not adhered to.

To Stevie my teacher and friend without whom none of this would have been possible. To Ian who kept my feet steady and my heart strong; and my lovely two: Fiona and Jessica.

CHAPTER ONE

~

Berlin 1990

Pulling on her leather coat, Sophia strode along Bellevue-strasse, jumping on the U-Bahn crammed with fresh tourists ready for a weekend of the city's particular magic. A group of drinkers lurched from one compartment to another, waving bottles and cans and growling out old songs about never-ending forests and mountains. Folding her long legs under the icy metal seat, Sophia burrowed into the worn coat, tucked her hair under the collar and thought about sex, as the night sky hung fog-mantled over the city and station signs and distant winding streets blurred.

Leaving Potsdamer Platz, they crossed the border where the Wall had just recently stood. The group roared, toasting one another with mouthfuls of supermarket *Schnapps*. An old woman, in matching nettle-green coat and handbag, sank further into her corner. She opened the bag just a crack. A flash of white. A pink nose nudged, then stained teeth chewed at the leather rim. One of the men prodded his mate. Pointed. The pair closed in. The woman zipped her bag shut as the drinker's mate grinned and spat. His phlegm landed, a gelid mound, between Sophia and the door as, with a squeal of brakes, the U-Bahn juddered to a halt at Friedrichstrasse. The woman stepped onto the platform as the group yodelled a discordant chorus. Sophia followed, smiling as the woman whispered '*Idioten*' to the rabbit in the bag.

The pavements were so full she had to dodge into the street to avoid the swarm. Talking, shouting, touching and laughing. Eating *Bratwurst* with *Sauerkraut*, the city folk drank *Glühwein* from a forest of market stalls that had sprung up along Unter den Linden even though it was only November. Why couldn't they stay at home and watch the news? They wanted, she supposed, to talk about their neighbours' new freedom. To laugh and stare. The market traders responded by hiking up prices. It was all too easy to encourage the flood of visitors that poured in from East Germany to traipse across the old border, then spend what little money they had.

There they were: pointing at the former checkpoint. Staring at the newly created window displays, forming orderly queues at the entrance, until someone took pity and told them *to open the door and go in*. Every face was fixed in an expression of wonder, as if they'd stepped through the door into a Disney theme park full of brand new fridges and American jeans.

Tonight though, crowds were welcome. Moving between them, Sophia kept her eyes firmly on the pavement, although every now and then she checked the edge of the throng for green uniforms that could spell danger.

A large guy trailing a wailing child collided with her and apologised profusely, his *Entschuldigung* pronounced with a throaty hum. What was that accent? Uneasy, she sidestepped down the next alley, pausing to catch breath and pull her hair back, wrapping the blue-black scarf tightly round her face. Near Rosmarinstrasse, she stopped again – stretching her neck to the sky: the distant boom of music was unmistakable. Heat tingled in her belly and between her legs.

There was the entrance, but a bouncer was leaning against the doorpost watching. She frowned and looked away; there'd been no mention of bouncers in the magazine flyer. Disappointment made her sour and grey. This guy could be a problem: he would remember things like her face. Her fingers burned with such longing that, almost moving against her will, she turned and, head down, dug out the entry fee. Inside the door, she handed over her worn leather coat; grabbed the numbered ticket and squeezed past a couple straining up against the wall. Both were moaning, swapping saliva and skin. The tight fist inside her stomach uncurled, opened, making her sigh as she made her way into the inky-black hall, signalling for a beer to avoid yelling through the booming music.

A swarm of bodies vibrated on the dance floor. Some in perfect rhythm, others touching: hand on shoulder, mouth to ear, leaning close to shout a word or two, weaving one way, swirling the other. Watching them she felt her body swell to a beat strong enough to pulse through bone. What would they see if they looked? A thin unyielding face or the dark-haired beauty Hajo had said she was? Long-limbed, supple with muscled arms and swimmer's legs. On a good day her eyes were deep blue, like a wolf – flecked with grey.

She checked the edge of the crowd for dealers: one figure joining another, drifting to the fringe, by the doorway, just far enough from the bright lights. The briefest of touches accompanied a nod, a hand to mouth, casually slipping the discreet pill between lips as the buyer swallowed his choice of drug with water or beer. White powder? Finding a clean surface in here to chop and inhale would be impossible. She preferred to inject, but only if the needle came in its plastic sanitised packaging. A cocaine fix was like magic: a buzzing, talking, fizzy-tingle that had walls bulging, the wind whispering crazy secrets to a moon that swung heavy and metallic in the sky. No, tonight she'd buy the white dots that warmed her icy blood enough to dance and, more importantly, feel. She nodded as they glanced towards her. Swapped money for five powdery circular fragments. Bought a glass of cold vodka and placed one ecstasy pill on her tongue.

Now the delicious wait. The smoky room would soon feel hot, thick as a creamy orgasm. Music would blast through loosening bone, slack and easy under deliciously hot, wet skin.

Spotlights swung across the crowd, winking silver to green. She drank until the floor became a sticky pool of sliding limbs, the night at its shuddering darkest. Then she danced, weaving her mind to the sound, moving like silk on water. Now she could see everything and nothing. There were no more boxed-in limitations. No more what she could, and what she could not do, just one long pounding wave of silver-green dancers moving closer.

From the edge of the crowd a slim-hipped stranger separated. His shoulders were broad, hips pushed forward, confident yet enquiring. Her nipples tightened, aching as she watched his shadow thicken moment by moment. He had a cruel full mouth that smiled above a determined chin. Blue eyes, hooded yet bold. Someone she recognised – yet a total stranger. As they danced, Sophia glanced up. His face should be less than symmetrical, the right eye tilting, slanting towards his right ear. But this young man was chiselled and perfect. How would he taste? She licked the downy fur on the back of his neck, slicked with sweat: bit down gently. He gasped, held her wrists and slid close, melting, before thrusting up hard against her.

It was always so easy – this glide from loose to electric, nothing more than motion and sensation. They melted from the crowd, hailed a taxi. In his apartment she undressed as he watched, one hand moving in practised rhythm. 'Kneel on the bed,' he told her. Oh. She could feel him, right there. Skin on skin. Deeper. Working with an intense, furious focus. She moaned, drifted in the white-pill dream. Muscles strained. She was swimming. Water above and below. No. She was lying on the bed. Not in water. The stranger was hunched above her, his face twisted tight. Eyes shut. She moved up/down, closed her eyes, swimming through bleached light that rippled across pale blue tiles lining the bottom of the pool. Raised her eyes above the surface. Noise. Row after row of children paraded to clapping hands. Eyes stared. Voices whispered, 'Faster. Turn now, turn.' She shot under-and-through in a practised arch. Dive. Dark shapes leaned over the pool edge, floating, dead. Dead as Diertha. Oh. Swim, swim deeper.

The stranger moaned. Jerked. Swore. Too soon, too

soon. He came, tucking his damp face in the curve of her neck like a child. Silence. A distorted clicking. Was that the distant splash of swimmers? She couldn't breathe, couldn't see. The water was blood. Something wet bumped against her shoulder. What was that bobbing white shape: a child's limb?

★★★

Panic: Sophia sat up sick and dizzy. She'd bitten her lip. Gagging, she slipped from the bed and fumbled her way into a strange bathroom. In the dark she trickled water, but not so much as to make a noise. Cupped her hands and rinsed out her mouth. Her jaw, head and shoulders were so tense they burned. Still dizzy, she sneaked back into the bedroom, dreading the possibility that she might have woken him. Thankfully the stranger with the cruel mouth, that mouth, was deep asleep. Sophia fingered her way around the silent room. The curtains were newly washed. A crack of light sneaked between the fabric to rest on a desk and chair, and – halleluiah, most of her clothes were strewn across a second chair by the window.

She peered, then fumbled around at the bottom of the bed to find her knickers. He looked young, so young, too bloody young – talking about banks, his lifeblood circulating numbers and money. At her age she should know better.

Pulling on her coat, she glanced over to the bed with a ready excuse should he wake (people to see, things to do, *anything*). Crept to the door and carefully released the latch.

Outside in the empty, dimly lit corridor, she leaned against the wall, tasted blood and, deciding against the lift, shoved open the fire exit and limped down the stairs, counting three floors of grey cement lit by a dull, flickering light. At last: out in the open. She spat into the gutter and inhaled the familiar smell of car fumes accompanied by the scent of fresh rain.

A cab was turning the corner into the next street. She whistled. The driver slowed, checking in his mirror to see if she was fit for his newly cleaned cab. The number plate was unknown. Good. She wasn't in her police uniform, no need to worry. Her hands weren't shaking, no giveaway signs of drugs or drink. Sophia tied her hair back with her scarf, wiped her mouth, just to make sure, and strode towards the waiting cab.

Home: instinctively she paused and remembered: spies, People's Police, Stasi? She knew what they could do and listened before opening the main door. Nothing, only the low hum of traffic from across the other side of the park, mixing with the slow air of a Sunday morning. Climbing the stairs to the top floor, she unlocked the apartment; double locked it from inside. Her clothes were gluey with sweat, smoke and the sickly sweet smell of sex. She peeled them off, leaving the pile on the floor and shivered her way to the bathroom, placing the four extra pills she'd bought in a plastic bottle marked Sleeping Pills. Her father might check. He did, she knew he did. Petrus the doctor, always right, always looking out for her. Only last month he'd found out about her secret dancing. She'd called him from a phone box, trying to hide the bruises on her stomach and legs by showing him her face. He'd forced the truth out. Now when he asked if she'd seen sense, she refused to answer.

Peering into the mirror, Sophia opened her mouth wide to stare at a blistering row of tooth marks along its right side. Christ. The purple circles under her eyes made her look like a vampire. Okay, one bruise on her shoulder. Minimal damage, she decided. Though god, it hurt like hell to pee.

Standing in the shower, eyes closed, face turned to the stream of cleansing water, she calmed. Washed her hair, inhaled the comforting normality of eucalyptus shampoo. Lately her dreams had been filled with milky faces that melted before she could see what they wanted. Diertha was one of them. Stupid Diertha, her cousin, roommate and bully at training camp, never seemed to leave her thoughts. During sleep, the ghostly voice told her things she didn't want to hear. 'They invited me, not you, to the head office,' Diertha would boast in her most annoying whiney voice. 'Your trainer was there. You know the one, little Sophi? Red face. Small hands? They kept me there all night, until I was bleeding.' Sometimes, she loomed above weighed down with reasons to kill Sophia as she struggled to wake.

Enough. She'd placed that time in the 'forgotten drawer'. Best to throw away the flimsy dance clothes right now – or at least the moment she was dry, and not go ever again as the nightmares were always worse when she took drugs. That thought had come and gone many times. Now, as before, it vaporised in the steam.

In the kitchen she made strong coffee, adding cream and stirring in three spoons of sugar, lapping up the nectar as dawn broke over a November Berlin. The ghostly voice inside her head wanted her to remember, but her father had insisted she forget, so she'd do what she always did to calm herself. She'd paint. The feel of the brush, the sensation of stroking wet oil to canvas, brought with it the burn of childhood love. Not true mother-love, that had been fleeting, hardly remembered. This love was for Frau Schöller who had cared for Sophia as if she were her own child; showing her how mix colour, how to take joy from simple things like the sun rising, the smell of newly baked bread. When Sophia painted, it was as if, for a short time, she found her way back to that memory.

Dragging the easel to the window, she angled it to face outward; squeezed oils onto the palette. Layering blue on green, she made the sea. That daub of grey was a distant whale, the dash of orange and white: a clown fish darting to safety inside his own anemone-home. Time crept from early morning to a rain-soaked afternoon before she stopped, dipping brushes in white spirit. Her mouth was healing fast so she rinsed with mouthwash, heated the last of the vegetable soup and drank a cup of thick sweet hot chocolate, a leftover of childhood comforts. Finally, when she believed she might sleep, Sophia limped to bed, leaving the light shining in the sitting room. Wrapped tight, eyes closed; she prayed '*Please, oh please, just let me sleep.*'

***

When the alarm began its penetrating ring, Sophia whacked the 'off' button and lay dozing in the warmth of the cosy bed, listening to the rain tap against the bedroom window. Wonderful. She'd slept well; something that often happened *after*.

The side lamp threw an arc of gentle light across the

bed and white rug. Shoving her feet in a pair of ratty old slippers, she opened the top right drawer where contents were precisely organised: white bras, folded chastely next to white pants and brown socks. The left drawer was filled with *other* underwear: satin, basque with ruched lace, ribbons and ties, black suspenders – stuff that just wouldn't fold – her secret life in black and purple.

In the closet, yellow police-issue shirts hung next to brown trousers, keeping company with the solitary spare police jacket. It made no difference that she'd easily earned a place on the informally dressed investigation team, and was often asked for to help with cases the Berlin police found impossible to solve – particularly those that involved people or officers from the GDR. Now, just after the Wall, the west Berlin police were only beginning to realise just how far the Stasi had penetrated every aspect of the eastern police force.

Sophia chose to wear her uniform. If working under-cover, she wore black. So what if her colleagues thought her a pedant unable to throw away the vestiges of a GDR childhood.

Showered, she dragged a brush through her hair until every strand was pulled into a neat, tight, bun. A thin face gazed sternly from the mirror. Make-up? She rarely wore any, was resigned to be whatever she was, although often she wasn't at all sure what that might be. Two skins, she decided, pulling on the uniform daffodil shirt, tucking her portion of the childhood friendship bracelet into her top pocket: two skins that chafed, occasionally moving as one when she was running, frightened or having sex. The pile of clothes still lay on the floor. Disgusting. Pulling on plastic gloves, she dumped everything into a tightly sealed bag.

A shrill buzzing. The bloody doorbell. She leaned forward, peering through the spy hole. No one?

'There's a letter for you, Frau Künstler, handwritten,' Frau Weiner yoo-hooed up the stairs. Out on the landing Sophia lifted her hand in a half wave before retreating and slamming the door. Already three letters made up a pile that sat unread on the kitchen table. Her address – 14 Tiergartenstrasse – written in a slanted, messy hand, a hand she knew only too well. She gulped down coffee with the last of the cream, shrugged on her green jacket and hugged the fabric tight. The safety of a uniform: *one of many*, not recognisable, not alone. The beige trousers weren't flattering but they hid her well, as did her cap with the insignia of Police Investigation Squad perched on the front. As she did every morning, she touched the medals that hung by the door. They clinked, a hollow sound against the wall.

Lifting the bag of washing, she ran downstairs, unlocked the mailbox and pushed the latest envelope to the back: out of sight out of mind. In the basement, she dumped the bag on top of her washing machine; turned and unlocked the door through to the garage. Sometimes she ran to work, loving the feel of hard concrete under her feet. But today, already late: she'd take the car. A broken bike, along with a mattress and chair, sat in the furthest corner of the garage, stinking of urine: a clear invitation for homeless drunkards. Right, that was it. The note she stuck on the residents' board wouldn't be so damn polite this time. Keeping the windows shut she drove out onto the street, along Kantstrasse towards the Orangerie Pavilion, and finally, left into Charlottenburg police headquarters.

No room in the already over-full car park. She reversed, drove furiously down towards Mollwitzstrasse, squeezing into a narrow space opposite the bakery. *Salzbrötchen*? The thought of the butter and salt roll made her mouth water. What the hell. She jogged across to the bakery and bought two.

Monday briefing was well underway. There was another bulky envelope on her desk, her name written in capital letters across the front. Why couldn't Maria leave her be? She listened with half an ear as Hajo, in a clean shirt and rumpled trousers, began to update them about the current investigation while, under the desk like a schoolgirl, she broke her salted roll into chunks. Hajo needed a haircut: thick dark curls nestled along the bottom of a strong neck. How delicious would it be to run her fingers through those curls? She lifted another section of roll to her mouth. Better not be too obvious about chewing.

They'd found a body in a lake at the park right across the road from her apartment. A girl? A woman? No one seemed sure. How difficult could it be?

'Sophia?' Hajo was glaring.

'What?' A bit of bread lodged itself in her throat.

'Take Ernst and get down there.' Her colleagues sniggered as she coughed.

Ernst was an arsehole. True to form he grinned and lifted his middle finger, wiggling it while Sophia caught Hajo's eye and smiled, showing her teeth. My god, he was grinning back, his green eyes seeing far too much. Lovely eyes: so strong, sure and steady. Her neck grew warm and she looked away. He straightened, broad shoulders stretching, leg muscle tightening under faded blue trousers, and dumped a fresh murder book in front of her, then leaned over. 'Keep your notes legible this time.' He was there, so close. *Ah.* Heat on her neck; he was breathing warm air on the spot between her ear and shoulder. Ernst made a rude comment, his mates dutifully giggled. 'Well?' Hajo straightened. 'What are you waiting for?'

Trying not to think: his mouth, her neck, Sophia drove back to her apartment where she could park for free as Ernst jabbered on about how work colleagues were only good for a shag and if Hajo wasn't available he'd be up for it. There must be one hundred ways to kill the little twerp: using him as a speed bump, reversing to make quite sure; leaving him in a very tight dark place; launching him into the path of a speeding car, or maybe just shooting him?

A small crowd had gathered on the footbridge that led to the moss-covered *Luiseninsel* island monument. The ambulance crew were moving the body to the water's edge; they looked relieved as Ernst began edging the crowd back. 'Ladies and gentlemen,' he shouted, 'your morning's entertainment is now over.' One spectator muttered about their walk being spoiled as Sophia slid down a muddy embankment.

'You shouldn't have moved her,' she said.

'Oh, you'd rather we simply assumed she was dead?' The paramedic had a smudge of black pondweed on the tip of an angular nose. Under a bright red and yellow striped hat quiet brown eyes assessed her.

'I need to know where she died.'

'Over there.' He pointed two foot into the shallow icy water. 'Stabbed in the stomach and neck.'

Sophia edged closer, then knelt as a pair of mud-stained ambulance staff began clearing a safe way for the stretcher to transport the body to the morgue. Icy black liquid seeped through her trousers making her knees feel as if they were bleeding. The body lay half submerged in mud. A muscled form twisted to spidered angles. Ratty hair floated in filthy water. The victim's face was half submerged. Sophia leaned closer. Freckles. A snub nose. A livid bruise under her left eye. No.

'Turn her onto her back. Careful I said, careful.'

Käthe? The water blurred. Pain in her chest. Breathe. Don't faint. No. Käthe wasn't here. She was in the other place; that long-ago home. Safe. Married. Happy. Content. All the things Sophia was not. This was someone else curled up like a bruised fist, the wretched shape horribly grey and wrinkled. What to do? Pretend this wasn't happening? Oh god. She touched her friend's hand. Ice cold. Her body was stiff, rigor mortis setting in, but the face was as familiar as if she'd seen her yesterday, not thirteen years ago.

***

Late. They were late! Out of the door, down the path, satchels swinging behind them. Sophi first. She was always first because she knew how to run. Oops. Damn. There it was, beetling between two houses. Run. Run faster.

'The bus!' Käthe's gasp was way too close. Sophi sped up, veered round the corner. Slid. Her left shoe! The shoe sailed through the air and landed smack bang in a deep puddle. Käthe barrelled into her back. It hurt. Sophi lurched forward. Her sock. Her foot. Käthe grabbed.

Pulled hard just as she began to fall.

'Help.' There'd be hell to pay. New blue shoes for a new year at school. Mama telling her how lucky she was. Papa telling her she was to keep them clean. Käthe was laughing. She had her hand over her mouth to hide it. Sophi wanted to thump her. Right on her perfect little nose. Make it bleed. But her own laughter came bubbling up, sneaking out her mouth as Käthe dashed to the nearest garden fence, broke a branch from a leafless shrub and poked at the puddle.

'Come to me, little fish,' she chanted, trying to hook the shoe which filled with brown water. 'Sophi, hold my bag.' Käthe leaned forward, a question mark shape with wild hair and freckles that dotted across a flat peevish face with raisin eyes. Her soft blue hat wobbled. Oh please don't let it fall. Käthe's shoes were old, so old you couldn't tell what colour they'd been. She didn't care about them, but she loved her new hat.

The bus had stopped at the end of the road. There was Maria! Her heart-shaped face and huge blue eyes that made boys write her stupid notes, pressed up to the window. Well, she could keep those dopy eyes, but one day Sophi would have hair just like Maria who was waving like a mad thing as the mothers marched the Kindergarten children to their seats, checked the list with the driver, then stood in a group on the pavement to wave.

'Put it on.' Käthe waved the shoe in her face. It was wet and cold. She strapped it tight and ran after Käthe whose arms wind-milled as she legged it towards the bus. Maria's face vanished, then she burst out of the sliding doors, grinning.

'Come on,' she yelled as the bus driver furiously beeped the horn. 'He can't drive because I'm keeping the doors open.'

'You three are nothing but trouble.' The bus driver closed the doors so fast Sophi's bum nearly stuck. They collapsed onto a bench seat screeching as the bus hiccupped and joined the slow traffic on the main road.

★★★

'Wake up.' Sophia tried to haul Käthe from the freezing mud. 'Dearest. Wake up.' The body slid from her fingers.

'You really shouldn't.' The paramedic had his hand on her arm. Käthe's nose was broken. Her dead eyes staring. Sophia leaned in and wrapped her arms around her friend's shoulders. She had to tell her how much she'd missed her. Ask her why she was here.

'You do realise she's dead?' The paramedic sounded worried. Perhaps he thought he'd have to carry them both up the bank? The thought made her gasp out a laugh.

'Let me do my job.' Sophia stroked matted hair back from that poor battered face, and closed her friend's eyes. Oh god. What to do? Had Käthe been trying to find her, even though she wasn't to be found? Father had said it was best to start again. Right from scratch. But what if Käthe had needed help? She should have been there, that's what friends did. Sophia brushed away tears, leaned forward, kissed her friend's bruised face and folded her hand over the sodden scrap of paper and small photo from Käthe's jacket pocket.

CHAPTER TWO

~

Mia wriggled on the metal seat and thought about chilblains, piles and her dead mother. It was way too early to be awake, and the shabby grey platform of the train station was freezing. When she was little, she'd imagined mother as a smiley face, not the hulking giant called Diertha, she'd been shown scowling into the camera. Every day Mia checked her thin stern face in the mirror, with its bug eyes and messy brown hair, and looked to see if her arms, like her mother's, were thickening to massive tree trunks. Stuff like that happened when you turned fourteen.

Everything in the West was supposed to be shiny, clean and new – stations and waiting rooms kept warm and made to look friendly. Well, this place was the same as home: full of dark shadows that seemed to float at the outer edges of your sight. You thought you were imagining them, but they were there. Mia had chosen a seat near the ticket office and pretended to fall asleep; but really, she was watching. Oma said she had the most amazing eyes, eyes like a princess, but she didn't feel like a princess now, just fed up and hungry. The train was supposed to have arrived ages ago. There was a narrow kiosk selling hot drinks and rolls, but she was too frightened to go and buy anything. Someone might decide to be nosy and ask why she wasn't in school; they'd find out where she lived and tell the police that she'd escaped. The Stasi would go to Oma's house and arrest her. Torture her. Put her in one of those awful cells everyone knew about: ice-cold rooms where you stood in water, windowless chambers where lights blinded you – lights that were never turned off. Perhaps they'd even go to Mia's school? Oma was all she had. OK, not her real grandmother. Grandmother Ulrike had died years ago. So had Horst, a grandfather she'd never even met. No one ever talked about Mia's father. It was like he didn't exist, though of course he did. You had to have a man and a lady to do sex; else she'd never have been born. It wasn't a nice thought: a huge mother naked with a father person.

She glared at the carefully dressed woman on the next bench whose hair was pulled back into a tight knot, on her neck an angry red birthmark spread out like a mushroom. Had she moved nearer? Mia glared harder. The woman edged back. Good. She wasn't going to cry, not here, not ever again, though it was hard to stay calm. Oma had told her what to do once she got to Berlin.

With a deep breath, Mia picked up her backpack and stomped over to the kiosk window. 'A coffee and roll please.' Typical. The girl serving behind the counter didn't even look up. She just waited while Mia sorted out the right money, before handing her a paper cup and roll. Mia warmed her hands against the hot liquid. She'd chosen a shiny roll topped with sugar-crystals. The crystals tasted sour. Yuck, salty. Good job the rest of it was buttery. She'd had to get off at Grünewald Station. The ticket collector said the train didn't go via Tiergarten Station, but headed off to Tegal Airport: no point going there.

Across the street, the name of the square made her smile: Schmetterlingsplatz – a funny name. Oops. She pulled her mouth down and chewed. People didn't smile when they were on their own. The coffee had finally cooled enough to drink, but she ached to be home so much it hurt like a bruise. She'd made up her mind weeks ago. Someone had to do something: and there was no one else but her. That morning Oma had stuffed money into her pocket, money they didn't have. Mia had edged her grandmother away, just about to say she didn't want the notes, when she realised Oma was shaking. Just like that she'd grown up. Terrified, clear-headed, she'd smiled brightly like nothing was wrong, like it wasn't a stupid time in the morning, and taken time to lift her bag, so that when they said goodbye Oma would be strong again. Able to wave with an impatient hand as if to say go on, hurry up; I've got loads to do. Mia blinked and drank the last of the lukewarm coffee. She had two addresses in West Berlin. She was to go the woman's address. If no one was there (she had to be absolutely certain), go to the other. Both people would help, Oma was sure, but she'd refused to say why the woman's address was better, or why she hadn't said anything about these two people ages ago, when things weren't so bad. It was so unfair. Mia slouched over to the nearest bin, threw her cup away and walked to the timetable display, running a finger along all the trains scheduled for Breden. Her watch said it was just after eleven. There was one due in ten minutes; she could go home, look after Oma and write to them instead.

★★★

Käthe's muscled, twisted shape had imprinted itself in Sophia's mind. Aged twelve, she'd been as skinny as an exclamation mark. Building such bulk on a frame like that would have been almost impossible. So she must have taken steroids. What to do? Someone should be caring for her. This was her old friend, not a stranger. Sophia had written to her once, so long ago, including a small photo of her in a uniform as a kind of joke. Käthe knew only The People's Police and Stasi. West Berlin Officers were nothing like them. She'd posted it as far away from home as she could get. Then waited, heart in mouth, for the Stasi's pre-dawn knock: her father's fury when he knew what she'd done. Now, as if to remind her of her past, Maria's bulky envelope emerged from under the pile of still-to-be-processed mail. Would it say something about Käthe? In her mind their faces stared. Käthe, sharp-eyed and coltish. Maria soft as lavender, yet stubborn as a mule when it suited. Oh, what was she to do? Käthe's parents would be wondering. Maria would be waiting for a call, and all Hajo could do was to stare at the lack of information on the murder board. There was no knife. No name. No address. No papers. No prints on file. If this continued for the next two days, the investigation would be put on hold. Father would approve. He'd say how things were better left unsaid; their lives safe as long as they kept the past and present separate. But now?

'She's from East Germany.' Sophia bent the envelope in half and shoved it in her coat pocket. She'd read what

Maria had to say first, then decide what to do.

'Oh?' Hajo turned.

'Her clothes, Hajo. Fake Levi jeans, and the jacket's from Intershop.' They'd believe her. She'd proved herself highly competent, if dogmatic.

'And you're sure you don't recognise her.'

Through the window and across the car park was the station gym. A lone figure struggled on the treadmill, his steps slow and heavy: the effort too much to bear. The scrap of paper in her pocket was her business. If she told, *they* would arrive just as father said. No one was safe. Everyone talked about a unified Germany, but there was no such thing.

'Sophia, can I have a word?'

Ernst coughed. The two officers from her team found their desks fascinating as she followed Hajo into his office. 'What's wrong?' He shut the door. All she had to do was ask for help. Explain how all her past was supposed to have disappeared, never to return. Käthe and Maria left behind. She could lean into him; let him try and understand. 'Sophia. You would say, wouldn't you?'

'Yes.' *No.* But how could he understand? She'd lived in fear of a thing so huge; you never knew where it began or ended.

'There's no reason to be frightened,' he said, and she wanted to cry because there was, and he would never, ever, comprehend.

★★★

People began to arrive, jostling for the best spot on the platform. Mia edged back and stood, bag ready, wondering what to do as, three minutes later, the Berlin Central train arrived. She had to get on, or consider herself a scaredy cat. She found a seat as far away from the nosy mushroom woman as possible and stared out the window. Massive cranes teetered over dangerous black holes. Men in white hats swarmed up metal frames. They looked like beetles building loads of new homes. Oh – there was a bit of the Wall again. It had been part of her life since forever and now, finally, the horrid thing had come down – she'd seen the party on TV. Oma said it had been a symbolic Wall, but that didn't make sense. What could be symbolic about a Wall? It was best not to listen when Oma started going on about communism and what East Germany was supposed to have been like. All Mia knew was that she hated the fear that sneaked up on everyone. No one talked, because everyone was terrified that something might get back to them. The dark shadows: Stasi, People's Police, *Inoffizielle Mitarbeiter.* The bus driver or your best friend might be informers. They'd report you for watching the wrong TV channel, phoning someone who lived in West Germany – even if that person was a relative. Anything reported was investigated until it became true. According to Oma people still watched. Her teachers, the shop assistants, their friends and neighbours, monitored their movements in case she and Oma did anything *unusual*, in case they packed up and left. Well, she just had. She'd walked to the local station and got on a train just like that, and look – Ta-da. Nothing had happened.

Only a few weeks ago Oma had made a real fuss about her friend's daughter crossing the old border, saying how foolish she was. OK, so Mia had listened to one part of her grandmother's warning and hadn't told her best friend. Now she wished she had because Gerda would definitely have come with her. Right then. Four stops before the place called Tiergarten. So far she'd counted one. Nosy woman had left the train at Zoologischer Garten, and now the carriage was full of people who looked different: the posh kind with sharp haircuts, perfectly ironed clothes and expensive leather bags. They didn't stare, but checked their own reflections in the window. One old lady made a fuss about her make-up, using a miniature silver hand-mirror. At Tiergarten, Mia dragged her worn bag across her shoulders and trudged out of the station looking for directions to the park.

★★★

Something had to be done. Sophia drove to Tiergarten Park. Someone must have seen something. In a homeless shelter an elderly drunk, bulbous nose poking from under what must once have been a button-up child's pink bonnet, admitted he'd seen a girl walking across the park that afternoon. A man in a long expensive woollen coat had spoken to her. The drunk only knew because he'd had a coat like that once – a likely story. Nevertheless, Sophia wrote everything down and pressed for details. The man had worn leather gloves and a soft, old-fashioned bowler. The young lady had seemed glad to see him. She'd smiled as they walked past the squat. 'Not that they noticed me. Not even a glance,' he whined.

Back home, Sophia dug out the scrap of paper and photo found in Käthe's pocket. The photo was as daft as the one she'd sent to her friend. Käthe crouched inside her ring, about to circle and hurl the disc. She'd squeezed her bulk into Lycra shorts and a tiny t-shirt with the GDR logo stretched impossibly wide across her massive chest. The note? Well, that had already been read a hundred times: her address written in Käthe's messy scrawl. Was it time to change jobs? Disappear? No. Please no.

'Just keep to the straight and narrow,' she muttered, opening the car door, peering at the imaginary chasm that would open if she didn't obey the rule of silence. Rules were good; they kept her safe and moving forward, but still … didn't she have to find out what had happened to her old friend?

The pile of useless furniture lay undisturbed in the corner of the garage. Sophia hunted round in the car for a scrap of paper. Maria's envelope! She tore a square from the back and wrote 'The rubbish in the garage must be moved IMMEDIATELY,' signing it with capitals. The twinge of intense pleasure was streaked with regret because maybe, sometimes, she wanted to be liked.

She stuck the note on the communal board inside the hallway and glanced up. Perfect – today was the tenants' quarterly meeting. The note would be dutifully read. Would someone mention her name? No. They'd drink coffee and eat Frau Weiner's biscuits whilst being efficiently propelled to discuss the mystery of the vanishing washing powder. Why, only last week Sophia had bought two boxes and placed one on Frau Weiner's washing machine.

In the washroom she stripped to bra and knickers, dumping her work clothes in the machine – before pulling on running trousers and top. Laced her shoes, unhooked the thinnest fleece and exited out of the side door.

***

Everyone was hurrying, no one just walked. Mia tried to work out exactly where she was standing, because if she knew where she was she'd know where to go. The street was crammed with cars trying to squeeze into every available space – it wasn't safe. Any moment now they'd miss a turn, forget to slam on their brakes and crash. Her hands were clammy. Breathing too fast she walked a few steps one way, turned, walked back, coming full circle. She was going to faint, scream, burst. Hang on, there it was. The golden angel statue, just to her left, not straight ahead as she'd been told it would be. Legs wobbling, wanting very badly to pee, she waited for the lights, hitched the bag securely over both shoulders and walked towards the statue.

The park was silent. Dead leaves lay slimy and rotten on the grass. The lakes were dirty black. On the surface of the nearest, spirals of green algae belched and popped. This was more like home: always quiet, everything just rotting away. Hang on, that was wrong. It had to be different here. There was all the building work she'd seen from the train, and, just to prove the point, over to her right a new red and yellow playground stood out from the dripping, fog-laden trees. There was a tiny child in a bright blue coat in the sandpit, digging with a spoon-sized yellow shovel. The child's mother was trying to convince the little girl that putting her hands in her mouth and eating sand, was going to give her tummy ache; far better to come home and have a hot chocolate and a biscuit?

Mia looked away. She wasn't lonely, she just didn't like being on her own. If Gerda were here they would have laughed, run over to the swings to dare each other: go higher, *higher* – until she'd go so high her heart would pretty much stop, because she'd imagine the swing going right over the bar. They'd forget all about finding people. Gerda would say: 'So what. Who cares?' and carry on swinging.

The people she was meant to find might have moved! Mia walked faster. It was all very well to worry, nothing she could do about it now. She was beginning to sound like Oma. Mia muttered the well-known words: 'That's just the way it is.' Dumb words that made no sense, particularly when sense was needed.

There was the golden statue. But it wasn't called 'Golden' or 'Angel' or even 'Statue'. Bloody hell, she'd got the wrong one. There were probably hundreds of statues that looked exactly the same, all over the city, in every nasty damp park. Plus whoever had built this one had been really thick because from where she was standing she couldn't even see the top. The plaque said 'The Victory Column'. What victory? She didn't know about any stupid victory.

Wait. Her instructions said: golden statue in the centre of Tiergarten Park, cross the park to Tiergartenstrasse. Right. OK. That was way over there, on the other side. Mia ran, weaving her way past trees, over the slippery mossy ground towards the street. She stopped, breathing hard, the straps on the bag were pulling and now she *really* needed to pee – but everything was okay because the sign on the corner read Tiergartenstrasse. She'd definitely find the house now. Mia walked all the way down the street on one side. She'd ring, or knock, and the door would open and everything would be just like she'd imagined it.

★★★

Crossing the road to the park, Sophia took the time to breathe and notice the late afternoon light. Dark and soft, she thought, stretching her arms up and looking at the sky. At such moments it seemed that everything was possible. Something new and wonderful could magically happen – like stepping into a new skin, escaping to a world where no one knew you and you could, really, truly, become someone else. She laughed: that chance had come and gone. Breath rasping in the cold air, Sophia eased into a slow run. Time to dream about Hajo biting her neck, undressing her while his eyes darkened, Hajo naked above her, the weight of him making her gasp, yet feel utterly secure.

All that heat would vanish when she told him she'd lied.

She was breathing too fast. Stop. A panic attack would bring helplessness, then fury at her own weakness. Focus on the one thing that calmed her – painting, blue on white, the coal-black depth of a winter sea, the possibility of mermaids that were strong and fearless, able to swim and never tire. The strangeness of time – why it dragged when she was on surveillance, or how it rushed out of the back door when she painted.

The evening light was dense and cloudy, thick enough to hide the golden angel perched on the Victory Column. Each time Sophia ran past she thought the statue, like

Diertha, was frozen in time, easy prey to the boom of aeroplanes and bird crap. Her cousin hadn't deserved her watery grave any more than Käthe. Was there a connection? No, absolutely not, but the voice in her mind said there was.

Bloody Diertha drowning herself when she realised she'd never make it as an Olympic star. Too fat and clumsy. Sophia lengthened her stride, relaxing into a comfortable rhythm through the park. A new shopping trolley blocked the entrance to the old bomb shelter. The stench of urine and beer leaked through the air. Thank god it wasn't her turn for this month's clean up. The residents griped, wept and (more often than not) crapped themselves before they were forced to leave. They might as well be dead. She could see no purpose to lurking, half-seen at street corners, outside off-licences, wanting drink, wanting drugs, wanting money.

No papers had been found near poor Käthe's body, and everyone in the GDR had papers.

And what about them: five unopened letters. More were likely to arrive: Maria had always been a horribly stubborn friend. How odd to forget someone so completely, only to remember, years later, their most annoying habits.

Doubly annoying because it was Sophia's past and she had every right to forget.

***

Mia couldn't find Number Fourteen. It was supposed to be right here. Number Sixteen stood next to an apartment block with Six, Eight and Ten printed on metal signs. She walked up the path and put her finger next to the buzzer of Number Eight. She could ask. She could say she was lost. Though maybe they'd get cross, think she was lying or something. Her hand edged away. On the corner between Klingerhoferstrasse and Tiergarten stood a gaping old warehouse; there were lights in the second-floor windows but it was a warehouse not a house. It was going to get dark soon. Tears started sliding down her face. She'd have to go home. Right now, before it got too dark to be safe. She turned, about to make her way back to the park, when the owner of Number Eight opened his window and glared at her across the front garden.

'What? Are you blind?' he said, as Mia mumbled on about being lost. 'Just open your eyes! It's on the corner. There.' He pointed to the warehouse. 'Clear as day: numbers eleven to fourteen.' He slammed the window shut. Beastly man. Oma was right, people were nosy, and rude, and they *did* watch though their curtains.

The warehouse on the corner had no door, just a garage grid. Mia walked round the side and saw a muddy pathway winding its way to the back of the building. She followed the path to a door where a line of names and numbers read like a magic spell: Eleven to Fourteen.

'Found you,' she whispered and pressed the buzzer. Nothing. The wintry light faded and the rain came. Mia sniffed. Now or never. She scuttled round the side to where some black bins had been lined up ready for col-lection. Tiptoed behind them and squatted: she wouldn't get pee on her best trousers, no one would come.

Pulling them up, doing up the zip on her coat, she slipped out from behind the bins just before she heard whistling that grew louder as a young man appeared round the corner. He didn't even look at her: just plonked his finger on Number Eleven, leaned near to the door and waited. He was wearing the exact same headphones she so wanted. A tinny whisper escaped as he moved his head to the beat. The door opened. A high-pitched voice called out: 'Hello?' from inside the building. There was a pause before the woman with the high voice said: 'Oh no you don't! I've already told you we don't want any free magazines, take them somewhere else and don't you leave them outside to mess up the pathway like you did last week.'

Mia ducked under the young man's arm and dodged into the hallway. There was a glimpse of a door opening on the left; the complaining voice repeated the same message as she jogged up the stairs. The young man replied that he had to eat and, just like everyone else, had to work delivering magazines whether people wanted them or not.

Apartment Fourteen was right at the top. Mia knocked, waited, then called, 'Frau Künstler!' When that didn't work, 'Cousin Sophia!' even though the name felt strange to say out loud. She placed her ear right to the door and listened. No one home. The voices downstairs continued to rise. She froze, waiting for the dreaded shout to come from below, the clatter of irritated feet coming up the stairs to throw her out. Doors opened, closed. Silence. Mia pulled a jumper out the bag, took off her coat and dragged the jumper over her head. Ten to five. She'd eat the last chocolate from home really slowly. Someone would come soon, and if they didn't she would knock on the door of Number Eleven. If, and only if, no one arrived.

★★★

The moment Sophia got home she'd phone Hajo. His trust was hard won; therefore infinitely rare and precious. The imagined feel of his lips would be nothing like those other men whose only pleasure was their own. He'd watch her, gently, patiently undressing her. Oh how she wished he didn't know where she'd been born, or see right through her. He probably knew she was lying. Only last week he'd asked her what the word '*Sobtrieks*' meant.

'No idea,' she'd said. It wasn't lying. He'd got the name wrong. *Sobotniks* had been the name of 'Communist Saturday' committees formed by housing associations.

'Are you sure?' He'd lifted his eyebrows, waited.

In the GDR, most committees included Stasi members or informers who swapped information for favours. Her father had joined their local group so that they could get the house re-painted.

Hajo had known she was lying then, so he'd know she was lying now.

Already on Klingerhoferstrasse, she had just enough time to decide what to have for supper: meat and cheese, along with a very large glass of wine. The cellar hummed with busy machines making the air warm and sticky. She fumbled with the set of keys from behind her machine and opened Frau Weiner's little washroom, took a cup from the nearly full powder box and swiftly locked up, set her machine to wash, collected her mail and climbed the stairs to her apartment.

Something lumpy and awkward lay on the floor next to her door. No one delivered anything upstairs unless you paid. A flash of fear: had her father come to leave her something and fallen? But he never visited without phoning first. Plus he was in perfect health.

Keeping the shape in sight, she rounded the last set of stairs to see the curved outline of a slight body curled up fast asleep beside a bag. Stepping over the lumpen shape, she reached for the bag – the shape moved. Sophia jammed her knee into the intruder's side, shoving her against the floor. Her mind registered *child* as the figure gasped and tried to wriggle free.

'No you don't.' She eased back a little, allowing the girl – she was definitely a girl (pink and purple fluffy jumper) – to sit up. Young, no more than thirteen at a guess. Brown hair, deep blue-grey eyes. A pale face: mouth opening like a baby bird.

'I wouldn't scream if I were you.' Sophia yanked the girl's arms up behind her as she searched the bag one-handed. There'd be a knife or drugs – something sharp and dangerous.

'OW. Give it back.' The girl tried to stand, making a wild grab. 'You're hurting.'

'How did you get in?'

If she questioned the girl there would be another report to write; she backed away, tossing the bag down the stairs.

'Get out before I change my mind and arrest you.'

The girl jumped, ran down the few steps, picked up her bag and reached slowly inside. Sophia's fingers tingled. She'd got it wrong, could easily have missed a well-hidden deadly sharp blade. Move towards the door. Keys out. Get in fast. Lock up. Call her colleagues. The child pulled out a tattered note. She held it out with a shaking hand.

'Please – I was waiting. I didn't know what else to do.'
Oh no, she'd started to cry.
'It's a note from your mother.'

CHAPTER THREE

~

This wasn't how it was supposed to be. Mia tried to stop crying, but her arms really hurt from being pulled. She should've gone to the other house; no one could be as awful as Frau Künstler, whose face turned a nasty beetroot as whoever she was phoning wasn't there. Mia was told to sit and wait – like a *dog* – while the woman went into the bathroom, coming out wearing a clean t-shirt. Mia didn't dare say anything rude like: 'You're too horrid to be my cousin.' She so wanted to, but Frau Künstler would have thrown her out – no doubt about it. Nasty people did things like that. It was dark outside and she wasn't allowed out after dark. Plus, even though she was hurt and tired and scared, she had to be here because Oma needed help.

She'd been given a drink, not hot chocolate but some kind of gross green tea.

'Go and clean yourself up.' The woman pointed to the bathroom. Mia went in, locked the door, poured the gunky tea down the sink and sat on the loo seat to cry. Crying made her stomach sore. Perhaps she could smash the cup? Smash everything? Wait. Oma always said there would be consequences. Mia took extra long. Washed and dried her face, neck and hands. Opened the cupboard, took out a bottle of pills, then another, and emptied the contents down the loo. Good, she wasn't crying anymore. She filled an empty bottle with the contents from another marked stomach settlers. That was better. Each time the pills were swapped she felt stronger and less afraid.

'Serves you right,' she muttered and squeezed the contents of a brand new tube of face lotion in the sink and ran water so the sticky paste glugged down the plughole. Finally there was only one half-filled bottle of sleeping pills left. They didn't look like the ones Oma took. Tiny, bleached, they lay on her cupped palm. Weird, there was an outline of a rabbit engraved on one side. Better to leave those in the right bottle. She didn't want to kill the cousin.

On the narrow windowsill sat a threadbare cream and blue friendship bracelet. It was damp, as if Frau Nasty had only just placed it there. Daisies had been sewn on at regular intervals, one was coming apart, the white thread straggling, turning brown. Still, it was pretty, and not what she expected of such an awful person. Frau Künstler looked just as Mia imagined: tall with dark hair and deep bluey/grey eyes. Muscly – but not like mother Diertha. A normal kind, like an athlete. Mia worried that, no matter what she did, she would grow into her mother: her genes expanding like a balloon. She'd stopped eating once, but Oma had found out and been so angry Mia had stuffed herself to say sorry. Then Oma got sick and no one noticed what Mia ate.

Nearby was a basket full of seriously cool hair scrunchies: furry caterpillar black, gold, red, purple and nearly twenty different blues – Mia's favourite colour. The forget-me-not one was best. She closed the cabinet door, and peered in the mirror. Her old hairgrip was rusty and bent. Only two of the five glass stones remained stuck to the metal. Pulling her hair back so it stretched skin, she wrapped the scrunchie tightly round. Wow. Much older and loads thinner, except her huge eyes stared back, red-rimmed, like a rat. Mia shoved the scrunchie in her pocket. It wasn't stealing. Sophia could have it back. No. That Woman could have it back, as soon as she said just one nice thing to her, just one.

Oma had promised Mia that both Nasty Woman and the other person, the grandfather would help, not to worry, not to even *think* they wouldn't. Grandfather couldn't be as horrid, he'd be nice. He'd make up for his mean daughter. She stuck her tongue out at her cloudy reflection: best not to feel frightened because she couldn't stay in here forever. Mia rinsed the sink and quietly slipped through the door, walking over to the window to peer out at the dark view over the city. Ugh, looking down made her feel queasy.

There was a walk-in kitchen opposite a settee and armchair that faced a really big TV. On the left a narrow hallway led to the bathroom and probably the cousin's bedroom. Her stomach still ached. Nasty's fault: she shouldn't have twisted her arm and pulled. If it hadn't been dark outside, she'd definitely have left and found a public phone box. Was there one nearby? Mia couldn't recall, but she had seen Sophia's number before she made her sit like a dog. She could get Oma to ring. Oma would say something really snipey and sharp. She did both really well, though much less now that she was so ill.

Edging nearer the window, Mia dared to look down.

The city was so busy. There were blurry bits of light that looked like bikes, or toy cars, going places – even though it was night-time. It made her feel unimportant and dizzy, a pinprick high above the roads and trains that could take her home. There was the park and look, there was the golden statue. One of its lights was broken. The angel was looking at her. Half in shadow, half out, *staring* – like it wanted to get her. Mia recoiled, bumped into the corner of a broad frame which wobbled: *oh please don't fall*. She clutched the corner and held on peering sideways. Nasty would come tearing in, any minute, eyes snapping, about to slice her into little pieces.

The painting was mostly just colours. They'd looked at stuff like that in class. Abstract art. Well, even she could paint better than this mess. Mia looked closer at the flashes of green in amongst the blue waves. Those could be fishes… Oh, maybe that blue blob was a mermaid, *there*, just behind the ocean's rock cave. Sophia was on the phone again. This time in her room, so she must have two phones. She was speaking quietly, as though she'd given up. Or even better: she was being *told off*. Mia poked the hidden blobby mermaid. Maybe she'd leave oily prints – and Sophia would notice, and be reminded, forever, how horrid she was.

★★★

The girl was prowling, and she'd bloody well told her to sit and wait. Petrus – seldom Father, never Dad – listened to her questions: who was this girl? Why hadn't he told her there was a child?

'Breathe,' she muttered as he waited her out: stay calm,

visualise Petrus, sleet-grey eyes, chiselled jaw, ridiculously long eyelashes, coat and all, disappearing into particles of dust, preferably inside a dustbin. Was this girl the reason Dagmar had stayed? No. Mia couldn't have been more important than her, could she? Sophia had burned to tell Petrus how hard she tried to do exactly as asked so as to get some small token of love in return. How she'd learned to accept the little offered, but longed for more. How everything started and ended with his refusal to speak the truth.

Silence; the silence he used best for keeping secrets.

Petrus knew about the child – she could hear it hiss down the telephone line like a whispered confession. Not the confession longed for: the moment he'd break his control and tell her he loved her.

'Mia?' Petrus spoke in an unusually gentle voice. 'Mia is here?'

There it was. One hundred per cent proof that he knew. Perhaps he'd even been expecting the girl. Sophia remembered his longwinded explanation about how so many things were better forgotten. Swathes of history cut away, hidden under the carpet. But a child?

'Sophia, do try and be kind. I'll be there as soon as I can,' he said – as if she weren't capable, as if she were an agent of destruction. No, that was wrong. The image of Käthe's muscled body returned. Wrenched out of shape. Her face beaten to a crimson, bloated pulp. Käthe's murderers were the agents of destruction. Muscles cramping and tightness in her chest, Sophia leaned down and reached for her toes. Her back twinged but she kept stretching until the muscle gave and she could rest her hands on the floor.

'Um. Frau Künstler, are you okay?' Mia's face blurred into view. Eyes met, topsy-turvy. The child's gaze was resentful, but something else lurked behind the anger. Amusement? Sophia straightened, felt dizzy and bit back a sharp reply. The child had said she was fourteen, her birthdate the twenty-eighth of February 1976. Fourteen? She looked a lot younger.

Be kind, Father had said, as if he might actually consider himself kind.

The girl slunk away and began inspecting her painting as though she had every right to look. Sophia slammed the hallway door so Mia jumped and moved away. Perhaps polite, or maybe matter-of-fact, would do.

'I really like your weird mer-thing,' Mia said.

Matter-of-fact would definitely do.

'Mia? That is your name isn't it? Well, I don't like people looking.' Her hands were shaking! What on earth was she to do with the girl until Petrus arrived? Feed her? Talk to her? She had things to do, letters to read, notes to make about Käthe's murder, plus the only teenagers she dealt with were high on glue, or so drunk they made no sense.

'Are you really fourteen?' She fetched plates from the cupboard, cut four slices of bread and put them on the table with cheese and *cervelat* from the fridge. Mia was certainly too young to drink wine, but that was all there was – the last green tea bag had been used.

'I'll be fifteen next year.' The girl glanced to see if her jibe had hit, then munched through the entire pack of cold sliced meat. 'Oma said you knew my mother?' She watched as Sophia pulled a second packet from the fridge and raised an eyebrow. 'Yes please.'

'And who was your mother?'

'Diertha. I *told you*. Your cousin.'

It wasn't possible. No one, least of all Diertha, had told her about a child. Not a whisper. There can't have been a baby in February '76. She had to get this right. No one had been allowed to get pregnant at training camp. Diertha hadn't looked pregnant, and she'd died in May, so how could a baby have simply disappeared to turn up years later claiming to be – what – her distant cousin?

Good lord. There was only one piece of bread left. She placed it, quite deliberately, on her own plate before trickling a little wine into Mia's glass. She wouldn't like it; kids didn't like the sour taste. Mia sniffed and sampled half a mouthful. She looked nothing like Diertha. This girl was soft and as delicate as half-baked bread. Diertha had been dark-skinned with mean pebble-brown eyes sat in wide fleshy cheekbones either side of a sharp nose. She would have relished the drama of taunting Sophia with the news that Dagmar had adopted her child and loved her more than she could ever love 'little Sophi'.

'Delicious.' Mia made a face as Sophia grinned, filling the glass to the top, watching as the child drank the lot in one gulp.

'Water?' No way was Sophia going to admit to a grudging respect.

Mia's thin face flushed from a pale grey to blotchy red. She wobbled with her plate to the sink, returning to the sofa to clutch the damn backpack, dig inside and pull out two wrinkled envelopes.

'What on earth do you want me to do with those?' If

Sophia never saw another envelope she'd be happy.

The girl didn't reply; she leaned, deliberately slowly, to place the letters carefully side by side. Sophia's name was written, in an old-fashioned gothic slant on the first, Petrus' on the second. That made a total of six letters – five from Maria, one from Dagmar. Six bloody letters.

'Oma wrote one for you. The other is for Herr Künstler,' Mia said.

Should she feel relieved, grateful, *honoured*, that her mother had deigned to write to her after so many years? Sophia took her time to drink her wine, butter the remaining slice of bread, and savour the long uncomfortable pause.

'She is your mother.' Mia sounded unsure about Sophia even having a mother. Spawn of the devil perhaps? Oh. There it was – a burn inside her heart, an irascible scorch from childhood. She wouldn't care if Dagmar loved this girl, replacing Sophia as if there truly had been so little love and it the simplest of things to let go. In the silence, as the TV flickered out its Monday repeat of Sunday's snail-paced soap *Lindenstrasse*, the thought came. Why not take Mia straight to her father? Okay, if she did he'd know she was incapable of looking after a child for one hour. Did that matter? Strangely it did, and anyway it was too late, like an owlet, the child's head had sunk to her chest. Asleep she looked too young to be anywhere other than tucked in bed with a cup of cocoa and teddy. Hard to imagine that she had managed to walk to the train station, catch a train, sneeze, without anyone holding her hand. Sophia gently propelled the muttering girl to the spare bedroom.

'Oh, for goodness sake hush, Mia,' she said. 'We'll have to sort everything out in the morning.'

The child curled, half under, half out the duvet, arms wrapped tightly around a pillow. She'd pulled off her filthy shoes and socks. They lay, a haphazard pattern of muddy white and red. Sophia leaned forward, about to place the glass on the bedside table, when the floor tilted: a peculiar sensation. The unfamiliar action of making this nuisance safe was upsetting, because this child, like her, had lost her way and become frightened in the city. What nonsense. Sophia hauled the duvet over Mia and shut the door.

Wait a minute. What if the girl woke and didn't know where she was? She'd call out, feel dread: so the door stayed half open. There was even less of a chance she'd wake if Sophia pressed the buzzer that opened the front door now, not later, when Petrus arrived.

She waited, flattening her letter against the landing banister. Running a finger along the curve of her mother's writing, tracing the imprint – Dagmar's plea for help, someone to care for Mia. Her fingers copied the angle of the pen, the weight of Dagmar's hand on the paper. She'd waited for her mother to come and save her from the crippling isolation Petrus demanded. Mother, she thought, *mother*. There was a faint memory of a home, a warm darkness, being tucked into a soft blanket. No. Home was here. In this city, this place she'd created as a fortress against the world. Wasn't it?

When Petrus arrived, she went to meet her impenetrable father. He was wearing his perfectly cut, soft grey winter coat and hat and holding his favourite umbrella. Handing it over, he preceded her up the stairs, paused to turn, full lips turned down in their usual unconscious grimace. He'd had a severe haircut, the box-like finish making his ears stand out like two pink shells. Had he ever loved her mother? Sophia thought not. He moved effortlessly through women, taking what they offered, giving less in return. Dagmar had been the mother of his child, nothing more. Expendable as soon as her waist thickened and her once lush hair thinned under the stress of motherhood.

'Sophia. Where is she?' Thick eyebrows rose to form an upside-down v before he gazed back up the staircase. Perhaps the girl should be poised there, pale and wanting, waiting for rescue? Annoying how the touch of the wooden handle, still warm from his hand, could ignite rage.

'Hello Father, Mia's asleep.' Such dark pleasure, such *Schadenfreude*, as his shoulders drooped.

'Ah, but where?' They had reached the apartment door and Petrus handed her his coat. He looked ridiculously well, grey hair and tanned skin offset by a deep-green pullover and pale-blue shirt collar, altogether too conscious of his own good looks.

She pointed to the spare-room door, but he hesitated. Was he afraid? Was Mia a dangerous reminder of the past? Sophia held her breath as he walked over to the bed, staring down at the sleeping child. A strand of dirty brown hair had fallen across the girl's thin nose, each time she breathed out it moved; gently flapping like a moth's wing. Petrus smoothed the errant hair back and leaned down to kiss the child's forehead. When he turned, there were tears in his eyes.

'Poor child,' he said, closing her door and making his way to the sitting room. What? Poor child? Spoilt brat was nearer the truth. Though why would she think that? Perhaps it was the way in which he had leaned, so carefully, to kiss her; his tall frame bending down, the harsh edge of him softening for this child as it never had for her.

Petrus glanced at Sophia's painting, keenly noting, no doubt, how amateur her brush style remained. Even though he'd not planned this visit, he would have brought a gift, something small yet expensive, a token designed to make her feel grateful and, at the same time, unworthy. As he finally took a seat, flicking an imaginary speck of dust from lovingly pressed trousers, she watched him take careful note of the two empty glasses, the dirty plates, the curled-up cheese rind.

'I thought I'd bring a little something,' he said and placed a pocket-sized gold box on the table. Lindt Pralines, her favourite. She'd imagine they were for her, though a small voice told her otherwise, and thanked him politely, making no move to open it before they began the old game, now a well-worn track: each waiting for the other to speak first. She could tell as he scanned the room, eyes resting on the letter that waited for him, that he was considering carefully what to say, weighing up the pros and cons. When he was ready to spin a half-truth, her father would lean forward, and, carefully manicured hands resting on knees, begin to weave his story. His version would wear well under questioning, but the tale would yield only a limited portion of the whole. He'd insist she be satisfied with breadcrumbs; grateful to be alive, grateful she had choices to make, grateful – to him.

Sophia leaned forward, a perfect imitation, hands on knees.

'Don't you lie,' she blurted, wanting him to do exactly that so that the Mia problem would go away, knowing she hadn't offered him a drink or anything to eat, and to him protocol was everything, rudeness the worst sin.

'Sophia? Really my dear, consider: when have I ever lied to you?' He leaned back, disappointment marring his handsome face.

Always, she thought, looking through the apartment window where the city lights shimmered. Always and every day. Down there, in between the light and darkness, a church bell tolled seven o'clock. A mother and child hurried along the pavement, the child's mittened hand tightly held.

'In any case,' he continued, 'you really are old enough to make up your own mind.'

And lie, just like you. Had she just said that out loud?

'Perhaps I could have something to drink before you begin your interminable questioning?' His hand shook as he took his glass. She had to look away. *Why* did she care that his hand was shaking? She tried to relax her neck and shoulders, carefully leaning back. It was always of far more use to note what Petrus did not say.

'Mia is the child of your cousin, Diertha.' He was talking slowly, as if she were thick, or, more likely, as if he were making it up on the spot. 'You know, of course, that Diertha died. No one really knew what state she was in after the birth. Suffice to say the child was kept at the hospital for some time. Afterwards Mia was cared for by Dagmar, soon after you and I had left the GDR.'

What baby? She'd never seen a baby. Oh please let it be a better story. One that made sense. Mia wasn't *his* child was she? No, that was crazy. Dagmar had come to the hospital just before Sophia was taken to West Germany. As her mother had tried to kiss her, Sophia turned away. Mothers were supposed to protect their children; hers had sent her into danger. Dagmar had placed Sophia's tattered childhood blanket on the bed as Sophia hated her with her eyes: she wasn't a child any more, the blanket wasn't wanted. She'd wanted a mother who fought for her. Not one who allowed her to be taken away. 'And you never thought to tell me?'

'There was no reason to.' His hand, placing the glass on the table, had steadied and she almost laughed in relief because she so needed to be reassured that this was just another silly family story that could be annihilated by a wave of his hand. She should tell him about Käthe's murder, not streets from here. See how he reacted to that, if his hands shook with a new fear. No. That was silly. He would only tell her to let others investigate, then add how lucky she was to have escaped; how that without his help years ago, she would have died.

'Tell me again,' she said, confident in role as investigator, 'why did we leave?'

Petrus sighed, leaning back to peer into his wine glass, perhaps he thought it too robust for his palate.

'Must we go through this?' he asked, as if the topic had been thoroughly examined, no corner left unturned.

Don't say a word or he'll never continue. Mouth clamped, Sophia stared at the table.

'You remember your final competition.' He was speaking slowly again, each vowel taking on a strange, almost hypnotic rhythm. 'The August '76 Montreal Olympics were the culmination of years of work.'

Oh yes. Red water, crowds roaring, paralysing fear.

'You became ill in the weeks directly after. You weren't able to train for months; they wouldn't have you back. Sophia, I've told you all this!'

'Tell me again.'

'Oh for goodness sake.' The slow talk began again, a kind of sing-song. 'You had inflamed ovaries. I wasn't aware how severe, until I took you to the athletes' treatment centre at Kreischa. We had to perform a laparotomy. My dear, how many times?'

'Just tell me.' Sophia glared. Why couldn't he say he'd acted out of love, not clinical concern?

He sighed, unbearably wearied at her bullying. 'In February '77, you were critical. The hospital wanted to protect their reputation. They were prepared to let you die rather than pay for expensive treatment. There was no guarantee of your return to professional level swimming. So I took you across the border.'

She remembered white walls streaked with red. Tearing pain. In her dreams the blood was hers. She couldn't stop the flow that leaked like tar. Petrus had driven them from Breden, past Leipzig and Potsdam, passing through the barrier at *Drewitz-Dreilinden* into West Berlin. He'd never explained why Dagmar hadn't accompanied them. All he had said was if Sophia had stayed she would have died. Father had saved her – what did he ask in return? For her to stay silent. Never contact anyone. Never mention where they came from or who they had been: she a swimmer, he a doctor. She'd thought her following amnesia had been a gift, now she wasn't sure.

'Now, where are Mia's things?' Petrus asked.

Wait. Nothing he was saying made sense. How had Diertha, aged sixteen in February '76, been allowed to have a child? Abortions had been routine. And, now she thought of it, how, in '77, had she and Petrus managed to cross the border with such apparent ease – when the barrier between the GDR and the West was so tightly manned? She'd ask Hajo when she rang him. He'd know what papers were needed. Never mind that he'd wonder why. Most importantly, right now, if her father took Mia she'd never know what this girl really wanted, plus Dagmar was asking for her. Her mother hadn't forgotten her.

'Mia's staying put.'

'Don't be ridiculous, she will be safer with me.' Petrus finished his wine, checked his watch and looked around the room as if he expected the child, hair brushed, shoes tied, jacket zipped, to simply arrive. 'You know I only came to collect her. It doesn't suit you to make a fuss; in any case the taxi is waiting.'

'Petrus, she's asleep.' Sophia watched a strange expression, similar to mild panic, appear momentarily on his face.

'So wake her.'

'No.'

'Sophia, imagine what might happen if you feel the need to go out on one of your excursions?'

'I'm not waking her.' She sounded like a truculent teenager; he knew just how to put her in her place. 'I'm a police officer. We're considered trustworthy.' Damn, now she was digging herself in by attempting to justify how capable she was.

'Why would you want her to stay, Sophia? You never have visitors.'

Did he watch her apartment door, make notes on who came and who went? How it hurt that he knew and didn't seem to care.

'I'm not going to wake her.'

'In that case.' Petrus made his way to the spare room, as if he would do the waking.

'She won't know who you are!' Sophia barred his way as an officer might.

'You are being utterly ridiculous.'

'She's a child, Petrus. Let her sleep.' How did he manage to reduce her to argument? As if she were capable of only a yes or no. A police officer with no mind of her own.

'Ah, Sophia,' he shook his head, turned away, 'very well, have it your own way.'

What? Why wasn't he arguing? Where was he going?

'Wait, just hang on a minute.'

'Make sure you give her breakfast. I'll be back in the morning.'

The front door closed. She could hear him making his way down the stairs. He'd left his damn umbrella. The gold inscription PK on the handle was cold. This never happened. Never. He won arguments. She should run after him. Tell him about poor dead Käthe. Tell him about Maria's letters. Say something between 'I hate you', 'I love you' and 'sorry'. Ask him to tell her if her mother ever loved her, if he truly thought of her as no more than a weighty responsibility, someone too damaged to ever be normal. Tell me, she'd say. Just tell me.

★★★

The first letter was annoyingly chatty. A new shop had opened with the latest fashions: American jeans, make-up and (best of all) scented soap. The ancient nightclub was about to be revamped into an all-night venue with a wine bar.

Just before Sophia's fifteenth birthday, on a rare break from sports camp and the endless cycle of competitions, the three of them (faces wallpapered with make-up) had sneaked in. They'd danced under the gloomy catacomb ceiling with half its lights broken. The music had been awful. A mix of illegal hip-hop dispersed with accepted rock by Dean Reed. Käthe had been obsessed with Dean who came from California, the place of beaches and blond boys, Maria mulling over who to date. If she'd stayed, Sophia would have been as Maria was now. Contented, settled in a place she knew as home.

Your mother is ill, Maria wrote. Come home. Well, she'd never held back. She must have seen Dagmar and forgotten how little care she'd shown her only daughter. Had it been different for Mia? As Maria droned on about family responsibility, Sophia thought of how the child had spoken of Dagmar with a fierce love, as if she'd been adored in return.

In the second letter, Maria described how Breden was changing, everyone waiting for the Wall to come down, everyone desperate for change. Jörg, her older brother, had a job. She didn't say what. Jörg had only been good at spying, the nasty little shit. Maria wasn't married, she worked as a nurse, had no children, wished she had – and when was Sophia coming? The third letter came straight to the point. If Sophia wasn't going to get in touch, Käthe was going to come over and get her.

The fourth was a frantic scribble: had she heard from Käthe? There it was, clear as day. Käthe had been minutes away, and someone had wanted her stopped.

Blaming exhaustion on her reluctance to read the final sizable envelope, she tiptoed to the spare bedroom.

The girl had wrapped herself in a duvet cocoon. Sophia listened to her breathing, heavy and regular, and found herself matching the child's rhythm. Her own childhood was remembered as deep water. A home filled with undercurrents. Over years, careful barbs had replaced words spoken with love. The mother Sophia remembered had, at first, been voluptuous: a young woman with dark hair and deep blue eyes framed by thick lashes. Gentle and obedient, she'd vanished inside Petrus' shadow, losing her light, changing to a thickly set woman with hopeless eyes and a pursed mouth, fading into resentful misery without much fight, leaving Sophia under her father's control. If she thought too hard beyond those watery images, a fluey sensation rippled across her skin, her past life stalking her.

She'd so wanted someone to shoulder her mother's consuming misery: someone to take a portion of the load. Maria's mother had done just that, she'd taken Sophia into her house when Dagmar's misery was too much to bear. As it did every time she painted, the soft memory of Frau Schöller emerged: thin with pale blue eyes and a shock of dark hair, paintbrush in her hand, focussed as she showed Sophia how to mix white and red to create the palest pink, or laughing as she attempted to rescue their latest cake disaster, hugging Sophia as she cried for a mother who wasn't there. The memory slipped and vanished as Mia turned over to sigh in her sleep.

The child had a slender face, and a slim athletic build. They'd said the same to Sophia many years ago when testing them for natural ability in sports: running, swimming and high jump, before measuring height, head, girth and arms, as the rest of the class giggled.

Like everyone else, she'd quaked at her turn – no one wanted to be tallest, or to have the biggest feet. Everything changed that day. She'd been given food vouchers for bananas and oranges – fruit only seen, never tasted. Sweet-smelling shampoo, medicines, vitamins and travel tokens. The sports coach had chosen her to swim for the GDR, a residential placement had been organised by the youth sports school. When Sophia left, age thirteen, to train at Hochberg training camp, Petrus had found another woman, and a new job far enough from home not to be bothered by his wife. He'd accepted opportunity as his due; never looking back, delighted to escape the turbulence of home.

Her hands were cold. Better not to remember. Better to know those enforced gaps were there for a reason, to protect and safeguard. Sophia made for her bed and curled up as her mind circled dark thoughts: strange waxy images of long shadows and zigzagging pool tiles. There was a smell of Wofasept cleaning liquid in the air, the bleachy stench from the changing rooms at school and swim club. After checking every window and door, finally admitting there was no source for the smell, she lay, unable to sleep, remembering what Petrus had told her. Why her mother never wrote, never came. Why she couldn't write to Maria. Why she'd had to make up a past. Why Petrus had said memory was a dangerous thing.

Damn. She'd forgotten to phone Hajo. Could she really disturb him now? The phone rang forever before his sleepy voice growled: 'It's past midnight.'

'Sorry.'

'Sophia?'

'A girl turned up on my doorstep.'

'What?' Hajo's voice sharpened, waking to listen.

'Her name's Mia. She's from my home town.' A voice inside her head was insisting she tell him about Käthe. But she couldn't. 'She says she's my niece,' Sophia took a deep breath, 'and I don't believe what my father is saying about her.' Zip it, she told herself. Don't say so much.

'How old is the girl?'

'She *says* she's fourteen, and that my mother is really ill.'

'Ah.'

'Hajo, I don't know what to do.' Burrowed under the duvet, the phone stuck to her ear, she imagined Hajo's arms tight around her; his warm shape spooned to hers.

'Families can be tricky.'

'Oh?'

'My father never said much that was truthful.'

'Really?' She would curl inside the sickle of Hajo's broad shoulders, as if he were an oak tree, a place of great safety. 'What about your mother?'

'She left him years ago.'

'Why?' Why hadn't her mother left Petrus? Why hadn't she found some happiness far away from his easy cruelty?

She wanted, quite suddenly, to cry.

'He was a prisoner of war in Russia. When he came back he'd changed.'

'What do you mean?' There was a long pause. She could hear his breathing, so close, just a millimetre away. Hajo, she thought. *Hajo.*

'Is this girl anything to do with your investigation?' He sounded annoyed, as if she'd prised out a distasteful memory.

'No,' Sophia said.

'Then why are you phoning?'

'I don't know what to think.' Why wasn't he here, warm in her bed, the heat of him burning her skin?

'Well, the child can't come to work with you, can she? So, you'll have to send her back, or take her to your father.'

'Her name's Mia.' She took a deep breath. Now or never. She did want to tell him. She really did.

'Goodnight, Sophia.' The phone clicked as he hung up.

CHAPTER FOUR

~

Running through the dense silent forests of home, Sophia tried to escape her dream and woke longing for her mother. What had Hajo's father done to make his mother able to leave when Dagmar could not? Stories about POW camps were similar to the Gulag. Soldiers placed in fields surrounded by barbed wire. Men reduced to drinking their own blood to survive. Petrus had had no such hardship. He'd chosen to seek out female company while Dagmar waited, stubbornly refusing to face reality.

The night's dream whispered of a confined room that stank of chlorine. Inside that room, a girl cut her skin. The fine slicing of metal against flesh released a line of pink bubbles. The girl's body was strong, so strong she wasn't able to control the heat that burned inside. Red dripped to the floor. No one was there to stop the whisper of the blade as it sliced through a freshly healed layer. The child's face seemed familiar, her eyes, nose, cheekbones mixed up portions of Maria, Diertha and Käthe. The sense of them was so strong she'd felt she could swim through their minds. Taste their sour thoughts.

Sophia tiptoed into the bathroom; twisted the shower tap. Wait a minute. The spare-room door was wide open, the room empty. Mia?

The girl *had* lied. No doubt she'd helped herself to money. No way was Sophia going to be taken in by one bedraggled *Ossi* camped out on her doorstep, behaving as if she were still in the GDR, bleating about how she was family, really she was.

Nothing had been taken. In fact, her visitor had tidied up. The hand towel, folded but damp, lay on the shelf in front of the shower-room window. A battered hairgrip by the sink displayed a partial set of fake diamonds. A strand of curly baby hair remained, stuck in between the two remaining diamonds and metal clasp.

The medicine cabinet had been rearranged. Her ecstasy tablets! Why was the bottle on the bottom shelf? She shook them onto her hand. Counted. Oh thank god. All there – but the girl had used up a whole tube of lotion; and Sophia's favourite hair scrunchie had vanished. Her friendship bracelet? No. Thank goodness. Where had the child gone? She glanced at the table. Maria's letters remained, stacked in a neat pile. When/if she saw the girl again she'd tell her a thing or two about messing around with other people's stuff.

She'd need sweet strong coffee before she rang father. He'd be livid, his voice controlled and quiet: Sophia should have woken, heard Mia or preferably stayed up all night to make sure.

'She took a taxi. Can you believe it! Rang from your phone using the list you keep there, and there she was, standing by the front door.' Petrus paused, adding rather inconsequently: 'I am cooking breakfast. Pancakes! The child wanted pancakes.'

Mia had sought to escape, as if she were afraid. Sophia put the phone down and stared at the neatly rolled umbrella. She didn't have pancakes, toast or cereal.

As the hot shower eased the tension in her shoulders, the morning circled back to just another day listening to the splash of water hitting the basin. Sophia ran soap suds along her left arm, feeling the narrow scaly ridges. Her mind shifted from denial to uncertainty. Käthe's voice, so easily recognised from many years ago, murmured: *Coward*.

Enough. If she didn't act now she never would. Dressed in jeans and a black sweater, she tried not to wince before dialling the station and asking to speak to Hajo. Really, it would be better to put her uniform on, stop being an idiot and go to work, but Käthe had been her friend. She'd take the leave she was due and take Mia home, then find out what had happened to Käthe the only way she knew how. She'd face them all: her mother, Maria and Käthe's parents; she owed them that at least. Hajo would be furious because she'd kept back vital information.

'Sophia?' Hajo paused. Sophia imagined his eyes searching the meeting room. 'Where are you? I need to talk to you about your home town.'

'What?' Hang on. What did Breden have to do with Hajo?

'You said the girl came from there.'

'The girl who was murdered?'

'No, Sophia, the girl who came to your apartment, Mia.' He sounded just like her father deliberately slowing down so stupid Sophia understood.

'Yes, she came from there.' She had to tell him about poor Käthe. *Had* to. 'Hajo, listen. I know her.' She couldn't even get that right. You couldn't know a dead person.

'Yes, you've explained – the girl is your niece.'

'No Hajo, *listen*.'

'I don't have time for this.' He was being deliberately sharp, the shared confidences of last night quite gone. 'We've been allocated three former GDR police precincts to inspect. Breden is on that list. I want you to go.'

She could hang up, pretend not to have heard.

'Sophia?'

If she pretended hard enough, perhaps his words would cease to exist. Her inspect Breden police station? She'd recognise people. People who'd worked for the Stasi.

'Hajo, her name's Käthe.' Her fingers were sore from gripping the phone.

'You said Mia?'

'Mia is my niece. Just shut up and *listen*.' She mimicked the stupid Sophia voice. 'I know who the dead girl is.'

'What?'

She heard his door close with a decisive click. Oh help. Better not tell him about the letters and how she'd not wanted to read them.

'Go on.'

'Her name's Käthe. Käthe Niedermann. From Breden. We were at primary school together. Me, Käthe, Maria. We did everything together, you know. Climb trees, build dens, sneak out when we shouldn't have.' She was blabbering on, letting the awful truth gain momentum. 'Hajo?' Oh, he was still there, breathing down the phone line. 'Mia has gone to my father's house. I'm going to drive over, then I'll drive Mia home.'

'Why didn't you tell me?'

'I was frightened.'

'Of *me*?' He sounded furious, as if her fear was worse than keeping secrets.

'No, Hajo. Of the Stasi.'

'There is no more Stasi, and if there was, what would they want with you?'

Everything. Nothing. 'They might have had something to do with Käthe's death.' She couldn't bring herself to tell him about the scrap of paper that bore her name and address. 'I have to find out.'

'Without telling me?'

'No. Yes. I was going to, just not yet.'

'Ah, well, that makes it all right, I suppose?'

She couldn't blame him for being angry. In his shoes she'd have fired an officer who withheld information. 'I'm sorry.'

'Sorry?'

'Yes, sorry.'

'Sophia, I'm not your bloody father.'

Perhaps she would be fired after all? She'd have to return home, to a place that terrified her, without even a badge to keep her safe.

'You're best placed to inspect the local police precinct, and, I suppose, find out about your friend.'

Bastard. This was why Hajo had been promoted so fast. He turned everything round to his advantage.

'Shall I send an officer to go with you?'

My god – that would be Ernst. 'No, I'll be fine.'

'You needn't come to the office. The case file and my instructions will come in the post. No, I know, I'm not daft – not to your apartment. What's your mother's address?' Hajo was tapping his pen on the receiver, a sure sign he'd lost patience.

'I don't know.' How embarrassing. Who didn't know their own mother's address?

'Sophia, you're a damn investigator – find out,' he answered, and she knew his eyes were rolling skyward. 'I'll let them know you're coming. Thursday? That gives you two days to be with your family. I'll tell the Breden police about our victim and ask them to assist you.'

He really had no idea. The People's Police could rewrite history to suit purpose, doctor police records so that each appeared unblemished. The knowledge made her fingers tingle.

It was already nine in the morning. The streets were quiet for the fifteen-minute lull before the shoppers arrived. She drove across Schifffahrtskanal heading past the Universitätsmedizin into Wedding. In March '77, following their escape, age sixteen and still living with her father, Sophia had been desperate to find a message from her mother. She'd steamed open Petrus' mail; trying to find answers. Imagining the unimaginable but wanting so much to read that Dagmar missed her. Holding the seal to the steaming kettle, she'd become expert at knowing how near or how far to go: so her fingers didn't burn, or the contents warp. Just close enough to slowly loosen glue. She'd sweated, a sharp metallic odour, like an animal caught on barbed wire, and learned to reseal each envelope perfectly. The only giveaway being that the paper didn't lie quite as flat as before. At first, finding nothing, she'd begun leafing through her father's treasured books on medical research. He might have hidden *those* letters, the ones she needed to read, inside books. She'd tried to find the key to unlock the desk drawer, and one day there it was – hidden inside a bowl filled with rancid potpourri. Barely pausing to breathe, she'd slotted the key into the miniscule lock, and the drawer had opened. Inside was a crisp pile of envelopes with her father's name clearly written.

The first had been from Ilse: her mother's replacement, the woman everyone had talked about. Sophia had seen her, once, after swimming practice. Ilse peering down at her as if she were some unpleasant portion of her lover's life. The letter didn't say that Ilse was coming to live with him (a thing of permanent dread). No, the note had been nothing more than a series of dates: one every month, right up to last month. No explanation, no love and greetings, nothing. The dates corresponded to the times her father was away on conferences. He'd told her where to call if she needed him, and how long it would take him to get back. She was told, 'Only phone in an emergency. You're old enough to cope on your own.'

Confused, Sophia had been about to put the letter back, when she saw the upside-down photo. She'd turned it over. Petrus naked. The back of his head straining back, his body bunched tight, bearing down into the girl's arched body. One hand-sized flushed breast visible. Ilse.

The front door had opened. Petrus calling her name. She'd slammed the drawer, turned the key, dumped it in the potpourri and – the day she turned seventeen – moved out. Her mother had said Petrus was a good for nothing. Well she'd been right. But, the worst of it was, you couldn't choose; parents just were.

Her father's house was next door to a popular Kindergarten grown from a brave venture to a business bursting
at the seams. Petrus helped out, a charitable pastime Sophia
found hard to place. He visited twice a year to talk about
being a doctor and how each person, little or grown up,
should be healthy. In addition to that he was happy to drop
everything and give advice should a child become ill. Naturally the mothers adored him, sending gifts: cakes, biscuits
and cards.

First thing in the morning the street was chock-a-block
with the day's drop-me-off routine. By nine it was all over
and the neighbourhood slowly unwound as noise levels
dropped with each departing parent and child. Now the
mini-students were inside, doing whatever they did when
the weather was too cold for outdoor morning play. Lights
shone from the window where a group of children fidgeted as they were kitted out in plastic aprons; most
clutched oversized paintbrushes that dripped pink, yellow
and red. One little blonde girl stared at her yellow brush
with such a focus that she caught Sophia's attention. The
child waved the paintbrush slowly through the air, then
shovelled it into her mouth.

Sophia shuddered and turned towards her father's front
door. No one, she thought, not even a dreamed-up whispery voice, was going to call her a coward.

Inside the porch the smell of burnt pancake lingered.
Petrus came to the door wearing a carefully tied, floral-
print apron, no doubt belonging to his current partner.
His eyes widened.

'Sophia? Aren't you supposed to be at work?' He reluctantly opened the door to the hallway, where Mia's jacket

hung next to his long coat, side by side with an assortment of fur and silk. Petrus' new lady, the latest in the string of hopefuls, was attempting to move in. Sophia knew only too well that the minute clothes started gathering, coats conveniently left until next time, the relationship was over.

Mia was chewing her way through a pile of oddly shaped pancakes drowning in treacle. She looked up; face tight, eyes huge and defiant. Her hair was tied back with the missing scrunchie but a number of wispy tendrils had escaped; they curled their way round her ears and slender pink neck, spoiling the intended statement. I dare you, her eyes said; I dare you.

'Yummy.' She waved her fork, a chunk of massacred pancake circling, pulling Petrus' attention where she wanted it. Clever girl. Sophia leaned against the door listening to the rise and fall of her voice. Those grubby jeans and purple hand-knitted jumper were far too young, but the child was undeniably pretty in a coltish way: long legs and arms, that silly baby hair twirling around a thin, stern face.

Her father was entranced. As he did with each new lover, he danced to attention, showering Mia with offers of chocolate spread, orange juice, biscuits. When she seemed taken by the offer of strawberry Nesquik, he sidestepped to the cupboard, reaching with surgeon's hands, long fingers, as slim as a girl's, to place the tub on the counter. Sophia glanced at her own bitten fingernails; put her hands behind her back. Who came to visit and drank strawberry milkshake? More to the point: how would she have reacted if he had focussed on her like that, just once, as she grew from child to woman?

Mia was a true professional. Shooting icy glances at Sophia whenever Petrus looked her way, she chattered enthusiastically about how long it had taken her to travel to Berlin. Petrus praised her heroic efforts and talked about Dagmar as if he'd seen her only days before, finding out what he needed without alarming the child. His face arranged, his eyes gentle and observant, he constituted a careful study of how to be kind – and Mia began to relax. There was no hint of the steel Sophia knew so well. His obsession with maintaining reputation with astute social climbing: one step forward, two back, never repeating the same mistake. He'd juggled his liaisons effortlessly; until Ilse, when, for a time, things changed. However, even during that strange, almost perpetual absence, he paid attention when Sophi swam. He'd become the pop-up version of 'proud father', carefully noting the envious glances of the other men, the coquettish heavy-lidded gaze from the mothers as Sophia tore along the length of the pool, leaping out to greet him.

That was before. She'd adapted. Become stronger. Able to survive.

Mia finished stuffing herself with pancakes, and there were no more questions to ask. In the silence Petrus cleared his throat and both turned, as if there were no way of avoiding it, to Sophia.

'Dagmar wrote to me, so I'll drive us there.' I'll find out who hurt you, Käthe, I will, she silently promised her dead friend.

Mia, about to hand her plate to Petrus, mistimed. The plate fell to the floor with a loud clunk.

'I've been given leave.' Not quite the truth. Father

needn't know about the inspection, or Käthe, yet. But she'd broken their bloody tight-knit chatter. Petrus pretended he hadn't heard; sweeping up the broken crockery before telling Mia she could phone Oma, leading the child away to the safety of his office. Was this what a wasp felt like before it stung its prey? She saw him touch Mia on the shoulder, leaning, as if, given the choice, he would have kissed her hair as he had the evening before.

'Everything will be all right, my darling child,' he said.

His darling? She wanted to kill him, anything to stop feeling pain at his easy love for this scrap of a girl.

'Sophia, why would you want to go back?' he asked, folding the cloth from the sink into perfect corners.

'She's my mother.'

'I am quite aware who she is.'

'You knew she was ill, didn't you?' How did he manage to reduce her to confused fury with such ease?

'Why must you be so objectionable?' He was watching, mouth curled, as if he'd eaten something that left a repulsive aftertaste.

'Whatever you decide makes no difference. Besides it'll be faster by car.' There, that was adult reasoning. Sophia stared at the floor. Eyes aching. Käthe was dead. Her mother was dying and her father saw no reason for her to return.

'Very well,' he said, 'but aren't you a little old to cry?'

★★★

On the phone Mia told Oma all about the early morning taxi drive across the city, the nervous wait watching the car headlamps sweep by. She said nothing about meeting

Sophia, or her terror that morning because at any moment Sophia might wake up and, like a man-eating bat, swoop down and snatch her. Oma didn't like that Mia had gone to Petrus' house. Why hadn't she stayed with Sophia? She sounded nervous, almost afraid, as if Petrus were danger-ous! Oma had that all the wrong way round. Now she didn't want to talk, so Mia went on and on how nice Petrus was, how clean his house was, how it looked out onto an avenue of linden trees.

'Maybe he's changed.' Oma didn't sound convinced.

'He made me pancakes!' She explained how she could hear some of the children playing a game of catch in the Kindergarten playroom next door. Oma tried to laugh; a dry rasping that had neither of them fooled.

She wanted to say how awful Sophia was, that she was mean, with eyes that seemed to see right into Mia's head. When Sophia smiled it was as though she had a big fat secret, something only she knew. She was skinny: Oma would say way too skinny, but privately Mia decided she wouldn't mind looking like that – rather than dumpy like Oma.

'Oma,' she said. 'How d'you describe a grin that's hate-ful, you know – not just nasty? You said it to me once.'

'Who's being unkind, sweetheart?'

'No one, Oma. It's just something I heard on the train.'

'What a thing to ask! I don't remember.'

'Yes you do.' It was better to keep her talking, to try to hear if she was all right.

'You mean: *Grinsen wie ein Honigkuchenpferd*?'

Yes. Grinning like a gingerbread horse! That was exactly how Sophia looked, except she didn't really look like a horse; which was a shame. Sophia didn't really know anything; she just pretended she did. When Petrus had told Mia about Sophia being a police officer, she'd been scared. Police were dangerous. They were the last people you went to for help.

'Oma,' she said. 'Promise you'll rest. Don't cook anything, okay? We'll be there really soon. We won't need supper. I love you.' And Oma was gone.

Maybe she could have a shower; her hair really needed washing. Better to wait until Petrus had sorted Sophia out. He'd been so kind but Mia had noticed the way his mouth tightened when he was irritated. She worried about Oma, but the worry was so old it had become part of her skin, working its way deep inside her shoulder joints, behind her eyes, inside her stomach. Oma was sick. Not just sick until she got better, but ill enough that she might not. When Mia was afraid about Oma dying, she thought straight ahead. One action came after the other. She edged the panic to a blue place she'd painted inside her head, a place where all terrors could go.

Petrus and Sophia were in the kitchen talking in loud tight voices. He'd send Nasty back to do her work, and Mia and Petrus would travel to Breden by train. She wasn't stupid. She knew that Oma could have phoned or written to Petrus, but had sent her instead – as though a letter or call wouldn't produce the same reaction. On the three-hour train home she'd buy a magazine and some chocolate. Better still, Petrus would pay. There'd be no Sophia to spoil it. Petrus was a doctor; he could make Oma better, no need to worry any more.

Mia trailed her hands over the soft leather that made

up the centre of his writing desk. Neat and tidy. Nothing to be frightened of. The shelves around the room were filled with medical books. She could be a doctor. Oma was taking more painkillers than she should. She'd have to tell Petrus. Even with those extra medicines, it took Oma ages to get out of bed and downstairs. Last week she'd been stuck in her bed all day without a hot drink or food. That night Mia had cried, hiding the sound by running Oma a bath. Now every morning she brought her coffee and biscuits. Oma's favourites: the ones with thick coffee icing.

Behind Petrus' desk was a picture of Sophia: young and smiling: her first day at work? It had to have been taken before she started arresting and beating people up, before she learned how to look so mean. There were no pictures of Diertha or Oma. No matter, soon there would be photos of Mia on that wall, pictures of her at school showing off her latest maths certificate.

One other photo looked familiar. A man in a dark green jumper held the hand of a girl who was showing her medal to the photographer: Sophia and her father. Mia couldn't remember where she'd seen it, but was sure she had. Next to it was a picture of Petrus with his arm around someone else. A woman. Not Oma, not Sophia, a young, slim, blonde woman who looked at him sideways like she knew exactly what she was doing. Mia looked at the back. No date, no name.

Mia put the picture back. She knew Petrus had left her grandmother. That didn't mean he was a bad person, did it? Nothing mattered as long as he came to help. Still, he didn't seem quite so nice any more.

★★★

The tea towel, rose pink with a recipe for dumpling stew, was old and faded, the list of instructions barely visible: grate two medium-sized potatoes, mix together with flour and semolina. Sophia dried, placing one plate on top of the other, before placing the tea towel on the radiator – imagining Mia, ear to door, scowling when she realised they were all going.

Driving home, heart pounding, the car full with Petrus' suitcase, medicines, and two silent passengers, she had just enough sense left to ask her father to write Dagmar's address on a scrap of paper.

'I won't be long.' She parked as near the garage as possible. She'd pack a bag and be back in ten minutes, tops. Jogging up the stairs gasping, 'Bloody hell, bloody hell,' at each step, she paused at the top to lean her head against the front door. Worst-case scenario, she'd be back by the weekend. Forget the whole mess and move on. She threw the mail into her workbag. Maria. She'd see Maria, and she'd see Frau Schöller. The thought made her giddy, as if at sea. What would Maria's mother do? She'd hug her tight, no doubt. She'd say how much she'd been missed as if the world were truly a better place now that Sophia was back. They'd talk about painting and how much improved Sophia was. Oh. What would they say about Käthe? Would they blame her, or be furious Sophia did nothing to save her friend, never mind that Sophia hadn't known Käthe was arriving. She'd have tell them and deal with whatever happened.

Sophia's running trousers and party gear went into an

overnight suitcase. The bathroom mirror reflected tired eyes as she yanked open the medicine cabinet and took out the bottle of ecstasy pills. Just in case.

'Hajo,' she said, when she was finally put through, 'I forgot. Get the lab to check Käthe's blood for steroids, will you.'

'What makes you think she was taking drugs?'

'Her muscles.' Steroids made you feel invincible and Käthe had fought her attackers with a ferocious strength. Her over-muscular body had been broken, bones snapped, muscles purple with bruising.

'Did you take steroids?'

'Hajo, what has that to do with anything?'

She had to repeat Dagmar's address three times. Did he want to annoy her? When she asked, he laughed as she closed her eyes, as if to catch the fleeting warmth of his humour. He was playing with her, knowing full well she'd only given him a portion of the truth.

Like father like daughter. The echo had her wincing and asking about travel expenses. Did Breden even had a hotel?

'Sophia?'

He was going to ask her why she couldn't, wouldn't, stay with Dagmar.

'I have the number of the hotel. You'll get reimbursement if you stay there, though I'll send a copy of the case file and inspection list to your mother's address.'

'Yes, all right.'

She called the hotel, requesting a single room, adding the possibility of a second reservation for her father. Downstairs Frau Weiner was delighted to have a visitor.

Less delighted when Sophia explained she wanted someone to cancel her milk order until the weekend. In the cellar, she chose her oldest running shoes, folded her working clothes straight from the dryer to the suitcase. Did she really need party clothes? An image of Hajo worked its way into her mind, watching from across a gloomy dance floor, undressing her with his eyes. Breden was a backwater town, but she'd take them, just in case. She stood quite still. It had happened. The thing to avoid at all cost, against all odds, was here.

CHAPTER FIVE

~

Mia craned forward, her thin nose poking into Sophia's side view so she had to lean forward to see if the road was clear.

'East Germany's totally different from West,' Mia said.

'Are you strapped in?'

'When the stupid Wall came down, loads of people just packed up and left. They just drove off, or got on the train. It was brilliant! My history teacher *walked*. She said she was going to trek through the forest right by the sentry points in a declaration of freedom, or something.' She paused, ignoring Sophia's repeated order to clip herself in.

Might Käthe have a child? The thought came from nowhere. No, Sophia decided. No.

'You're a police officer, aren't you?' The girl blushed when Sophia turned, but her eyes were calculating. 'They're really, like, nasty.'

'I like arresting people.' There, that would shut her up.

'No you don't, or you would've arrested me. What else do you do?'

'I'm a detective. I investigate missing people, theft, murder.' How had this child managed to turn her snipe into nonsense?

'Oh. Are you going to investigate stuff in Breden?'

'I am.' Sophia glanced right. Petrus was studiously gazing out of the window, hands folded casually on his lap. 'I'm going to see my mother, and then I'm going to find out about someone else.' His hands locked, white-fingered, tense. He took a slow breath in and carefully relaxed.

'Is the person *dead*?'

'Very.'

'Did you know them?'

'Yes, I did.'

'That's really bad.' She paused, clearly at a loss about whether to continue. 'Anyway, Gerda would have liked travelling across the border. We could've pretended it was still, you know, dangerous. Not allowed.' Mia made it sound like a great adventure, something not to be missed.

'You've only been away one night!' How had Dagmar looked after this impossible child? And what should she call her mother? Dagmar, Mama, Mother? She hadn't been the best of mothers. Was that Petrus' fault? Sophia wasn't sure. All she remembered was a huge brown sadness that had filled every corner of the house.

The atmosphere in the car was chilly. Mia finally silent. Christ. Could the girl read her mind? Sense how much she didn't want to see Dagmar? Sophia imagined Mia's eyes burning holes in the back of her neck. No. She hadn't said a bad word about her bloody Oma, so she couldn't know. Belatedly the realisation sank in that she'd inadvertently suggested that best friend Gerda might not be missing Mia. After that it seemed like basic survival to shut up, tune out and concentrate on driving.

She'd call her mother 'Dagmar', like someone she didn't

know and was politely indifferent to. She'd ask her 'why did you choose Mia over me?' No, too childish. She'd say: 'Why did you decide to stay in Breden when you could have had a better life with me?' That sounded just as bad. She was driving into her own shadow, drifting nearer a darkness that fell softly across her waking life, compromising the light.

Petrus began a new conversation, steering comments away from anything that might prove upsetting. He talked about studying medicine and how much he'd enjoyed his time as a student. Sophia imagined him dark-haired and handsome, taking his pick of the young girls as he worked his way through university into an early marriage. Dagmar had been beautiful. Sophia had seen pictures of her creamy-skinned mother, dark eyes and a steady smile, tucked into the lee of her father's arm, waiting for life to begin.

Mia didn't manage to hold on to her caustic silence for long. She followed Petrus' lecture with a detailed account of her science lessons. Petrus twisted so he could see her. Sophia opened the window a crack. The air from the road smelled of petrol and damp. Each car they passed left a trail of spit, an oiled ripple on the tarmac. Sophia's fingers tingled. Could someone be aware of her imminent arrival? Nonsense. That was the kind of ridiculous notion her father fed her. I'm going to find out who hurt you, she promised Käthe. I'll be the friend I should have been.

As they neared Potsdam, Petrus finally broached the subject of Dagmar's health. Mia's chatter stumbled and slowed. Dagmar was always tired, always in pain. She took too many painkillers, even when Mia *told* her she shouldn't. She wouldn't go to the doctor anymore; Mia had to collect her medicines from the pharmacist.

'She's really stubborn,' Mia began to list all Dagmar's medication. Perhaps her mother's inability to accept a failed marriage now centred on not accepting how ill she was? Somewhere in all the mess Dagmar had got it right. She'd brought Mia up, focussed on the child so that the result was a strong, healthy young woman. Sophia caught her father's eye as he gently shook his head, making some half-baked joke about doctors and prescriptions always sounding worse than they really were. Mia's face blurred out of focus: perilously close to tears. Indicating right, Sophia said it was high time they stopped for a coffee break.

Petrus took their orders and Sophia walked over to the shop to glance at the newspapers and to stretch her legs. Mia followed but paused to look at a wilting display of pink and white roses followed by a hideously overpriced checked tablecloth. Should she stop her, or let Mia waste money? About to suggest they look somewhere less ridiculously priced, closer to Breden, she noticed paired hairgrips displayed near the counter: twin dragonflies decorated in silver, blue and green. Beautiful. She paid, relieved to see the child frown – and stomp back to the table.

Eating cheesecake with some kind of pink jelly on top, Mia explained she'd wanted to buy Oma a present, something pretty, but the flowers were droopy and the tablecloth boring.

'I'll buy you flowers,' Petrus smiled. The nearby all-female table beamed and nudged one another. 'I'm sure they have some fresh bunches if one asks nicely.'

Such a joy to see her father sandwiched between

wanting to please the child but not wanting to appear in Breden with flowers and give the wrong message. Petrus, just like herself, would have to work out how to deal with Dagmar.

Sophia waited until he'd left before handing Mia the hairgrips wrapped in white paper. She shouldn't have bought them. Mia might not like them, might not like receiving them from someone as unpopular as herself. The girl leaned forward and held them gently, turning them round so the greens and blues glistened under the bright lights.

'They're beautiful,' she said. 'Blue's like, my top favourite colour.' She fidgeted, reaching out, as if she wanted to shake Sophia's hand or perhaps even hug her. Sophia leaned back. Petrus was standing by the shop entrance watching, a colossal bunch of pink roses in his hands, his eyes dark and questioning.

'Well, anything to stop you taking mine,' Sophia said, absurdly relieved when Mia laughed. Now one dragonfly perched in the girl's dark hair, poised as if it were just about to fly away.

They arrived at six, Mia squashed in between the two front seats as she directed Sophia through a maze of back alleys. Not the home she remembered. Dagmar would have had to move as she had no husband, no money, only a dependent child. The darkness was broken by the occasional yellow streetlight that illuminated expanding circles of rotting tarmac. Sophia half expected to recognise the corners and alleyways but the landscape was unfamiliar. Looming pipelines zigzagged above them, a conduit for gas or water. A factory wall tilted dangerously near the road. Pine cones, petrol, wet wood and chlorine: the smell of home in a place she'd studiously forgotten. On either side of the street formerly grand town houses sagged, their opalescent, stained-glass windows proclaiming better times. On the corner, newly built flats ballooned with damp. Dirt-streaked they squatted, a sad monument to the lack of maintenance afforded to communist housing.

Sophia parked the car inside a horseshoe of functional, two-up, two-down lodgings. Lights came on in the neighbouring homes. My god, any minute now the welcome committee would come out with sharpened pitchforks. One door opened and, as if on cue, curtains twitched to one side, showing each neighbour's dark profile.

A short, heavy-set woman came out to stand, then lean, on the narrow doorframe. Mia scrambled from the car and ran toward Dagmar, hugging her. Dagmar's arms encircled the child, her head lowered and she kissed her. Hot tears welled up in Sophia's eyes. She blinked and took a deep breath.

'Oma,' Mia said. 'They're here.' She pointed dramatically to the car. Petrus was undoing his seatbelt, reluctantly leaning back to get the flowers, taking forever to find them and straighten the paper wrapping. Sophia gritted her teeth, got out and slammed the door. Bugger Petrus. Bugger everything. The curtains twitched again; a single yet united motion that had her on the brink of hysterical laughter.

'Sophia.' Petrus was waiting for her to open the boot, his soft blood-red scarf a beacon in the dreary street. 'Would you please carry these?' He pointed to his bag and Mia's muddied backpack. Their eyes met as Sophia turned away. Let him carry it. Mia was busy trying to get her grandmother inside. She answered Dagmar's questions – Have you eaten? Are you well? Have they looked after you? – with gentle reassurance, her voice calm and sure; as if she had learnt some time ago how much love Oma needed.

Dagmar leaned against the door and looked across the front garden at Sophia, who froze – one hand on the gate.

'Child,' she said, holding out her hand.

Sophia remembered a gentle young woman from the distant past, before the advent of a silent unapproachable mother. This mother had aged. Her dark hair, gone to grey, had been cut short and left unkempt. Her skin was waxy and loose. Old skin. Sophia stared down the narrow path. Mother, she wanted to say. But she wasn't her mother's child, had never been. If she looked up now she'd die, because this wasn't her mother, this was someone else.

'Coward,' a voice whispered in her head. Her mother's hand wasn't held out after all; it was stroking Mia's hair in a slow, gentle, caress. *Mia* was encircled in Dagmar's arms. Mia was the child. The name had never been meant for her. Sick with disappointment, she remembered her mother's emotional games from long ago and looked her in the eye.

'Dagmar,' she said, making her eyes say that she understood. Oh yes, she understood.

'Sophi.' How could her mother's voice be gentle, yet so full of pain? Sophia let go of the gate. Walk? Run the other way? She was at the front door. Dagmar was holding her hand, stroking it as if it were something precious. 'Sophi,' her mother said, 'my Sophi.'

Dagmar's hands were cold. Mia was staring. Was her mother *crying*? Sophia put an arm carefully around her wobbling shoulders, leading her into the house, past a dark sitting room, a window that looked out onto a scrap of garden, a kitchen that smelled of yeast, cinnamon and something else she couldn't name.

'Sit down, Mama.'

Her mother wavered as Petrus waved the bunch of flowers around like a traffic warden. Sophia found a vase; Dagmar's eyes followed her to the cupboard, back to the sink, while Mia talked at a hundred miles an hour. Who wanted what, she asked, rinsing cups, making coffee and fiddling around with a homemade apple and cinnamon cake, Sophia's absolute favourite. The same cake had been baked for her each time she came home from training camp. She turned. Dagmar waited.

'Thank you, mama.' Sophia forced a smile as Dagmar leaned, her hands shaking on the back of the kitchen chair. Mia's face was flushed, eyes glistening with more expected tears, and something caught deep in Sophia's stomach; a forgotten chord, unpractised and flat.

'Mia. Stop. Why don't you take the cake into the sitting room?'

Mia threw her a red-faced grateful look. 'And phone what's-her-name? Gerda? We'll be fine,' she added as Mia blinked. 'Go on.'

The front door burst open and a frizzy-haired, stoutly built girl dashed in and grabbed Mia. The two danced, Gerda shrieking – what was Berlin like? Had she seen anyone famous? Did people in Berlin have loads of money? Why hadn't she *told* her? Eventually, Mia shoved her friend in front of her, introducing Petrus and Sophia to her best, *best* friend.

★★★

Even with the lights on, the sitting room was overwhelmingly gloomy. Surely only someone very depressed could have chosen to decorate walls brown. It seemed that, as the years passed, the furniture and the resident had grown darker.

Sophia spotted it as Mia and Gerda disappeared up the stairs, heads close together. Her childhood comforter, a much-loved cream mohair rug with plaited edging, folded over the back of the armchair. Dagmar picked it up, swayed, then leaned forward, placing the small rug in Sophia's waiting hands, before she sank into the settee where she sat, head back, breathing in, out, slow and deep, hands pulling at each other in her lap, those melancholy eyes fixed on her daughter. Sophia folded the soft fabric into her hands, smelling conditioner, soap and childhood. Her mother had remembered; she'd washed the fraying comforter to welcome her daughter home.

'Dearest, did Käthe find you?' Dagmar's laboured breathing was dispersed by the girls' animated chatter, muffled through the ceiling.

Oh lord, what to say? She couldn't blurt out how Käthe was dead, and the reason she'd come back was to find out who had hurt her friend, not to see her mother. Dearest, her mother had called her dearest. This soft woman and the other mother were opposites. Which was right?

'No, Mama, Mia found me.'

'Mia is a good girl. You must tell Käthe and Maria

you're back; they so want to see you.'

'Yes, yes, I will.' The girls' voices rose and fell: the occasional short question, a shriek of laughter, a pause.

'Sophi, you've grown beautiful.' Dagmar's eyes were fixed, as if she wanted to savour the sight of her daughter. The girls clattered downstairs with rushed explanations: they were just going to Gerda's house, for a while, they'd be back soon – okay? Mia looked at Dagmar, at Sophia. Her mouth opened to ask again. Sophia nodded and she whirled out of the door. Dagmar twisted her hands and whimpered. Her skin was grey, tinged with yellow. Barely conscious, she'd slumped forward.

'Mama,' Sophia leaned close, 'when did you take your pills?' Her muttered response made no sense. 'Your pills?' Sophia repeated. Where the hell was Petrus? 'It's all right. Everything will be fine, don't worry.' Oh god, the peculiar odour that seeped from her mother's skin, something like rotting pear, was the smell of death.

'Sophia?' Her father was there. There wasn't enough air in the room. She was going to faint, the air was turning red; she could see it swirling round and round behind her eyes.

'Hold her head and stop behaving like a child.' Petrus' voice was far away. 'Dagmar? I'm going to call the hospital. Sophia for goodness' sake, stop shaking, these will take away a little of that pain.'

'I'm not going anywhere,' Dagmar muttered as Sophia moved closer. Her mother's breath was putrid. Sophia retched.

'Pull yourself together!' Petrus snapped, and she was holding her mother, easing her up gently; touching bones as delicate as a bird's, cradling her head so Dagmar could swallow the medication with water. Her mother's hair was soft and clean and smelt of eucalyptus.

Sophia felt her eyes burn. Tears leaked their way down her neck, soaking into her fleece. She remained silent as Dagmar gulped down four pills, lowered her mother's head and stumbled up the stairs into the bathroom.

'Fuck this.'

Scooping cold water on her face, she dragged a towel from the rail, glaring into the mirror at red eyes and an expression that was a police officer's disapproving mask. If she held the towel over her mouth, she wasn't crying.

Petrus was standing by the window, one hand pulling back the curtain, watching the street as Dagmar's breath laboured in the darkness. A dark shape stretched out from the corner of the street, a thin profile against the mackerel-grey night. Sophia moved to her father's side just as the shadow melted and Dagmar farted, rolling onto her side, grunting as she sank further into a medicated sleep. Sophia winced. Petrus looked round and she edged nearer, needing reassurance, a modest gesture of solidarity. He laid a hand on her shoulder for no more than a moment. There was an expression of terror on his face before he dropped his arm and moved away, crossing the room to close the curtains with a decisive sweep.

In the hallway, she searched for Gerda's home number, eventually finding it on a list stuck to the kitchen wall. Frau Rentsch (Elke) was delighted to have little (*little?*) Mia stay the night. Yes, of course, Mia could stay as long as she wanted; it was no trouble at all. Thank goodness someone had come; really, they had all worried how Dagmar would care for the child when she herself was so ill.

Dagmar had not only baked cake, but also supper. Petrus joined Sophia in spooning the hot potato and sausage straight from the warm baking dish. Deliciously creamy, well-flavoured food, a taste from another time and, even in the bleakness of the moment, Sophia felt vivid and alive. It was as if the house and town had been waiting. Yes, she'd see Maria and explain, and there was Hajo's awful insistence she inspect the police precinct, but now that she was here, she was capable of anything, all manner of things could happen. She could find out why they had left without Dagmar. Why she'd become so ill. Athletes were supposed to be strong and healthy, but she'd nearly died. The imagined victories played out in her mind. The Wall was down. She could do what she liked.

Stop. That was stupid thinking. Nothing had changed. Nothing. But still, she'd find who had killed Käthe and make them pay, she would, she really would.

When the phone rang, Petrus motioned her to stay. She couldn't hear the conversation. More than likely it was Mia being awkward, asking to come home. Petrus was too soft, he'd probably agree, and the girl shouldn't see her grandmother so sick. Sophia moved to the door. Petrus' voice was tense and controlled. Not Mia. He wouldn't talk like that to her.

'No, nothing has changed,' he said. 'I'm simply here to help Dagmar, nothing more.'

Who was he speaking to?

'I'll be staying,' he said to her. 'You go to the hotel.'

'What about Dagmar?'

'Sophia, I am a doctor. Go on, I'll see you in the morning.'

'And Mia?' What if the child wanted to come home? Petrus didn't have a car.

'Just go. I'll call you if I need to get her.' Petrus looked worn, as if life had suddenly caught up with him.

'Are you certain?' Everything was slipping from known to strange.

'Sophia, *go.*'

She found a blanket to tuck around Dagmar, and leaned in, touching her lips against her mother's parched cheek. Petrus moved about upstairs, no doubt deciding where to sleep: his wife's bed, Mia's room? While he was safely busy she called the operator, reciting her police identification code so the woman had authority to retrieve the caller's number. She jotted it down on a scrap of paper then dialled, certain Ilse would answer – and then what? What could she say to Dagmar's nemesis? A woman with lustrous blonde hair, so different from Dagmar's brown. Delicate hands, like a child's. Sophia remembered seeing Ilse's glossy black shoes with ice-pick heels on the few occasions they'd met, either at Sophia's swimming class, or the few times her father had visited her at training camp. 'And who is this?' Ilse had asked; clearly displeased that Sophia even existed.

'Petrus? What now?' A *man's* voice, thick with annoyance. 'Just keep me informed and nothing will happen, is that clear?'

Sophia replaced the phone. She was sweating, the toxic vinegary stench of fear she'd smelled on herself when she'd found her father's secret mail.

Outside the air tasted of burnt plastic, so different from the night fumes of Berlin. To her the evening smelled of old pain: the suffering that had been ripened and preserved by the vaguely named 'Department of Technical Interception'. Its workers went to great trouble to gather 'dissident' scent specimens for agents who compiled a smells register. She knew exactly how the Stasi did their collecting. A cotton wool pad pressed to the victim's groin. A sterile dust cloth placed on a car seat to collect the terrified smell of whoever sat there. All interrogation chairs had been fitted with dust sheets, which, once removed, would be folded and the centre piece cut then lifted with tweezers to be stored in a jar.

Earlier that year the Berlin police force had been deployed en masse to manage the crowds that stormed the headquarters of the Ministry for State Security, or Stasi, in Berlin-Lichtenberg. That day Sophia broke from the riot line, took off her work jacket and slipped inside rooms filled with ripped paper. The office shredders had done what they could. When the motors burned out, the employees started tearing reports by hand.

One room had been filled with jam-jars, each containing a scrap of pickled yellow cloth. Sophia had greeted the glass jars like old friends. Her training group's scent was here somewhere, tucked into a corner or on some anonymous shelf, preserved forever. There would be a fragment of Diertha's perfume, the cloying cheap spray she'd used, along with her sweat. Sophia had walked through Stasi headquarters shaking, furious yet excited, looking for the file that bore her own name, the jar with her scent. And there it was –alphabetically arranged under the code name 'Torpedo' given to her when she was a swimmer. A tribute to how fast she'd moved from junior swimming club to training camp, then international league. In the chaos she'd easily slipped the jar into her coat pocket – hers to keep. At home she'd smashed the jar, taking great satisfaction in grinding glass to powder, burning the square of cloth in the kitchen sink.

Käthe's death changed everything. Sophia wasn't going to clean up anymore, nor covertly destroy evidence. This time she'd investigate and find. The knowledge was thrilling, powerful as a hit of speed, better, because it was doing something good. She'd ask Maria about Käthe, and then she'd know what her friend had been doing.

Now, pulling into the car park of Breden's only hotel, Sophia realised she wasn't thinking straight. The person Petrus called must have been one of his old friends or colleagues, but it hadn't sounded the kind of thing a friend or colleague would say. Maybe Ilse would know? Sophia could find her. Question her. Make her talk. Did she work in a surgery or hospital? Would she be sitting at home, right now, with her perfect husband and children who knew nothing? Sophia could hunt her down; make her life a misery of questions. Wait. It didn't make sense. Petrus had received a call from a man here. In Breden. The person had known what number to call. Oh God. Her father had stayed in touch with people who lived here, not just Ilse. Other people.

The side of the hotel facing the car park was scrawled with graffiti. Black/blue swirls and scribbles claiming ownership. Tribal warfare or proclamation against the broken dictatorship? Not so long ago the scribbler would have been interrogated, locked up for days until he (or she) admitted to the crime. Sophia closed the car boot, checked into the hotel and unpacked. Placing her few possessions in the measly cupboard, and there it was, loitering in the bathroom - Ilse's perfume, sharp, yet sweet, like an echo of her father's desire.

***

The entrance would have been so easily missed: the filthy glass door leading to a seedy hallway, a make-shift wine bar and suspicious bouncer who took her money. No need for a stamp. She was utterly recognisable as a stranger.

Unable to settle, the hotel room shrinking as questions circled: where to go first, who to ask, how to tell Käthe's mother her only child was dead? Sophia had searched through her suitcase. Pocketed a pill, and walked. It had been so much easier to imagine perfect lives for Käthe and Maria, to hate Dagmar rather than feel panic, even dread, as her mother managed alone, year after year. Worse, her mother had struggled to bring up a child that wasn't hers. Had Dagmar agreed Sophia should not be contacted? Had there been some kind of deal that kept her mother away? The child offered up as compensation for staying put? It was exactly the kind of thing her father would have done.

Down the winding stairway, the underground cata-comb stank of piss and sweat, the rounded brickwork pock-marked from years of smoke. A group of young men in tight black jeans gathered around a pool table. Under the low-hung lamp studs glinted against the shell pink of their ears. An angular girl with a severely cut fringe prowled the area. A small gold ring hung from her beaky left nostril. Her mean black eyes focussed on Sophia. She paused, licked her lips and leaned into the arms of the nearest male. The man laughed and placed his right hand between her legs. A wave of heat uncurled in Sophia's belly. She turned away. Damn. Too late.

'*Hello* stranger.' The man edged the girl to one side and cupped his hand over his balls. 'Fancy a fuck?' he called to accompanying whistles.

'I might, if you were a man.' She noted his red face, the flash of anger, his mate's roaring laughter, and made a note to take care walking back.

'Lager,' she said, as the barman's small eyes zeroed in on her small breasts. He looked away when she stared back. People were edging round the dance floor, you couldn't call it dancing. A single green strobe lit a filthy mirror ball. The floor was a dizzying patchwork of black and white triangles. Two scrawny young men, all elbows and knees, competed, each catapulting higher than the other. One had a black Mohican, the other a chain attached from ear to nose; it glinted in the light. In the far corner an emaciated girl, in a tiny black t-shirt dress, danced alone, the words 'Sex Kitten' were inscribed in gold across a non-existent cleavage. Her movements were slow and sad, eyes pin-hole black, her neck a mess of toothy love bites.

The white pill nestled in Sophia's pocket as she watched the room fill. Men arrived after the bars closed; found their usual spots near the bar. Chased beer with schnapps. Their narrowed eyes followed the girl. Her child-like waist, her tiny pointed breasts, her tight slit – prepubescent, clearly wet, they might imagine, for each of them. No, she'd not take the pill tonight; she'd watch and wait. Maybe she'd recognise someone? When the music changed from heavy metal to dance, a thickly set man with yellow hair sprouting from his ears tried to get her attention, but he was drunk and mean with the utter boredom of a small town.

Someone was causing a ruckus in the hallway upstairs. The pool table crowd flowed up the stairway, eager for a fight. Perhaps it was time to leave before any police came, though it would be good to get a look at them. Nothing. One by one the players returned to their game. Lost in the darkness and sound, Sophia knew herself an older version of the emaciated girl, lonely, sad, at ease only in places such as these.

Maria! No, it couldn't be, but it was. Clearly the ruckus had been Maria no doubt insisting she come in without paying. She had her arms crossed, just as she'd done as a child when Sophia did something wrong. This Maria was twisted into someone with a thick waist, puffy face and skin the colour of an old tea bag. She wore a blue faded sweater and cord trousers. The hem on the right leg had frayed. Worse, she'd cut her formerly amazing black hair dead short. All that remained were blunt ends of grey. Aged twelve, Sophia had decided that when she grew older and stopped swimming, she would dye her own wispy middle-length hair jet-black: just like her friend's. Oh god, she was going to have to tell her about Käthe.

Maria tapped her foot: thirteen years of waiting stretched between them.

'Maria.' Sophia said, ignoring the twist of sympathy in her belly; her voice a thin wail above the music. Maria didn't know, if she had she wouldn't look so angry, she'd be sad. 'What on earth have you done to your hair?'

The barman laughed as Maria raised an eyebrow, a

rehearsed movement, and took a pack of cigarettes and lighter from her back pocket. Lit the tip, inhaled, and deliberately blew a long stream of smoke into Sophia's face. They'd promised each other they'd never smoke, *never*.

'Sophi, all grown up,' she said, 'or is it Sophia?'

There was time to walk away from this grotesque version, and not look back, not once. Sophia took a step. Maria winced. She wasn't scared, was she? No: she'd always been so much stronger. So able to joke or laugh about the things Sophia feared.

'It's Sophia.' Automatically she checked the room to see if anyone was paying too much attention, and inclined her head towards the doorway.

'Right. I didn't plan to stay.' Maria ran a self-conscious hand through her hair.

Outside in the freezing air, Sophia tried to place this woman with the girl she'd known. 'How did you know I was here?'

'Don't be so stupid.'

Why was Maria being so awful? 'I'm not.'

'Not what?'

'Stupid.'

'I rang the hotel, but they said you'd gone out.' Maria paused. 'Then I followed you. I thought you were coming to see me.'

'How did you know I was back?'

'Everyone knows.' Maria shrugged, as if such information were commonplace.

'How?'

'Oh, come on! You arrived at your mother's house and

someone phoned me. Sophi, Käthe did find you, didn't she? Tell me, has something happened?'

CHAPTER SIX

~

The two green-finned mermaids laughed, combed their black hair and gossiped - which was the brightest coral to wear? What was the best way of braiding seaweed?

'Shut up,' Sophia tried to turn over. How could a double bed be so uncomfortable? The fitted sheets made her feel like a tinned sardine. Just before dawn the mermaid faces darkened against the endless rise and fall of the ocean. One looked very much like Maria. They began to ask questions, just as Maria had done the night before, questions that bothered her. Come on, the Maria mermaid mocked, stop pretending you're above feeling pain, we were friends once, open my last envelope, read what's in it. *Think.*

When she'd told Maria that Käthe was dead, her friend had turned white and nearly fainted. Sophie had had to run back into the bar and ask for a glass of brandy, anything to revive her. Back in the warm, with the music wailing and everyone staring as her friend sobbed, Sophia had offered comfort. Later, as they walked back to the hotel, Maria had explained why they had hatched a plan. Dagmar was ill, Mia a child. They wanted Sophia to help. After three attempts at writing, Käthe had agreed to go in person, while Maria waited and worried.

There was more to it than that. Käthe's death made no sense. Maria wasn't telling her everything. Sophia had tried not to think about Petrus and that phone call, but what was clear was that Petrus had known about Mia, so he must have known that Dagmar was ill. He was a doctor and doctors were trained to heal. Petrus had always been distant, a patriarch not given to weakness. Now he was changing to a dark and sinister shadow.

Thank god first light brought with it reassuringly human chatter. Through the slightly opened window the cooks and cleaners could be heard organising their morning: who was doing what, how many guests were staying in the hotel? There'd been a complaint about the lack of towels.

'What about this awful bed?' The bedclothes gave just enough for her to turn on the side lamp. It was still too early to ring the house to ask how Dagmar was. She'd call room service and ask for coffee, cream and lots of sugar. It was the very least they could do after providing her with such a bad night's sleep. Fortified, she'd stop avoiding a past that seemed to run full tilt towards her, and open the final letter. Then she'd go and meet Maria in the arranged place.

A migraine waited, a slow beat at the base of her skull. Great. Life couldn't get any better. There wasn't time to be ill; so another idea would have to replace pain, a lighter picture. A cactus opening to the sun? That solitary flower she'd seen growing in white sand during her holiday last year: a painting trip in Sardinia. Might help, anything was worth a try. Even now the thought of white sand warmed her. Memory, though. Nothing more. Bringing any of that whiteness home, and onto a canvas, had proved impossible. The colours had changed from molten gold to cool water, and frustratingly, layer after layer of turquoise and green had appeared. She'd ended up painting her usual freezing ocean.

She needed caffeine and gallons of water. Even better: a new brain. The young voice on the end of the receiver told her, yes, they were attending to her request. Although, didn't madam realise the time?

No one called her *madam*.

***

Each sheet of paper (there were five) had the stamp 'Ministry for State Security' printed clearly on the top right corner. Stasi documentation. So there *was* more to Maria's explanation than simply trying to find her for Dagmar, or the child. Wait. Why was her father's name 'Dr Künstler', printed here, alongside the code name 'Romeo'?

Petrus had a code name. Did that mean he'd been involved with the Stasi? Oh please, she prayed. Please no. Hands shaking she answered the door to a bleary-eyed girl clutching a tray. Poured. Ladled in sugar. Drank.

'MfS' was 'Ministry for State Security'. She was holding a Stasi file with details of a 'discussion' between Herr Schenke, 'Code name Wolf', and Dr Künstler.

Wolf and Romeo? She'd laugh if she didn't feel so sick.

Herr Schenke/Wolf, reported that the Stasi had needed no persuasion to secure Romeo's medical services as a doctor in charge of athletes' care. His daughter was a potential GDR star swimmer, he was happy to be involved. Compromising photographic evidence of Agent

Hammerman and Dr Künstler had been handed to Frau Hammerman, to deal with as she saw fit. The hair of the back of Sophia's arms fizzed as her mind slid from the word 'intercourse' and 'medical services'. This was worse than anything. Her father. A member of the Stasi and a doctor.

That phone call? The man saying 'keep me informed' might that have been the other person, the one named Schenke?

Dr Ilse Hammerman's name was followed by: 'Informer on Special Mission'. Ilse hadn't simply been an informer. 'Special Mission' employees were paid to prime useful contacts who'd end up owing their lives, and the lives of their families, to the Stasi. So she hadn't been annoyed to meet the young Sophia. The meeting had been planned. Ilse would have kept tabs on whoever Sophia talked to, her training partners at swim club, Maria and all her friends in Breden.

Back inside that time, Sophia imagined Ilse bending over her desk, hair falling like angel hair across her shoulder, writing her report. Her delicate shaping of letters in a spiky left-sloping script, listing the names of who had said what and why. Ilse would have known how her relationship with Petrus affected Dagmar. She would have known when Sophia and Petrus left the GDR. Wait. Ilse could have had them stopped and brought back. Why hadn't she?

'Research Programme 08 – State Planning Theme 14.25'. What? No. She couldn't breathe. Those codes for the 'GDR Sports Association' had been cut from her memory like rancid cheese. Gone. Never to come back.

Spots danced right, then left. Coffee spilled. She wasn't going to be sick. She wasn't. 'Training and use of supportive means in order to increase performance' made her dash to the toilet and vomit. The taste in her mouth was metallic, bitter.

When she trained, they gave her pills. Supportive vitamins to make her stronger, though everyone knew the pills were not just vitamins. The injections came later. Nail-biting rushes of pure adrenaline, the sensation of unlimited power. The page rustled in her hand. There was a long list of athletes' names, steroid doses next to each. Fourth from the top was hers.

Her head hurt. She could put everything back. Reseal the envelope. Shove it in the bin. End of.

From the sink of Sophia's memory poor muscle-bound Diertha grunted her way through weight training. As her cousin, Diertha had been asked to look out for Sophia, not bully her. Unused to water, in death Diertha had appeared lumpen on the surface of Hochberg Lake, something other than human. Another image: the razorblade Sophia had kept so many years ago. Would it still be there? Waiting; in between the seat fixing and wall of both changing rooms? School and camp? That blade, her true friend, tucked away, secret and safe as she swam; learning to tighten her arm curve, how to manipulate hand flow. Would it have rusted into the wood leaving a square brown stain; that stain the only proof she had of being that girl.

Through the hotel window the sky was black, as if all signs of daybreak had been imagined. Her past was catching up. Petrus had told her not to look back. What manner of horror would appear if she looked further? A father who saved you couldn't also be the one who'd created harm, could he?

What to do? Phone Hajo? At five am? He would say she was crazy. The GDR beast couldn't be easily explained, and he so liked to have everything broken down into manageable chunks.

She rang his home number, fingers crossed; please don't let him be angry or worse, have someone else in his bed.

'Hajo?'

'Christ almighty, Sophia. This is getting to be a habit of yours. What time is it?'

'Early. Sorry.'

'And.'

'I've a letter from an old school friend. Maria? I told you about her.'

'Why would I need to know about her?'

He wasn't making it easy. Perhaps it would be better to apologise, put the phone down and ring later. 'She's sent me Stasi reports about my father and me.' There she'd said it. At least he couldn't accuse her of withholding anything more.

'Wait. Look, just give me a minute to make a coffee. I'll call you back.'

'No. No. Listen.' Damn him.

She put the phone carefully back in the receiver. Her migraine wasn't waiting, pain boomed up her neck into her eyes. Let it come, do its damnedest. Drinking the oversweet coffee in one gulp, she dressed. Sod waiting. She'd go running even though it was still dark. Running was like being with a friend, the steady rhythm a settling thing. She'd think about the contents in the envelope. The names and drugs were only one part of 'Theme 14.25', the monster the GDR had created. Under each layer of code and subterfuge, an abomination hunkered.

Outside the air was cold and damp, promising yet another grey day. A perfect morning for curses, the ones kept for running on grim days like these. Curses that made her believe she wasn't as driven or as lonely as she was. Clouds idled over the town, brown with pollution and dust from Berlin. Eventually they would drift on to Potsdam, or further to Warsaw.

Today she'd follow the Weisse Elster River to the childhood meeting place she and Maria had used: their tree that hosted the absurd informers' post-box Maria's brother had so diligently built in woodwork class.

Apart from the hotel staff and two drivers who gawked as they passed, there was no one about. Focussing on avoiding potholes, Sophia reached the river's edge. There, stretching out ahead was the partially frosted footpath. Beautiful, quiet, the tight icy air simply melted away. Running was better than having a friend because, rather than chatter, it offered solace. What to do? Who and what to investigate? Her father? Ilse? Yes, but what about those questions she'd need to ask the police about Käthe. Who might have reason to harm her, or had her murder simply been a mugging? Käthe had been coming to find her and been murdered before she arrived, so she was central to everything. Could Sophia investigate herself?

Added to the mix were Mia and Dagmar. Someone would have to look after the girl. Her father would find someone suitable. Finding willing female assistance came naturally to him. He liked company as much as he craved adoration. A weight of sadness, loss, and something else, burned: her father's lies about being involved with the Stasi. She'd not known he'd treated athletes. Not seen him at sports camp. He'd known all that had happened to her and never said. Feet thudded against the ground, a dry heat scraped behind her eyes. Bloody hell – the migraine was following. She'd have to take pills and soon.

Circling back to cross the Elster via a narrow bridge she tripped, grabbed at the wooden railing, and laughed, leaning on the rail to get her breath back. This was it! Their hiding place: weeping birches, one on either side, bent their naked branches towards the water. On the far side sombre fir trees grew and thickened into a silent, frozen forest. One overhanging birch was leaning, heavy, about to fall (she remembered it standing). The sky brightened as she stood, breathing in the past, unfolding a wintery blue layer that seemed, this early in the day, to be streaked with a mushroom grey. Leaning further over the rail, peering into the darkness under the bridge, Sophia barely registered the impulse before climbing over and sliding down the embankment. Here it was, by the main birch root. Lean forward, stretch one hand round the base – there, perfectly intact, between the bark and the stone wall, was Jörg Schöller's informer's mail-drop – still resembling an innocuous wooden bird box.

Above were the branches they'd climbed to watch Maria's much-hated brother fumble in his pocket for his payment: a pack of cheap American cigarettes. He'd check: a quick glance right left, puff on his fag and strut up and down in what he imagined was true Stasi style: thin chest out, knees high, chin jutting. Slicking back overlong hair, he'd preen to an invisible mirror and finally stuff his latest report in the box as they, Sophia and Maria, shook with silent laughter high above him in the branches. Should his mother have caught him, there'd have been hell to pay.

She craned around to look inside, but the angle was wrong and her feet weren't steady. There might be a report. A note would be useful, just to prove that things were how she remembered. Carefully she inserted two fingers. The box was wet, slimy, and empty. No. Wait. There it was, stuck to the base, wrapped in revolting soggy cling-film. She scraped her fingers against the rotting wood, pulled it out and wiped the worst of the slime on her trousers before opening and reading: 'Sophia. I know you're back. So come and see me, M.' the date, carefully written in the top left-hand corner, was yesterday.

A noise (a twig snapping?) made her slip and land awkwardly on one knee.

'I knew you'd look.' Maria was standing near the tree, her face a pale moon in the gloomy light. She pulled out her pack of cigarettes and lit up, blowing smoke out across the mud-coloured river. 'You know, Käthe was always talking about you. How you'd won this or that medal. How you'd managed to get out and not be hooked on steroids.' Maria drew savagely on her fag as Sophia winced, imagined the grey smoke turning her friend's lungs to mush.

'I'm sorry.' She did still take drugs, just not steroids. How strange it was to care what this aged version of Maria thought of her.

'Did Käthe have papers, like the ones I sent?' asked Maria.

'I told you. Käthe didn't find me,' Sophia stared at her feet, encased in green slime – they'd be a nightmare to clean, 'I found her.'

'Did she have the *papers*?'

'What papers? She just had a photo and a scrap of paper with my address in her jacket pocket.'

'Are you sure?'

'Why would I lie?'

'Yes, why would you?' Maria started climbing the bank, 'I don't suppose you or any of your colleagues has thought to tell Käthe's mother?'

No. That was Sophia's dreaded task. 'Maria? Where are you going? I thought you wanted to talk here!'

'Home. As if you care.'

What reason did Maria have to be so hateful? Sophia wanted to thump her as she had done when they were girls and argued. Maria would glower, thump her back and everything would be fine again. They walked silently through the old corn market and turned right to where the house stood mid-terrace in a long line of grey. Each terrace was a mirror image of front garden, neatly painted gate and door. Behind the dark buildings, orderly vegetable gardens bordered onto a second terrace. The pattern continued all the way to the wooden summerhouses that would, at this time of year, be empty and cold, waiting for the warmer weather.

'Well, are you coming in?'

Sophia's heart began to thump. Maria's mother, Frau Schöller, would be there, any moment now, dressed in her blue dressing gown, short black hair that curled – no matter how she tried to make it straight. She'd have a smudge of red or blue paint on her pointed nose, even though she'd only just woken up. She'd greet Sophia like a long-lost friend – like her own kin. She'd understand how much Sophia had cared for Käthe, how the shock of finding her had made her feel faint, as if all manner of horrors had joined forces. Her eyes brimmed; she'd talk to this second mother about why Maria was being so awful. She'd hug Frau Schöller, and be comforted.

The narrow hall was, as always, lined with pictures: a silver wolf howled at a blood-red moon. Sophia leaned closer: the delicate layering of oil was amazing. There were grey clouds and pale specks of rain, bright against the distant black and yellow glow that suggested thunder. Something was wrong. The wolf was staring with merciless eyes.

Why wasn't Frau Schöller taking her hand, her arm, holding her, making her welcome? There was only foul-tempered Maria standing in a kitchen surrounded by white walls stained with circles of brown mould. Worse: she was reaching, with the casualness of a long-time smoker, to light another bloody cigarette. Sophia watched the smoke drift slowly towards the ceiling. She'd have to open a window or she'd start feeling sick.

Maria flicked ash into an old coffee cup and sat down, cupping her chin in her hand. The damp in the room shifted, closing in. 'I've been trying to contact you for over a year,' she said. 'Whether you like it or not, I needed you to come back and help. I didn't know what else to do, and, now the Wall is down, I have to do something.' Maria was staring at the table, as if the dents and stains held answers. 'Sophi, Käthe wasn't the person you remember.'

'Oh?'

'She got herself in a mess after they threw her out of the discus team.'

'What?'

'She couldn't carry on without steroids, so she started running supplies across the border to pay for her drugs.'

Sophia imagined her old friend, a muscled shadow between trees, hiding in goods trains, walking through the night, afraid of everything on the outside, yet even more scared of what was inside.

'I've been collecting paperwork,' Maria said.

'But why?'

'Someone should pay for her and my mother's death.'

She'd misheard. Maria was being stupid, trying to get at her any way she could, but a small voice in her mind whispered – who would do it that way? No one joked about their mother's death.

'Sophi, you must have heard?'

'For god's sake, Maria, why would you say such a thing?' Sophia pulled out a chair, sat down heavily. Everything was wrong. Käthe and Maria had been the lucky ones, her friends who had everything, the ones who'd been safe. 'What happened?'

Maria disappeared. Sophia was about to follow when she heard her rummaging around in the sitting room; when she returned she was holding out some sort of large box wrapped in worn tissue-paper.

'Mum wanted you to have this before you disappeared over the border without telling me.' She laughed: a sound like sandpaper on wood. 'Some best friend you were.'

Sophia lifted one corner. A silverfish darted out to

weave round her wrist. She squealed. Maria really laughed, and – just like that, thirteen years melted away, leaving them flushed and awkward, glances meeting only to slide away. Oh, she'd have to take care. This was a dangerous weakness. A long-ago friendship, filled with joy, turned to grief. Sophia turned the gift the right way up. The painting was perfect: a dazzling mix of green and blue. Frau Schöller's artistic style, her flair, was in her confident brush-stroke and a use of colour Sophia could only dream of.

A sliver of blue – a mermaid! – swam with a shoal of angelfish; a guardian in the deep water. The seaweed drifted and spun, and look – just there, around the black outline of a rock, a pairs of eyes played hide and seek: a second mermaid?

'How did she die?' Sophia was crying, dripping onto the picture. She'd ruin it if she didn't stop

Maria lit yet another fag. Her mother had sold her pictures. Never too many to risk being noticed by the government. Making money for individual gain was capitalistic, so a jail offence. Jörg wanted to study to be journalist, Maria as a nurse. Because Frau Schöller had been an artist, her children were forced to train for manual work, complying with communist policy: complete change of class and profession.

'Jörg was furious.' Maria avoided looking at Sophia. 'He thought because he was working for them, he'd be treated differently.'

Jörg. Sophia thought. Where was the creepy little shit with his scribbled reports that had earned him points and cigarettes? Maria was keeping that information quiet. This was his fault, his failing.

One of Frau Schöller's landscape paintings was chosen by the council to hang in Breden town hall the day Ulbricht came to visit. He so liked her style that more pictures were commissioned. She was told to paint portraits of the great GDR leaders: Ulbricht and Honecker. They loved her pastoral scenes: mountains covered in cowslips, cathedrals and lakes, forests under a muted light. Her work, Maria said, was on display all around East German government buildings, in the town hall, the museum and library. She'd been hailed as a GDR success story, but told to keep what they called her silly nonsense: the dark shadows that crept under doors, the mermaid pictures Sophia loved, to herself. By chance an informer had gone to the opening of a new art gallery in West Berlin, he'd been following a defector, one of Frau Schöller's 'nonsense' paintings had been on the wall, priced and clearly for sale.

It would have been early when the Stasi came. No one awake to hear the first knock on the door – or the second with more force than necessary. Maria and Jörg panicking, Frau Schöller trying to calm everyone down, trying to explain, to protect her children from the officers who turned the house upside down. She would have been terrified when they took her to the waiting van. Even so, Maria said, Jörg had been certain it was all a mistake. Someone had given the officers the wrong name, the wrong address, anything but this. Initially there had been hope – plans for her imminent release, promises made. Every hope vanished when the Stasi told them they had records of how many of her paintings had been bought by Westerners.

'Your father tried to help,' Maria said. 'He collected

enough money to buy her passage to the West, but she died before they got the paperwork, or so they said. Our food parcels weren't getting through so she had almost nothing to eat, and she became ill.' Maria paused, the effort of obliterating the image of her dying mother apparent on her face.

'I should have told you about Mum in one of the letters, but it didn't seem right, plus you never answered.' Maria placed a mug of black tea on the kitchen table. 'You do remember how ill you were when you left? Your father did tell you?'

Pain, red and deep inside her stomach. A wet bruising that wouldn't ease. Sophia remembered sinking; disappearing inside the bruise. Being bundled, shaking with cold, into the back seat of Petrus' car. The endless drive through pine trees where the moonlight had drawn wolfish shadow-shapes across the top of the car. Sophia had woken at home. Maria had been holding her hand, telling her nonsense about school, while Frau Schöller painted a picture to make her well again. Frau Schöller who had called Sophia and Maria her dark mermaids and loved them for who they were.

'Don't you remember?' Maria was holding her hand. Her skin felt like rough leather, yet Sophia held on. She'd been trying to paint this exact image for years, re-working the blue sea and that bloody mermaid behind her cold grey jagged stone. Trying to get back to somewhere where someone loved her. 'Mum said the sports doctors wanted you to die. They said that was easier for everyone – as you'd never swim again.'

In that place of pain, white walls were painted with

blood. Faces melted in a milky distortion, as if an invisible hand had smeared their features. Eyes stared. Mouths opened. No words came other than a curious wailing.

'I remember,' she said, desperate to put some distance between herself and the memory of that awful sound. She was here, not there, wasn't she?

As well as painting make-believe, Frau Schöller had painted the darkness that had begun to creep into their lives. Her realistic depictions of the town had included shapes that edged out from behind doorways, eyes that watched from behind darkened windows. All that time Sophia had watched and learned how to mix oils – how to layer colour onto colour. How to paint what she saw, what she imagined and what she knew. She'd pretended so hard Maria's mother was really hers, and listened to the truth that Frau Schöller spoke. A truth that was often uncomfortable and dangerous. When she left for training camp, Frau Schöller warned her about vitamins they handed out there. She'd heard they were something more. She'd been gentle when Sophia cried; telling her that Dagmar did love her, it was only that her mother's heart had been broken. It would mend, she'd said, one day it would mend. Sophia had been comforted, grateful to the world for giving her this one person.

'I'm sorry, Sophi,' Maria said. 'I haven't asked about Dagmar, or about the child. It's a lot for Mia to take, especially at thirteen – when you know what's going on.'

'Mia's fourteen.' She'd been utterly wrong about Käthe and Maria's lives. Perhaps she could make amends, help in some small way. The wooden picture frame had begun to flake; she'd varnish it as soon as she got home. Make it perfect and whole again. 'She's Diertha's child! Can you believe it? I had no idea.'

'Are you sure she's fourteen?' Maria lit yet another cigarette.

'Maria, it doesn't matter.' Sophia glanced up to see Maria staring, a sad expression on her worn face. 'I need to know about Käthe.'

'She was going to ask you to help her, but I don't think you could have done anything. The steroids were making her really crazy. It was as if she, Käthe, wasn't there any more.'

Every time they competed, Sophia felt invincible. Before the games the drugs had to be stopped to avoid anyone being caught with them still in their system. When they were stopped, her skin felt sullied, as if it could never be clean. Stomach cramps induced vomiting. After the games came the slow decline of resilience and strength until drugs were handed out again.

'Where was she getting paperwork from?' Sophia asked as Maria bent over the sink, her hands automatically scrubbing, drying, and finally placing the worn crockery in a cupboard high on the wall.

'Me. I've papers on doping: Theme 14.25,' Maria said. 'Käthe took a few. Not from Hochberg, the training camp you went to. I sent those to you. I worked in sport centres as a nurse.' Her friend's face moved from helpful to calculating. 'I'm at the hospital now, but I'll show you the reports, if you like? But I want your promise of help before I do.'

'Maria, how did you get my address?'

'I asked Dagmar of course. So, will you promise?'

'You know I can't.'

'You're a Western police officer. You have contacts.'

'I have to talk to my boss first.' She'd be named as a former athlete who was doped. Well, she didn't care about that, but that wasn't all. If there was any way to discredit her, a way to silence her, the people who wanted all secrets to remain just so would link her to the Stasi. She'd never work as a police officer again. What to do. Walk away?

'Why do you need permission?'

'If you want anything to happen, your papers have to be properly recorded and investigated. Not handed over to me as a bribe.' She couldn't walk away, but she could leave this to her colleagues to find and act on. Käthe was dead and Maria had asked for help, so she'd help and she'd do it properly.

★★★

As she walked the short distance to the hotel, Sophia wondered how she'd got it all so wrong. In the bathroom, waiting for the water heat: a distant drone. The phone! She dashed through to the bedroom, and bashed her toe on the leg of the bed. *Shit.* Hajo.

'Stasi reports?' Hajo yawned loudly into the receiver.

'Hang on a minute.' She put the phone down and wrapped a towel around her, the mean width of it only just reached. 'My father.'

'Yes, you said your father has a Stasi file. Hang on, was he involved with them?'

'Both.' He'd be rubbing a hand through slept-in hair, leaving the stubble ridged like a wiry question mark; burly shoulders would be leaning against the back of his chair as he drank his coffee.

'And what about you?'

'No! Of course not.' How to tell him she didn't know anything, but at the same time, knew so much. 'But there's a list of athletes who were given steroids, and I'm on that list.'

'Well, you were an athlete, but what did your father do for the Stasi?'

What should she do? Tell him? Don't tell him?

'He had a code name.' She'd had a code name, but she couldn't say it, not yet.

'Really?'

'Yes.' Why wasn't Hajo here in this room, a solid force. Even with his focus on detail and sensible explanation, he'd be a comfort. 'I don't know what to do.'

'Sophia, you know I said my father was imprisoned in Siberia? Well, when he came back, we ignored his strangeness. My mother imagined he'd fit back into a normal life.' There was a pause. Please don't stop, she prayed. Tell me.

'He always went out late, so I decided to have him followed.'

'And?'

'I'm just trying to say you're not the only one with difficult parents.'

Difficult parents were one thing. A father who worked for the Stasi, another. 'What happened?'

'He was picking up young girls.'

'How young?'

'Very young. I told him what would happen if he continued, and, well, he left the next day.'

'Oh, Hajo.'

'I was bloody glad he'd gone. So, let's get on with this. What was your father's code name?'

'*Romeo.*'

'Not very original.' He laughed – a deep thrilling sound.

'It's awful. He had a mistress. I found a photo years ago in his desk. I just didn't pay it attention.'

'Why would you?'

'I should have.' She should have paid attention right from the start. Not listened to her father's fabrication, his absolute way of explaining things so that his seemed the only logic. She could have asked questions, used her skills to find out more. Instead she'd been father's little puppet, afraid of her own shadow.

Sophia dragged the phone lead from behind the bedside cabinet and moved to the window.

'I'll need to look at that list.' Hajo said.

'I know.'

'And did you find any more about our victim?'

'She was coming to find me.'

'Oh?'

'Maria had been trying to contact me by letter. I didn't answer, so Käthe came instead.' It hurt to say that she was to blame for her friend's death. 'She had papers for me, stuff about the practice of doping athletes. More names.' There was a crackling sound. Damn, she'd sat on the envelope. The paper was warm and basin-shaped. A corner of one sheet had ripped. It read 'Ministry for State Sec'.

'You'll need to speak to Käthe's parents sooner than later, ask them.'

Hajo the pedant was back, ticking his to-do list.

'Have you any test results?'

'Not yet, but we will.' He paused. 'By the way, I've sent you the inspection list. It should arrive at your mother's today. The chief of police, Inspector Martin Rathmann, is an old friend from college; you can ask him for whatever you need.'

What? He was asking her to trust an old friend, someone who'd worked for years in this town? Her head really hurt.

'Are you serious?' Bloody Hajo. Why couldn't he come to Breden and do his own stupid inspection? He and Martin could talk about old times together; they could put the world to rights.

'Why wouldn't I be? Martin's a solid bloke.'

'You're being an idiot, Hajo. Your old mate's been living in Breden for years.'

Martin Rathmann would have had contact with the Stasi, it was impossible not to. Now he'd be told to inform on his Eastern colleagues as part of his reconciliation package, ending with his retirement. Somewhere in the police station was a record of every trip Käthe had made, every arrest. Those reports were the ones being systematically burned.

'What about your old friend?' Hajo asked.

He had a point. Maria was an old friend. She'd summoned Sophia home as if she had every right, as if Sophia would do something with the collected information. Who to trust? She should tell Hajo about Maria's proposed deal. Her friend could be weaving a web in which to catch her, so she would be forced to do whatever Maria wanted. Worse – what might the connection between Herr

Schenke and her father uncover?

It seemed like a very good idea to dump the papers on the floor and lie down. The shower was running. In a few moments the water would be hot enough to loosen knotted muscle. Could she really survive here until Thursday?

CHAPTER SEVEN

~

Gerda was in one of her moods. As soon they got to school, she flounced across the car park and ran up the stairs to the main hallway to catch up with beaky-nose Tessa – who did everything Gerda told her to do. Tessa made a rude sign at Mia who trailed slowly behind. As they stood outside the classroom waiting to go in, Gerda deliberately turned away.

Gerda had said she was going to ignore her all day – because Mia had gone to Berlin without her. Mia had stared out of the window of the school bus and imagined the hours turning into a day, a week, a whole term where she wouldn't have a best friend. Better to disappear quietly, without a fuss. Be totally unnoticeable. What made it worse was that they'd had so much fun last night. Hardly sleeping – just talking. Gerda's mum pausing outside the door every so often; meaning they had to shove their giggling faces into the old smelly cushions.

Waiting by the classroom door, ignoring the treacher-ous heat building behind her eyes, she thought rather fiercely about Berlin and the things she'd *not* told Gerda. How she'd cried, instead of being brave. How the park had seemed spooky – although it had just been damp and dirty.

She'd lied, saying that Sophia had been nice. Making up how she'd been invited into her apartment and asked a million questions about Oma and her home town. It had sounded so much better that way.

It was maths, and maths was easy. The numbers fitted together into neat solutions with clear answers. Herr Stringer said she was a good student and, well, it was great to be good at *something*. Mia walked over to a desk as far away from Gerda and the others as she could and sat on her own, ignoring their thick-headed whispers. Best to pretend today was just another day.

As the teacher began to talk, Gerda sidled away from Tessa to come back to sit by Mia. She whispered: 'You missed the worst homework' and dug her elbow into Mia's side. It really hurt. Mia shoved her back even harder, and just like that everything was all right and they were friends again.

Mia had woken really early, thinking, deciding that she was going to make sure Oma got better. Before Gerda starting chattering, she'd thought up a list. First, and most important, Petrus had to stay– he was a doctor and he could make sure that Oma had the right medicine. Second, when Oma was better, Petrus could go back to Berlin. Third was Sophia. The problem was it was difficult to decide whether she was Nasty Woman any more. Maybe not, because of the dragonfly hairgrips, and the thing that had happened in Oma's kitchen. It was as though Sophia knew when Mia was feeling upset. Not only that, she knew what to do about it. Weird. Though even weirder was Petrus and Sophia's disagreeing about everything. She'd heard them arguing that night in Berlin, when they thought she was fast asleep. She'd so very nearly got up, but the bed had been warm and she'd been so tired. Sophia acted as if she had a secret, something she had kept forever, but didn't want. Petrus was like all the older people here, afraid to say too much, careful, because you never knew who might be listening. Which one should she trust? Maybe Oma only hated Petrus because he'd left. Maybe Sophia wasn't really nasty? Mia really needed to trust someone because Oma was ill and Oma was all she had. Today she'd talk to Petrus. She'd ask him straight out: what is going to happen to me and Oma?

The teacher told them to get out their books and turn to page twenty-one. Algebra? Easy-peasy. Mia touched her dragonfly. Gerda had hassled like crazy to borrow the second one but she had said No Way.

What about her birth certificate? How daft not to have thought of it before. She'd find it and then she'd know who her father was and perhaps ask him if he'd help.

Herr Stringer was collecting in last week's homework. He paused by Mia's desk, smiled and welcomed her back. They'd all missed her, he said. Yeah right, a likely story. Mia smiled politely, and bent down to fill out the answers in her book.

Gerda had actually done her homework. Mia waited until she'd handed it in with a dramatic flourish, Herr Stringer sighing as he took the messy scrap of paper.

'Gerda,' she whispered. 'Have you ever seen your birth certificate?'

'No. Don't be stupid! Why?'

Before the Wall came down it was different; even Gerda did her work, and at the start of each day the class had to stand as their teacher marched in. He would call out: 'For Peace and Socialism, are you prepared?'

They had to reply: 'Yes, always prepared.'

God, it had been so embarrassing. Mia was sure they were the only people in the world to have done such moronic things. Gerda had always made a face, screwing up her eyes, sucking in lips while Mia had kept her expression blank, mouth tight. You got into real trouble if you made fun of stuff like that. She'd finished. Best to re-check though, just to make sure. Gerda chewed her lip: her exercise book was covered in inky blotches and streaks where she'd half-heartedly attempted to write (mostly the wrong) solutions.

There were new questions on the board. Nudging Gerda, Mia placed her book sideways. Gerda began to copy furiously as Mia slowly wrote out the new exercises. Gerda was only lazy because Elke, like so many mums, worried about everything. Was the weather too hot or too cold? Did Gerda's room need cleaning again? Should Gerda walk to school or catch the bus? She went on and on about how much school work they had. Imagine having her as a mother! Oma wasn't like that at all. She didn't freak out at the smallest thing, like not cleaning her room or eating in the sitting room. In fact, recently she'd not been bothered by anything other than trying to get up in the morning, or trying to cook supper.

The thought just sneaked in, uninvited, treacherous. Oma was really ill. What if she were going to die? There would be no one to look after Mia. No one at all. They might give Oma the wrong medicine. Hook her up to the wrong machine. Give her an injection she didn't need, the injection they gave to old people that doctors couldn't be bothered to treat.

She couldn't breathe. Her pencil had drawn dark squiggles across the page. Gerda stopped writing and stared. The stupid pencil gave a dry crack and snapped. The numbers on the page blurred – eight became zero, four dissolved, and from a long way off she heard Gerda say: 'Herr Stringer. There's something wrong with Mia.' The teacher was putting his hands on her shoulders, gently pulling her to her feet saying: 'Perhaps you should go and see the nurse?'

Everyone stared. Mia heard Tessa giggle just as their teacher told her to be quiet, and the class to get on with their work.

The corridor was silent. Mia's shoes squeaked all the way to the girls' toilet. What to do? She couldn't turn up at the nurse's room crying like they used to in primary school. The school toilets were awful. If you *had* to pee, you had to squat on the toy seat and risk having someone haul themselves up and peer down at you, laughing, making gagging noises. Worst was if you had your period. If that happened, you could go to the nurse's room and ask to use theirs, but then, of course, everyone knew.

She leaned over the baby-size sink and ran cold water over her hands, face and neck. She couldn't stop crying. Should she phone Sophia? Petrus? Who would help? Who could she trust? Not Gerda who took her friendship away whenever she felt like it. Not Petrus, not Sophia. Then who? Mia counted to ten, twenty, fifty. What should she to do? Phone Oma? Well, that was just stupid. Oma would be in hospital by now. She'd thought everything would be all right as soon as she'd got help. Well, it wasn't. It was worse, because they weren't pretending anymore. Oma was going to die and no one would want to look after her. She sat on the floor with her head between her knees and sobbed.

Sophia. Sophia would come if she were asked. Somehow she just knew she would. Petrus was the one who knew how to make Oma better, but Sophia? Since being so horrid that first night, she'd been kinder, more like a big sister. The thought brought on a fresh wave of sobbing. The door opened. Gerda was holding her tight, saying everything would be all right. Mia hugged her back and tried to believe what she said as a new voice, clear and icy – like *Sophia's* – told her to stop being childish: nothing would ever be the same again.

'You really need to blow your nose.' Gerda leaned away, peering in the mirror to check that no concealed spot was about to erupt from her already pitted skin. She scowled. 'Mia, you can stay with us you know.'

Mia tried to smile. She'd give anything to go home and hide in her bed, in her own room and pretend that everything was quiet and safe. Gerda's room was jangly, a total mess of make-up, concealer, hairbrushes and face lotion, chucked all over the place as Gerda went from one fashion extreme to the other. Mia would rather die than tell her she liked having stuff folded away – neat and tidy.

She opened the door but paused, looking back at Gerda, busy squeezing a zit.

'I'm going to ask Nurse to call Sophia. She'll come and get me, I know she will. She'll take me to the hospital. D'you want to come?' Gerda would say no, no one wanted to sit for hours in a room that smelt of pee and disinfectant. Once Mia was at the hospital she'd ask Petrus what was going to happen. She'd watch him really carefully and see if Oma was right, and he wasn't the nice grandfather Mia wanted him to be. Plus, she'd try and get to know Sophia better. She'd be really polite and then, when they were talking, she'd dare to ask her about Diertha, and who her father might be. She'd be a detective, just like Sophia. She'd put clues together. It was better to have a plan than nothing at all.

They went together to the nurse's office, Gerda obviously happy in the knowledge that she was missing the rest of maths. As they walked down the corridor, she began doing an incredibly daft imitation of Herr Stingy telling Tessa to be quiet.

'Silence!' she hissed, waving her arms, eyes bulging from her sockets, and Mia choked out a laugh.

***

Sophia smiled her version of friendly at the young couple sitting by the main window that looked out to a narrow cobbled street. The hotel breakfast room had been redecorated, leaving a faint tang of fresh paint. Perhaps as a way of showing new guests how much had changed since the Wall came down?

The couple greeted her with nods and smiles, continuing to eat as Sophia chose a table by a different window, as far away as possible without seeming rude.

She'd slept, sprawled on the top of the bed with the shower running. Now it was nearly mid-morning and she'd only just managed to convince the hotel staff to let her in the breakfast room by pointing out that the two lovebirds were still eating.

Through the window, just to the right, the street opened out into a rustic, pretty market place. Although there was no market today, the shops surrounding the square were busy. The couple whispered, leaning close. How *sweet*. The young man, apple-cheeked with severely back-combed pale hair, spread soft cheese onto a corner section of toast. He offered it to his love. The dark-haired girl giggled. She tried to sneak it back towards him with: 'Don't be such a silly.'

Her creamy skin and sharp nose contrasted rather oddly with her soft brown eyes. The young man tried it again and they laughed, glancing sideways at Sophia, who pretended not to notice how young they were and how doltishly in love. They were just like children playing with a sparkly new toy. New toys were easily dented; they broke, or simply lost their dazzle.

She helped herself to rolls, ham and a miniscule bowl of what looked like strawberry jam. She wanted nothing more than to find Petrus and make him tell her everything, an action that would produce nothing but lies, or silence. So, she played her favourite game of pretend. The one in which she was a person who travelled the world. Someone who was, at this very moment, waiting for her husband to come down to breakfast: a model husband of course, one who never lost his sparkle. There would be a different life, a better one, full of friends, fun and laughter – perhaps even love. Hajo's green eyes, keen and searching, made her belly hot with longing. He'd trusted her to be a capable officer, shown her how to take criticism and when not to snap as others laughed, or teased her. Somehow he had become a beacon. A point to which she turned, knowing that his was the right way.

Petrus's sly voice breathed in her ear: careful, don't lose yourself. Keep to the straight and narrow. Stick to the rules. Rules are good; they keep you safe and moving forward.

What, she wondered, gazing out at the street, would it be like to rest her body against Hajo's backbone, to hold tight, be one, a half that needed the other. Like a half of an orange, or a lemon? What a daft idea. She'd be a fruit with thorns and, rather than thinking of love, she'd think about work and act as would any other police officer. She'd investigate and find out facts and proof, as she always did. But where to start? So many ideas battled for first place.

The last thing she'd written in her police-issue note-book was 'How do I tell Käthe's parents?' Pathetic, hardly investigative detail. The words 'Romeo and Herr Schenke?' made her queasy. She had to think like a police officer, not a scared child who had fled the GDR.

Rules, that was it. Rules were wonderfully simple. She'd write a 'to-do' list, not a rambling, incoherent mess of panicky thought.

One: the awful duty to go to Käthe's parents and tell them about their daughter. Two: collect her post and check specific detail about her visit to the police station. Three: find that sneaky little shit Jörg. Four: the files Maria had spoken about needed to be secured. Five: Petrus, how involved was he? Could he have had a part in Käthe's death? No. He couldn't be, but could Herr Schenke have been the man on the phone? Six: find Käthe's paperwork. All of it. Every last scrap so that she could truly know what had happened to her.

Time to get a move on. Hajo was a stickler for rules. He'd have to decide if her involvement as a former athlete rendered her unable to pursue any investigation, and if he did, she'd be told to go home.

'I won't though. I'll stay here and get every one of you,' she muttered, knowing she might have to convince Maria to hand over any papers without a true promise, then keep them safe from the GDR police until Hajo sent in a team. He would. When she revealed the extent of the monster she was facing, he'd believe and act.

A slim young woman with a razor sharp blonde bob moved energetically across the dining room, heading towards Sophia with a neatly folded note in her hand. Apologising for the disturbance, she explained there'd been a call from the secretary at Town School 13. Someone called Mia Künstler was in the school sickroom. She needed collecting. Was it possible that Frau Künstler could go?

Had Mia actually asked for her? She'd been unkind to the child. Hurt her when she came asking for help. Nearly refused her entry. It was only the fact that she'd recognised Dagmar's handwriting that made her listen to the child's explanation that night. She may have been unkind, but knew only too well what it was like to be unwanted, to be a responsibility rather than a joy. She'd bought the child hairgrips. Did that make her care? No, but somehow Mia was never far from her thoughts.

Sophia took the well-remembered bus route from her

childhood address to her former school: drive across town, turn right at the town hall, take the main road and turn left into the school car park. She'd collect Mia from the sick room and take her to the hospital, then go straight to Käthe's parents.

Strange that every turning took her through unknown backstreets into a new housing estate where one block of flats followed another. As she crawled along, peering out of the window for anything that looked like a road sign, a round woman in a pale lavender housecoat leaned out of her window and shouted, 'Clear off!' Sophia turned and parked directly beneath the window, leaned out and stared up at the house until the woman ducked inside and shut the window with a bang. Sophia laughed. Better to mock them. To be more as she really was. Fearless. Strong. She leaned back and closed her eyes, tracing the childhood route. Petrus, harassed, already late – telling her to hurry up; Dagmar, holding out a mid-morning snack. Cake or biscuits?

The memory of a kiss? Her mother's lips whispering against her hair? That had never happened, had it?

Close the front gate. Turn right. Cross over the road. She began driving in the direction she imagined was correct. There it was! The shortcut via Maria's house. No way was she going to look at the sweetshop, nor glance at her friend's home. Frau Schöller was gone, so she'd have to make sure Maria was there when she spoke with Jörg. As a child, she'd been afraid of his constant vigilance, sneaking after her and Maria when they didn't want him. He'd cornered her once. She'd been waiting for Maria, and there he was, grinning, sallow-faced and sharp-eyed. He'd come close until there was no space left between her, the brick wall, and him. He'd reached into his trousers and taken out something that (to her terrified child mind) looked purple, swollen and angry. He'd rubbed it, then forced her to touch it. As she did he'd groaned, swearing a long line of filthy words as white pudding came out. How she'd enjoy seeing his face when he realised there were no similarities now to the girl she'd been.

★★★

Stuck in a sea of concrete, with a flat roof that filled with water in the winter and smelt of dead things in the summer, Town School 13 was exactly as remembered. At the furthest side of the car park, silver birch trees grew. Her story trees: reaching up so much higher than before.

In her final summer at primary school, the teachers, too exhausted to conjure up adventurous themes, had told them to paint or draw one aspect of their school life. Sophia had covered the page with earthy brown before drawing grey and silver tree roots stretching for miles under the school's concrete icing. The idea had developed, as they skipped and played, because the adults had seemed as distant as the moon. They'd talked in pairs or tight white clusters. She'd painted her people white because they were quiet and frightened. To give them somewhere safe she'd drawn the grown-ups an underground world, sketching the groups a way to communicate by linking tree roots so that people, like the trees, could have silent, private conversations. The teacher hadn't liked it. She'd placed the picture on the homework table and, as everyone's work went on display, Sophia's disappeared. Eventually she'd spied her trees branching out from the classroom bin.

Sophia stretched, hands reaching up to the sky, spine snapping. 'Bloody teachers.'

In the entrance hall, the same low table and three apricot-coloured chairs sat on a circle of brown carpet, an island in an ocean of linoleum. On the table stood the ever-present flower display; each petal bristling. Woe betide any student who came too close. High on the facing wall hung portraits of past headmasters. Each moustached face gazed into space, looking important and serious. Maria had made rude faces at them. Sophia glanced round, screwed up her face, and poked out her tongue.

The sharp-featured receptionist didn't seem to need a name. She glanced at Sophia who had her hair tied back as usual, black boots done up tight, wishing belatedly that she'd worn her uniform.

'Mia Künstler,' the woman said, inspecting her perfect manicure, 'is on her way.'

It was quiet, the kind of silence that descends only momentarily on a school. A hush that indicates all are doing what they're supposed to be doing. Mia had better hurry up. The thought of being in the building when the break bell rang was faintly terrifying.

Three full minutes crawled by, the clock-hand moving ominously nearer break-time. Time to find Mia. She knew the way to the nurse's room; had been there often enough with bumps, bruises, and, occasionally, tears. Striding past the display boards, boots squeaking loudly, Sophia slowed and moved on with care, balancing on her toes. The displays were great, better than in her day when they'd had pictures of their leaders lining the corridor. Now a recent trip to Leipzig was presented as a story in photos. Outside St Nicholas Church, groups of children turned to the camera and stood, arms wrapped round each other, eyes searching for evidence (a chip in the wall from a bullet?) of the famous Monday freedom demonstrations.

The last board glinted, caught her eye. A shimmering purple headline: 'Our Famous Students' listed the names of head girls and boys, was followed by the names and pictures of pupils who had gone on to do great things. Gudrun (Gudi) Neuberg had become a Professor of Biochemistry.

There was the same picture she had tucked in her pocket. Käthe Niedermann, crouched inside her ring, arms flexing, about to circle before hurling the disc. Oh shit, they didn't know she was dead. Sophia flinched, bit her bottom lip. Squeezed into Lycra, the GDR logo stretched across her chest, her muscled body made her look like a cartoon figure – a dancing hippo. Poor Käthe who'd done nothing more than try and be the best.

For goodness' sake. Please no. Where had they found it? Stuck between photos of the two-hundred metre runners, Padma and Miep, was a picture of Sophia and her father. Petrus was standing tall, as if the world were spinning on the axis of himself and the child. The girl held up a medal with ribbon. The medal glinted in the sun. She was smiling.

Sophia peeled the photo from the display. It came away with a sucking noise. The backing paper ripped as she tried to smooth it back into place. The folded picture fitted neatly into her trouser pocket.

Outside, the playground air was cool enough to calm hot skin. She gazed around: how everything had changed, but, at the same time, remained exactly the same.

The bell rang; a jarring drone. Children poured out of classrooms. Chattering and jostling, they raced to the canteen and further out into the playground. Sophia, arms by her sides, became an island in the tide. What if she moved sideways? A child's backpack dug into her back. Ouch. These weren't students, this was a rioting crowd.

Four feet from her original spot, Sophia now faced a pale blue building with double doors. A teacher, wearing a dark jacket and contrasting green tie, emerged from one of the bungalows. To avoid being asked who she was Sophia ducked inside the doors. This was the nurse's room, no question. Next to the toilets would be a door that opened to a waiting area and the sick bay.

The hallway was old and dry and *wrong*. A distant clicking from the other side of the double doors was followed by the smell of chlorine. The world tilted. The tingling sensation that had begun in her fingers now ran up both arms. She edged sideways toward the second set of doors. Opened them and stared at blue and white tiles winking through a yawning expanse of white water.

Head down, legs splayed, she sat on a moving floor, forcing breath in and out. Bright rippling water. The beefy red-veined face of her swimming coach. Hands clapping. Mother smiling. She was going to puke. Sophia crawled. Hunched over the toilet with its child-sized rim, she retched, listened. No sounds. No voices. Just the click click of chlorine dripping into whiteness. Everything was wrong; she couldn't be frightened of water and chlorine? It was all coming back. She remembered him: the beefy-faced man at the edge of the pool. He'd hurt her. Just as

Jörg had, only much worse, because there had been nowhere to hide, and he could make her do whatever he wanted.

Sometime later, mouth rinsed, the tingling in her hands was replaced by an almost welcome headache. The things that had happened at sport camp, the instances she'd imagined forgotten, were not forgotten at all. She'd simply changed them to become part of what she did now. The drugs she took when she went dancing had replaced the steroids that her coach insisted she swallow, her dancing – a form of swimming. And sex? Well, she'd never dared to love. An image caught at her. Lying beneath her last partner as he laboured, intent on his release, just as the beefy-faced man had done when she was still a child.

Oh please. Where was her safe place? The place to hide, the room where everything was neat and tidy and made sense. Sophia tried to stand, but the world tipped sideways before tilting the opposite way as she edged along the wall, past the door, into the changing rooms. She counted: one, two, three – stopping at the fourth cubicle to implore the world to stand still before she found the cramped seat, and fainted.

Child hands. Touching her. Someone was trying to suffocate her. At the same time those hands pulled her back from the comfortable nothingness. Sophia tried to swipe them away.

Mia's voice ballooned through the mist.

'Stop being so dense and breathe into this,' the Mia voice ordered, and a paper bag was placed around her mouth. Sophia breathed in a mouthful of breadcrumbs and spat.

'Bloody hell, get off.' A crumb lodged itself in the back of her throat. She coughed. Someone was holding her hand. Mia. Sophia grabbed and held on.

Outside the cubicle the school nurse hovered and fussed: 'Dear. I *am* the nurse,' she repeated, trying ineffectually to get the girl out of the way. Mia had somehow managed to get Sophia's trousers wet. The girl mopped the damp patch enthusiastically with a square towel. A pink flannel appeared. Mia placed it across Sophia's forehead; the cool of it was utter bliss.

'Mia. How long have I been here?' Thank god the child had found her. She wanted to weep with the weight of remembering.

'Ages. I was waiting, and some of my class found you. What were you doing?' Mia leaned closer, eye to eye. 'Now listen. I'll let you sit here for a few minutes, but you're going to have to get up or they're going to carry you out in a stretcher.' With that she vanished.

In that moment of stillness Sophia knew she had to let go of her father's orders. She had to discover what had happened to her while she was a child swimmer. Perhaps once she knew, she'd be free? Reaching to the left, her fingers inched down the crack that separated bench from wall. Ah, there it was, rusting quietly in between the damp brickwork and cement.

The blade came away from its hiding place with little resistance, settling in her hand just as if it had come home. Silently she told Petrus she was sorry, but she had to risk everything, because she wanted, so much, to be able to live. And then she began to remember.

CHAPTER EIGHT

~

Hochberg 1973

Her body folded sideways on the narrow bench (feet high so no one would see) Sophi relaxed into the smell of damp tiles, old urine and sweat. She let her head sink to her knees, waiting to make sure no one had noticed she'd stayed behind. The changing cubicle remained blissfully silent and warm, as if the narrow space was just for her. However, she was a child inside the body of a giant – and couldn't stretch out without either breaking through the door or reaching high over the cubicle wall.

The cleaners were mopping the pool sides with Wolfasept: a mixture of bleach and soap. Soon they'd move on to the men's changing room, leaving (as if by prior agreement) her private space until last.

As the overwhelming smell of bleach drifted in through the main door, Sophi raised her head, sniffing the familiar scent, the scent of the place that had become home. Soon she'd shower. As long as they were out there, she was alone with no surveillance, no one watching or listening – free and silent as the stars.

She flexed her broad shoulders round and back, pulling back bone, moving thick muscle, as much as the space allowed; placed her feet on the floor. Next to her sat a box of plasters. Innocently skin-coloured, they were her secret companions, accompanying her where no one else could. Sophi lifted the box. Shook it gently. Only three left; somehow she'd have to get more. Her fingers were thick and clumsy as she fumbled to take one out. A prickle of tension began at the base of her neck and she reminded herself: it's all right – you're made of saltwater and speed: a torpedo under the waves, inside the tide you can move through water. You're a dark mermaid.

The plaster slipped, floating towards the bench, falling through the gap in the wood to the floor. In a flash, she seized it from the wet tiles just before the adhesive soaked up damp and became useless.

One of the cleaners had already moved to the men's changing room. Not long, she didn't have long. To her left, between the wall and the seat, was just enough space to keep and hide the blade. She wedged two fingers into the gap and the razor slid into her greedy fingers; ready to soothe, cut, let tension out.

There'd been another injection. The sting: needle-breaking flesh, heralding a wild roaring speed one hour later. Her trainer had smirked and preened, nodding to the others as she muscled through the water, making it clear she was a winner. The plans he had to ride on her success story were common knowledge. He'd been bragging about an even bigger car, a holiday abroad after the first International Swimming Federation Championship in Yugoslavia, and the whispered promise of a place in politics. Yes, he was happy letting her take more pills, working her even harder.

Sophi turned over her right arm, running fingers gently across the ridged scars that were healing; though not fast enough. She'd had sidelong glances from the other girls, and couldn't risk more attention.

The still damp swimming costume stuck to her back. It had become overstretched and worn with use, so she'd ask for another. Pulling down the straps, Sophi looked at her breasts – pink perched jellies with a thick brown raisin stuck on top. The muscle on her torso and arms took up so much room she could be anything between boy and girl. Her stomach was flat and toned, but a line of thick hair wormed down from her belly button; spreading a forest between her legs. She didn't look there. Maybe so much hair was normal – maybe. Other things happened there. Sometimes she swelled, grew hot, tingling so badly that she had to run, hide in the toilet and rub, tension rising, squeezing as she groaned. Heat bursting into her stomach and heart, making her cry out and moments later; weep.

She let others do that to her now: girls with clever fingers and tongues; wet and slippery, whispering or groaning. Boys and men that grunted and made crude promises as they prodded their *thing* hard up inside her.

Sophi was forgetting who she was.

Her periods had started three months ago and she couldn't get used to the cramps that came with it, nor the strange object she was supposed to shove deep in there to hold her blood.

Thirteen years old and she thought she was going mad with wanting. She wanted to die, to live, run, dance, swim, never stop doing sex until she was loose and deliciously spent – and that never lasted.

Sophi traced a cut along her left breast, the thin slice releasing a trail of wet red bubbles that popped across her skin, opening up a stream that drifted towards her nipple. She sighed; this weave of metal on soft flesh was delicious, tension easing to a soft, gentle whisper.

Along with injections there were now even more pills. Pills that would stop her monthly bleed: their golden girl couldn't miss training, not for anything. She'd asked her father about the vitamins once. Papa said not to worry, they weren't going to make her ill. Part of her whispered it was treacherous and wrong. Now, whenever she went home, she looked in his medical books and knew the drug she was taking was called Oral-Turinabol. The book said the tablets, one pink, one blue, were chlordehydromethyl-testosterone. So far she'd looked testosterone up in the dictionary, and freaked when it said how men had it. They were injecting her to make her strong, more like a man. That was why she grew hair on her face, and swelled up, down there. Of course Papa was a good doctor, he didn't know about the things that happened, the secret things in the white room, underground, far away from the normal training centre.

Sophi slid her hand across the red cut, licked her finger, gently rubbing spit across the wound, cleaning away the blood. She cut another line just below and leaned back, eyes closed, swimming in a purple rapture.

Clumsy. Fast. She pulled the costume down to her thighs, drawing a finger through thick hair until it was inside her. The relief was instant, a long trembling shudder that had her gasping and crying out, hips dipping up and down as if the boy were there with her. She cried, tears dripping on her burning face and bent down, about to pick up the wet costume.

The last cut was deeper than she realised. Sophi heard waves breaking on a stone beach, the grating pebbles heaving sand under foam. A hush as the white swill eddied and swung from left to right, milling, waiting for the next wave.

She woke slumped against the concrete wall, cold and pimpled, costume on the floor. There was someone tapping on the cubicle door, tentative but persistent. A woman's voice called 'Are you all right?' In the distance came the echo of another call, but this time it came from a voice used to being obeyed.

'Künstler, Sophia Künstler. Where the hell are you?'

She scrambled to her feet, shaking. 'I'm right here, about to shower.'

Thank god. Her trainer slammed the outside door. He wouldn't come in because the cleaning women were here. Sophi had a flash of his face above hers: red veins bulging. Lips tight. Eyes closed. Sweating. Panting.

She opened the door and stared into the eyes of the woman who stood, hand on her mop, about to knock again. Stare them down, she thought. Stare them down. The woman's eyes slid to Sophi's breasts and she swayed, put her hand over her mouth, eyes widening, backing away as the handle of the mop slapped against the floor.

Sophi closed the door and sat down again. It was all right. Everything was all right. She picked up the swimming costume and the nearly empty plaster box, placing the blade carefully back in its home and left the cubicle, walking calmly to the shower block. Eyes firmly on the ground as the woman mopped the floor. It suited them both to ignore what had happened. The code was simple: look after yourself, see nothing.

Calm, she dried and dressed. The plasters pulled as they held each cut together – healing. Now she was ready to face *him* with a plausible excuse.

The cleaning woman was crying. Sophi touched her shoulder, the crisp feel of dry cotton, comforting, unfamiliar, so far away from all she knew. Alone, she turned towards the dark music that evening was sure to bring.

***

1990

Time to leave the changing room. No way was she letting the nurse check her blood pressure or whatever it was she wanted to check. Mia's open mouth. The muttered, 'Are you insane? You can't drive the car, you just fainted,' made absolutely no difference. No doctors or nurses, thank you. There had been quite enough of them before. Plus there were stronger medicines back in the hotel room, though amazingly any signs of a headache had fled.

The girl was blessedly silent all the way to the hospital. They visited the pharmacy and gift shop to buy stomach settlers, a bottle of water and a glossy knitting magazine for Dagmar. Mia tried to convince Sophia to come to the ward. No, better not, she'd calm herself, drink her water and try to ignore the fact that her mother was lying, desperately ill, on the other side of the swinging doors.

The corridor grew dark under a low hanging cloud as she worked up the courage to go and face Käthe's parents.

A nurse rushed round the corner with a pile of notes under her arm. The file on the bottom had tilted to show the words: 'Methylated Androgen': steroids.

A feral young girl was pelting through the woods with a group of athletes whose feet streamed across the ground. Running until their lungs were about to burst. The young girl was her. The young Sophia climbed a tree, laughing as one or two joined her. Others mated – that was the only word for it, mated – by the tree roots, their gasps and groans making the others roar with laughter. The climbers leaped from the branches to rip young sapling trees from the ground with their bare hands. *Baumausrissen*, they'd called it. *Baumausrissen*. A test of who was the strongest.

Clutching her half-empty bottle of water, Sophia ran for the safety of her car. A brown file lay across the dip in the passenger seat: Dagmar's medical notes. Petrus must have tried to find her and put the papers in the car – but he didn't have a key. Head down, she drove to the hotel, locked the door and wedged the back of a chair under the door handle; she wasn't going anywhere until she'd calmed and felt herself again.

Dagmar's medical notes would be routine, but best take look, keep an eye on everything father did. In July '75, the doctor had prescribed low-level painkillers; in November antidepressants. She'd known her mother suffered from depression, but Dagmar had been better when they left in '77, Petrus had said so. More appointments followed, closer together: February to May '77. So, yet again, he'd lied, Dagmar hadn't been better at all.

The doctor's cautious notations described 'acute episodes of agitation' following an order for 'necessary' interrogation. What? Stasi interrogation? The interrogation order was signed by 'Romeo'. No. Was it possible that Petrus orchestrated such an action the day he and Sophia left the GDR? A deliberate ruse to keep the Stasi focussed on Dagmar rather than himself? Had Dagmar been interrogated because they'd escaped? Somewhere, in the midst of reading, Sophia began to weep.

She'd left Breden thinking Dagmar didn't care. Her mother had been ill, terrified of what would follow if her husband and daughter fled, but she'd stayed to face the Stasi and their never-ending questions. Why? Because her mother had loved her and wanted her to be safe? Or was it something else? Hang on, the timeline didn't make sense. Diertha had died in May '76. Petrus had told her how 'Dagmar cared for the child soon after we left'. What? While she was being interrogated? It didn't seem possible. Would the hospital have agreed to such a thing? More confusing were the dates. Diertha had drowned *before* the games, not after, so how long had Dagmar been caring for a child?

The Montreal Olympics had been in August '76; Sophia had come home triumphant with gold. She remembered cheering crowds. Smiles and damp handshakes from important people she didn't know. Then a hospital, and feeling very ill. Had she seen Dagmar during that time? Yes, there was a brief memory of a pale-faced mother bending down to kiss her, but how could she not have known about Diertha's six-month-old child?

In the drawer by the bed the ruinous blade waited. Picking it up again, she gently ran a finger along the rusty pitted metal. Useless. The disintegrating alloy, just like the one at home, was singing the same strange song of pain and wild release, of deliciously silent places where no one ever found you. She rubbed her nail against the flat edge and sniffed. Unmistakable: miniscule particles of her thirteen-year-old blood had turned as dirty as brown rust.

Her past inside 'Theme 14.25' was slowly unravelling. As she tried to catch hold of it only portions emerged, bright and perfectly assembled: as a scene on the inside of a toy snowstorm shaker. No moment seemed to connect with the others so as to make sense – and she so liked making sense. It was vital no one knew about this ancient secret relic. Or the new blade that sat, year in year out, in the bedside drawer in Berlin, a silver reminder that she was never ever going back to being a part of the machine that had moulded her from child to programmed athlete.

She'd forgotten the beefy-faced man. His rapid, stale breath as he edged his tongue between her clenched teeth. He'd drive his penis into her, time and again so she bled. When she cried out he'd come: jerking, labouring. Grunts, wet gasps spilling from his open mouth, eyes closed, head back, his neck stretching up to the sky. Now she remembered the silver blade. The bite of that knife as it cut away hope, sliced away her childhood – leaving nothing but a machine that did her trainer's bidding.

It was useless re-reading everything. The more she read the angrier she became. She whispered 'sorry' to Käthe. She simply couldn't face visiting her parents, and worse, by now they'd undoubtedly already know. But she couldn't stay here and think, she had to do something.

CHAPTER NINE

~

Petrus was speaking in his too-cheerful grown-up voice; the one he'd used when Oma refused to get in the car. Everything was 'all right', he said, so straightaway Mia knew it wasn't. They'd been at the hospital for hours. Oma had fallen asleep in the metal bed with a plastic under-sheet that burped each time she moved. There were tubes coming out of her arm but, worst of all, Oma looked and smelled like a dead person.

Dead. If she didn't stop thinking about it Right Now, she'd start crying and wake her. Better to think about Sophia, bad-tempered, pig-headed Sophia, who had got lost in the school while Mia waited by the car in the parking area like a complete idiot. Her friends had been just about to come out for break. Gerda would've seen her and thought she was lying about going to the hospital.

She'd had to go back to the medical room and wait – all over again. It had to have been *her* class that went into the changing rooms to get ready for games. Someone (thank god not Gerda or Tessa) found Sophia and rang the nurse. Mia had run to see what was happening. Everyone had stared, then chattered excitedly: this was the perfect excuse not to go out to games. They couldn't get changed now, could they? Mia explained that the fainting woman was Frau Künstler, but the teacher had given her a funny look – as if he knew who she was. 'Stop gawping,' he'd snapped at the class, 'Out! Out to the sports field.' Then, when everyone complained about going out in their school clothes, he'd glared at her like it was *her* fault Sophia had just sat there puking.

The puke was gross. The cleaners had mopped it up so Mia saw no reason why they couldn't leave right away, but Nurse spoiled everything. She said they couldn't move the patient. They had to call an ambulance because, according to school rules, only fully trained staff should carry her. Being transported on a stretcher might not be a problem for Sophia: she could just disappear. Walk away like she'd done years ago, leaving Oma and her to survive on her own. Mia had to face everyone the next morning.

Sophia had got better fast, it was like she couldn't bear to be weak: fainting one moment, forcing herself to get up and walk the next. The problem was – she wasn't better at all. She'd sat in the car, sweaty and pale, not looking at her shaking hands. Mia realised that Nurse had been right, so she'd stared straight ahead and kept her mouth shut tight. If Sophia could pretend she was fine, well, Mia could pretend even better. She'd been pretending *normal* for as long as she could remember.

When they finally got to the hospital, Sophia hadn't said a thing about being sick or fainting. She'd bought a magazine because Mia asked her to and turned around and left. Just like that. So now the school puking thing was their secret.

Mia sat by Oma's bed and thought about secrets. Her

newest one, the one she'd made last night, was that there was no way, no *way*, she could live with Gerda. Everyone thought that was the answer but it wasn't. She'd have to share her room. Put up with Gerda's mental moods and pretend to agree with her: because if she didn't she'd be told to leave, and that was worse than anything. Mia knew what it felt like when you weren't wanted. She'd learned to get through grey days when no one called and Oma sat silent in the sitting room. Not even answering when Mia asked about supper, TV or going out. It seemed, at those times, that Gerda wasn't there either. Not ever. She'd be out with her new friends, leaving no message and Mia's heart would beat way too fast. The world would stretch to an edgeless panicky nothing. The scary feeling would stick like glue and burrow into her. It made her ache with longing for something she didn't know, because she didn't know what belonging felt like. The feeling could be kept under control as long as she kept talking, reading or watching TV. During those in-between times when she was tired, alone and quiet, the greyness would come back. Gradually it had settled deep inside her. Hardening layer by layer – until the outside was as brittle as a walnut shell.

'Mia?'

'Yes, Oma. I'm right here.'

'Dearest.' Oma's hands were papery dry.

'I'll get you something to drink.'

'No. Listen to me'

'But you have to drink so you can get well.' Her grandmother's voice was different. Frightened but stern, like she was going to tell her off for not being in school.

'Darling, listen.'

'Yes, Oma.' She sank back onto the nasty plastic chair ready for the lecture.

'I don't want you to believe any of Petrus' nonsense while I'm away from home.'

'What nonsense?' This wasn't a lecture, this was worse.

'About Sophia, or Diertha and that sport centre.'

'But he hasn't said anything.'

'He will, and you're not to listen, because he'll lie.'

'Oma!'

'Mia, if I don't get better, Sophia is the one you should listen to.'

'You will get better, you *will*.'

'If I don't, I want you to live with her, not with your grandfather.'

'No.' She was crying, the grey panicky feeling welling so she couldn't breathe. 'Sophia doesn't like me.'

'Yes, she does.'

'She doesn't.' She was wailing loud enough to make Petrus look over.

'Quieten down child. I don't want him to hear.'

'Hear what?' Oma must be delirious. Was it the painkillers she was taking?

'I don't trust him.'

'But he's my grandfather!'

'Even grandfathers can be bad.'

'You should tell me why, Oma.'

'Not now, dearest, the nurse is coming. Just promise me.'

The nurse had a load of medicines. She made a fuss of giving Oma each tablet, making sure she took every one, and drank all the water. Mia kissed her and said she promised. She'd do what she'd been told, Oma should try to sleep. It was as if *she* were the adult and Oma the child. She didn't want to look at Petrus in case he saw how frightened she was, so she followed the nurse out into the corridor and asked what they were giving Oma to make her think such mad things. Nurse said she wouldn't tell her because she was too young. Mia could ask Dr Künstler if she wanted to know more.

What was she supposed to do? Mia went back and gazed around the ward. Most of the patients were old and wrinkled, sitting or lying in bed like dried prunes.

'I have chocolates for you,' one lady piped, holding out three gold wrapped Christmas bells. Her hands were so thin Mia could see blue veins and red bruises where she'd had injections.

'Thank you,' she said and pretended to unwrap and eat them as she smiled. She'd wait until she was home before throwing them away.

Petrus was nodding at whatever the other doctor was saying. They were too far away for Mia to hear, so she walked to the nearby window. Petrus glanced over and smiled his 'nothing to worry about' smile. Oma was right. He was sneaky. He could smile like that but you knew it wasn't real. What if Oma never came out of hospital? The thought squeezed at her tummy as she stared fiercely towards the car park. No crying. Not now. She had to be grown up because she had a bigger secret than any of them. She knew now that Petrus wasn't the person he said he was. He was hiding something, and, no matter what, Mia was going to find out what it was, and what had happened to her mother. The truth. Not the fairy tale version Oma told her: her mother had floated away to heaven, somewhere that was stuffed full of stupid pink clouds and angels. Then she was going to find her father. Even if her father didn't want her – it wouldn't matter. Up until now, even with those long silences and the grey feelings, she had Oma and Oma had her, but now? Mia didn't know. She felt safe with Sophia, but really, Sophia didn't like her and she wasn't interested in looking after anyone, she'd probably laugh if Mia asked her to. She wanted to ask, because she was really scared.

She had to stay with Petrus until Oma was better. She'd use the time to investigate. She wouldn't make a fuss. She'd go to school every single day, taking the bus so as to not need a lift. She'd cook, clean and work hard at making Sophia like her just a little bit. Once Petrus had got used to her, she'd make him tell her how and why Diertha died, and who her father was – because he knew, she was certain of that. And then she'd find out if what he said was true. Oh dear. It all sounded confusing, as if she didn't have a clue where to start.

Everything was normal outside. People hurried from one building to the next. Cars parked; others drove away with people who had families waiting for them at home. Mia had no one. Petrus might feel responsible, but he didn't actually care. He'd said how Sophia wasn't reliable. How she disappeared for days without contacting him. How he'd had to go and get her the time she was in trouble with a man. He seemed to like talking about how irresponsible she was. Sophia hadn't waited for Mia at school, he said, because she didn't care about any of them; only about herself, but Mia knew better. Sophia *was* upset her mother was so ill. She just didn't know what to do about it, and she'd bought Mia the dragonfly hairgrips. People who didn't care wouldn't do such a thing.

Wiping her eyes with her sleeve, Mia turned away from the window. Oma was snoring. The lady in the next bed had fallen asleep sitting up, her scarecrow head wobbled to and fro as she breathed.

'Come along, my dear,' Petrus said, his best smiley pretend face fixed like a mask. 'I have ordered a taxi.'

On the way home she decided that she was now the best at keeping secrets. She knew about Petrus being untrustworthy, his affair with that blonde woman, the one in the photo in his office, and the shared (fainting-puking) secret with Sophia. Plus her secret plan. All that knowing definitely made her a better secret-keeper than Oma, which was good news. Now she had to think like a detective. Every bit of information would help to make people tell her about her father. She had to start looking straight away.

At home Petrus turned the heating up so high the house creaked and popped. He made hot chocolate. In a croaky voice she whispered, 'Thank you' and took her drink upstairs. Petrus would think she was going to her own room, but she wasn't.

Oma's bedroom didn't smell of her normal favourite biscuity perfume; it smelled of being ill. What to do first? Pack a clean nightdress? Start looking for clues about Petrus, or her father? Find Oma's favourite book? That was easy – it was there, with its pretty cover of blue shells, on the bedside cabinet, *The Shell Seekers* by a lady called Rosamund Pilcher. She'd take it to the hospital and read a whole chapter out loud. There was a clean nightdress in the drawer, and some massive old-people's knickers. Okay, so whatever happened, she wasn't going to get old, and if she did – she'd never ever wear knickers like that.

The greyness was coming, reaching out its soft fingers.

She had to make plans, plans were better than doing nothing; they were the only way to avoid other people arranging your life for you. She opened the desk drawer; searching through receipts and old half-empty medicine boxes. The plastic container for false teeth made her feel queasy. If Petrus came up now, he'd tell her off. She could say she was packing clothes for Oma. That was true. She could also tell him to mind his own damn business because Oma was hers, not his. He'd left her alone with nothing, nothing to help her stay happy and nothing to help her stay well.

Head leaning on the bedclothes, the stench of panic seeping through the mattress and blankets, Mia wept. How could she even think of going to live somewhere else? Oma might get better. Oma would get better, and anyway no one wanted her. Petrus would leave right now if she ever *ever* said anything bad to him about being selfish, cruel or not caring for Oma when he should have.

There were sounds from the kitchen: Petrus cooking supper, Petrus trying to look after her. She had to calm down because it could be a lot worse – like having supper at Gerda's house with a long inquisition about Sophia, the changing rooms and that disgusting sick.

'Come on, Mia,' she muttered. 'Get a grip.'

Her school reports and baby photos were in the bottom drawer. Mia in nappies, in braces, oh dear: at camp – worse, in the bath. Seriously cringe-worthy to see Oma had kept every story she'd written about the pets she'd wanted. A hamster, a rabbit, that kitten she'd seen at Tessa's house. Whatever the animal, the answer was always N.O. No. No pets. Not today, not tomorrow, not ever. Help. There was that doltish picture of her make-believe puppy called Pip.

At the very bottom, underneath all the baby stuff, she found a faded envelope dated February 28th, 1976. Her birthdate! The 6 looked like it had been a 7. The top bit scrubbed too hard with a rubber until the paper came away. She peered closer. No way could the people who recorded things like a baby's arrival have got it wrong, it was just dirt. A dark bit of one of the photos had stuck to the envelope and smudged it – that was all. Inside were three more photos of a baby wrapped in a towel. The baby looked like an ugly worm. Nothing else. No mention of her, or her mother's name, or which hospital.

She waited for Petrus to walk in and disapprove of her sneaking. When he did it would all be over, though from the racket he was making, he seemed to be happy: clanking pans, banging cupboards open and closed as he rooted round the kitchen.

There had to be a birth certificate with her name on it. It was a legal document so you didn't exist without having one. Mia pinched the skin on her arm until it bruised. There, that was proof she existed. Proof she wasn't just a ghost or something. Wait a minute. Sophia would have access to records. The police could do what they wanted, they could look at anything. Even better, investigators were taught how to find things other people tried to keep hidden. Mia could be super nice to Sophia, then watch and find out how she went about investigating the dead person she'd mentioned. By watching, she'd learn how to find things. Sophia might be willing to help if she believed that by finding Mia's father, neither she nor Petrus would have to look after her. Sophia wasn't daft though. She'd know that a father who hadn't contacted his daughter in fourteen years was unlikely to want her now. Mia would have to be really careful how she asked, if she asked.

The closet, where Oma kept her clothes and shoes, was the last place to look. The scent, lavender and dust, was achingly familiar, Mia's stomach tightened and tears welled. She brushed them aside. Now was not the time to cry. It was dark, but she could make out the shapes of shoes, an umbrella, a vase (furry with dust) and something that looked like an old shoebox. Picking up the box, she emptied the contents onto the bed. Photographs of girls in swimsuits poured over the dark blue bedspread and slid over the edge onto the floor.

Petrus called, 'Supper, Mia! Ten minutes!'

The girls were wearing GDR swimsuits. Mia had her own black costume shoved at the bottom of her swimming bag. They could wear what they liked until they joined a sports group; after that they had to wear costumes with a logo. She picked up a group photo: young athletes in track-suits with patterned waves interlacing pale blue and white, spelling DDR. Oma had made Mia promise to tell her when the sports trainers were coming to her school. On those days Mia stayed at home. At first it had been great to skive. Oma had shown her how to make cakes and biscuits; they'd played cards for hours before the TV went on. Then her school friends started to tease. They said she was a cissy, someone who was afraid of games. Mia loved running, but most of all she loved to swim. The silence, the cool water on her skin made her tingle – in a good way. The next time the trainers came, she asked to go to school. Oma refused. She'd lost one daughter, she said. She wasn't going to lose another. Except that made no sense because Mia wasn't her daughter.

The girls grinned at her. A medal dangled from each neck. Written on the back of one photo was the name Käthe Niedermann, another: Sophia Montreal Olympics 1976. Sophia had been a swimmer. Mia knew that, but a famous one? Mia turned the box upside down, just to make sure there was nothing else. One crumpled photo fell out. Not a swimmer. A young-looking Petrus, talking to a man Mia recognised as the chief of police. He'd come to tell the class about not talking to strangers when she was in primary school. The date on the back said 1976, the year she was born! Why did Petrus know the chief of police? Maybe Oma hadn't been muddled at all. She'd keep the photo and ask Sophia, just as soon as she could.

Thank goodness there wasn't anything else, apart from a mouldy old swimming cap that had stuck to the cardboard. When she pulled at the cap, circular bits stuck to her fingers, plastic that had wrinkled and congealed like old skin. One print had fallen between the wall and the bedpost. Mia dug her fingers round it and pulled. Sophia. Happy and confident, standing next to her father and holding out her latest medals.

She should've worked this out ages ago. The same picture was on the wall in Petrus' house, and the display board in the school corridor. No one actually looked at them.

The pictures were just there, like boring old desks and blackboards. That's why her teacher had looked funny when Sophia fainted. He'd known who she was.

Who was Sophia investigating? Someone's death she said. No, not death, their murder. Maybe Diertha? That wasn't right; her mother had been dead for ages. If someone from here was dead, well everyone would have been talking about it. Maybe Sophia had found something else?

Petrus was on the phone, so she waited, sitting on the top step to listen and find out who he was talking to, but he was only leaving another message for Sophia. Speaking slowly, as if he were afraid that whatever he said she'd misunderstand. Perhaps she ought to call Gerda. In fact if she didn't ring there'd be another day of silence, another day of being ignored. Gerda would ask why Mia wasn't coming over, followed by the dreaded question: when was Mia going to move in?

'No one told me Sophia was an Olympic swimmer.' She blurted as Petrus put the phone down. He'd not answer truthfully, but she'd got his attention. Right. Now or never. *Ask* him. 'Oma's going to die, isn't she?'

Petrus flinched. He'd rolled up his sleeves to do the cooking, and had Oma's old flower print apron tied very tight around his waist. The apron was too big. It wrapped round him twice, the ties doubled into an elaborate bow at the front – right across a faded tulip print. His eyes said 'yes' but his face was carefully arranged to be safe and comforting. He was going to say, 'Oma will be fine'. He was going to reassure her, lie, just like Oma said. He'd pretend, anything to make her feel better, and briefly she felt glad, because even though she knew all the bad things in the world, she didn't want to hear them.

But he didn't.

He spoke the words. The ones she didn't dare think. Oma was going to die. Not today, not perhaps for a while, but it was only a matter of time. Mia wanted to ask if that matter-of-time was long enough for her to grow up, but she didn't. He said the staff and doctors at the hospital were making her comfortable, taking away the worst pain so that Oma could manage better. She could even come home – as long as Petrus stayed, and he would (he promised) as long as they needed him.

'What about me?' There. She'd said it. Now he'd say she'd be better off staying here, with the people she knew like Gerda and her mother.

He said she should do what Oma wanted. Well, that wasn't possible. Even though Oma had said what she thought was best, Mia couldn't stay with Sophia at the hotel; so that was that. Oma had said Petrus was cruel. She'd said that when he left her she'd been glad, really glad – but when Oma was sad, she acted like one of those old black-and-white movie stars, the ones who stared out the window, just waiting for someone to come and make everything better. When Mia grew up, she wasn't going to spend one second bothering to look out the window for someone who wasn't there.

Petrus said after things were sorted (what he meant was once Oma was dead) she was to make up her own mind. She could come back with him to Berlin, if she wanted, and go to a new school; when the time was right. Mia cried until her head felt empty and wrung out. She wanted to ask why he had come only now – when it was all too late, but she was crying too hard, and something told her not to say anything about Oma, or her warning, just pretend to trust him. For now, until she had proof that he was bad.

'I want to. Come to Berlin, with you I mean,' she said. Before he could be suspicious of her and say he'd already made arrangements, arrangements that couldn't be changed: like her living with Gerda, or going to boarding school. Grown-ups were like that; they offered something and, just like that, took it away. Petrus smiled and kissed the top of her head. It made her cry again, a weak, tired sobbing, because Oma kissed her just the same.

'Petrus,' she had to ask, to see what he said, 'what about Sophia and her investigation?'

'Dearest, what investigation?' Petrus found a piece of kitchen roll and handed it to her.

'The one she came to do.'

'That really is of no importance. She won't stay for long.'

He was avoiding her question, but her nose was blocked, her eyes sore and aching, and all she wanted to do was to curl up under her duvet and pretend everything was fine.

'Won't Sophia mind?'

'You coming to live with me? No. Sophia won't even notice.'

That didn't sound right. No matter how awkward Sophia was, Mia couldn't imagine her ignoring the fact that Mia was living in Berlin. 'Would I be able to see her?' she asked, and Petrus' face changed to tight, angry and really scary. When he saw her staring he moved his face back to smiley again. All at once Mia was one hundred per cent certain that she couldn't trust him. He could change from angry to nice, just like that. 'I mean, just sometimes, you know, as she's my cousin,' she added, to make him think she wasn't really bothered.

'She's not the sort of person you want to rely on.'

'Why not?' Oh dear, she didn't want to make him angry again, but Sophia was a detective so people must rely on her all the time, or else she'd be fired. Mia wasn't stupid.

'My dear child, Sophia has something called traumatic amnesia,' he said. 'She had a serious illness when she was sixteen and nearly died. She remembers some things, not everything. She might, for instance, forget to collect you, like she did at your school today.'

'She wasn't late. She was sick.' Why did he say 'my dear child' like that? It made her feel small and stupid.

'Sadly, that is part of the illness. When she sees something that makes her remember, she's sick and can't cope.'

That made more sense. Sophia had been really sick, but she hadn't fallen apart like Petrus said she would. She'd pulled herself together and been really strong. Even if the awful memories made her scared, she'd got on with it. The awful memories must be about training, though why were they bad? Sophia had looked happy in her photos. Maybe the bad thing had happened at sports school? Maybe it was to do with Mia's mother? Had Sophia seen Diertha drowned in the lake? If Mia saw something gross like that she'd definitely have traumatic amnesia.

Sophia wasn't *Nasty* anymore. In fact Mia had to admit

she was beginning to admire her, like someone she might look up to. Sophia wasn't the person Petrus said she was.

Dinner was awful: soggy potatoes and thick cream cheese. The cheese stuck to the top of her mouth as she chewed and tried to swallow. Despite that, she ate it all. Petrus might start going on about her eating properly, like Oma, and she didn't want him to think her a nuisance. When he offered her more, she said no, shaking her head to emphasise the point, and told him about Sophia's picture being on the school display board. Instead of looking pleased, like a normal father would his face did the angry tight thing again, before he turned away to gaze out the kitchen window. There was nothing to look at out there, just a dingy street light that lit up a portion of their garden and the pavement.

It was all so confusing. Even with his two faces, Petrus made her feel cared for. He was quiet and careful, as if she were a delicate piece of china, something important that could break, but maybe that was him just pretending. Oma had said so little about what he'd been like when he lived in Breden. What if he were one of the Stasi? That wasn't so difficult to believe. Pretty much everyone who lived here was linked to them in some way, mostly because they had to. But what if he was one of the awful ones they showed on Western TV? Men and women who'd done terrible things: torturing people to make them say stuff, admit to stories that weren't even true. She checked to make sure the photo was safe in her back pocket, cleared the table and washed up so she had time to think. When she'd finished and went along to the sitting room, Petrus stood up, like she was a visitor in her own house. Mia felt angry and scared all over again, but she didn't say anything. He poured her a glass of wine that tasted of old sunshine and ripe pears and made her throat tingle. He'd changed into brown trousers and a grey jumper that looked expensive. Maybe *she'd* get some new clothes when she went to live in Berlin? A sharp voice told her to stop being so stupid. If Petrus were that bad he'd never look after her. He could be saying he would because he needed to be here to get rid of Oma, because Oma knew things about him.

She had to tell Oma to be really careful, not to take any medicine unless she was sure it was safe. She'd talk to her in the morning. First thing. She'd make Oma tell her what it was that Petrus had done all those years ago, and then she'd tell Sophia.

Later, in bed, woozy from the wine, she whispered her love across the town to the hospital bed, 'I love you Oma. I love you,' and fell into to a dream of mouldy changing rooms, Oma shouting at Petrus, the nurses' sneaking looks that said they all knew exactly what was happening: Sophia fainting.

No. Wait.

Mia sat up so fast she felt dizzy. Sophia had gone back to the swimming pool where she first trained. That was why she'd fainted – her memory was coming back properly, not so as she couldn't cope. This time she was remembering and carrying on as if she wanted to know. Something really bad had happened. Maybe a long time ago or maybe just recently in Berlin. Whichever, Mia needed to know. She wouldn't tell Petrus. She'd help Sophia in her investigation, and maybe Sophia would help her?

This time she fell asleep busily planning just how to find out about Sophia's past, and how to get Sophia to help her find out who her father was, and glad, so glad she was wrapped in her own duvet in her own bed, safe at least for tonight.

★★★

Sophia walked silently across the badly lit hospital car park, through the side entrance and along corridors where strip lighting flickered and droned, finally turning into the ward where her mother lay babbling, half-crazy in a yellow morphine haze. Having spent the entire evening inside an endless circle of blame and sadness, Sophia picked at her guilt, a scab which never healed, her heart refusing to let the problem go. How could she have left Dagmar with no family to protect her, no way to earn money? No way to be safe?

'Mama?' Her mother's arm felt like unbaked dough, damp, slightly warm and sticky. Dagmar sobbed and called out: 'Mia?'

'No Mama. It's me, Sophia.'

'Sophia,' she said. 'Little Sophi. Where are you?'

'I'm here, Mama, right here.'

'Sophi?' Dagmar, eyes closed, clutched her hand. 'Don't go.'

'I'm not going anywhere.' Did her mother imagine she was a child again?

Dagmar whimpered, pulled her closer, her sickly breath making Sophia turn her face away. 'They'll get you, child, just like they got Diertha.'

Was the warning for the present day, or the voice Sophia

remembered from the past? The echo she'd laughed away – glad to escape, ignoring her mother's peevish caution.

'Mama, wake up. What are you talking about? Who will hurt me?' Dagmar pulled at the needle in her arm until it tore. Sophia stopped her, placing her hand over the needle, holding her still. 'Stop it. Wake up.'

'Sophia?' Her mother opened her eyes, took in where she was and finally calmed. 'I was dreaming. What are you doing here?'

'I wanted to see you.'

'Has something happened to Mia?'

'No, Mama, Mia's fine.' How could the child trump everything with such ease?

'Don't leave her with your father.'

'Why ever not?

'Sophi.'

'Lie still, Mama, your arm's bleeding.' Sophia found a wad of tissues and wrapped them around the redness. 'That's better.' She was blathering when she needed to tell her mother that she loved her, and that she understood.

'Promise me.'

'Promise?'

'You'll look after her.'

'Yes, I'll look after her.' Right now she'd promise the world away to give her mother peace. She'd wanted to say that she understood, but all Dagmar could think about was the child. Well, if she didn't say it now she never would. 'I'm so sorry for leaving you on your own, Mama.'

'It was never your choice, dearest.'

'Maybe not then, but I could have come back.'

'That's nonsense thinking. Now child, listen to me.

When you visit the police station, you find your file and read it.'

'Mama! How did you know I was going there?'

'The nurses have been moaning about how my daughter is going to make their husbands lose their jobs.'

'They're probably right.'

'I said – if their husbands were filthy Stasi, they deserved to go.' Dagmar smiled. Here was the mother remembered from childhood: strong, unbowed. Sophia leaned down to kiss her; Dagmar's arms formed an arc around her.

'Mama, why should I read my file?'

'I was wrong not to tell you, dearest child.'

'Tell me what?' Her mother's arms were slack, eyes closing. 'Tell me what?'

★★★

The bouncer took Sophia's entry fee with a disconcertingly friendly grunt. The filthy staircase, the young men who played pool, remained unchanged. The young man who'd leered, now pointedly ignored her. The anorexic sex kitten was nowhere to be seen; instead, groups of garishly clad aged hopefuls milled around the bar. Some dared the dance floor. An old couple moved in an antiquated dance routine. The brittle, painfully slender woman wore a long black dress with sequined glass diamonds that sparkled as she waltzed. Her partner, an aging turtle of a man, leaned – his forehead curling over the top of her head. Both concentrated fiercely on their movements.

'Half price drinks with your ticket.' The bartender was wearing a smart jacket, white shirt and magenta bow tie. 'Dance night,' he continued with false cheer.

Why had she been so foolish to take the white pill? Her pulse raced. Her head ached.

Nothing here was *right*. The hall should be dark and anonymous, the dance floor filled with that strange breed of nocturnal folk with whom she felt so at ease, the sort of people that didn't notice who one was. A group of men were drinking schnapps as a dare. They turned, stared at her, nudged each other and tipped back the next shot to cheers and muttered gossip. One man had dark blue eyes. He was tall. Black hair cut short and neat. Perhaps he would do? No. She turned her back and drank beer as the room slowly filled. The schnapps group lurched onto the dance floor. Arms hooked, they sang along to Madonna's hit 'Like a Virgin', circling first one way, then the other. Two staggered off to the bathroom amid roars of laughter. The man with dark blue eyes was standing at the bar. He smiled, raised his glass. Sophia looked away. Yes? No? She so needed to forget. To feel and not think, just for a few hours.

On her left a crowd of women wiggled around a pile of purple and vivid green handbags. Dressed in denim jackets, their bright short skirts were an unkindness to burgeoning cellulite. One ample woman had a silver tiara in her hair. The coterie tittered, glanced over toward the men, jutted hips, pushed breasts out and wisecracked to ever increasing mirth. A drink appeared at her side. She nodded her thanks to blue eyes who shook his head and pointed.

Hajo! Images collided. A blade. The beefy-faced man. Hajo. She was high on drugs and he was her boss. Where to escape? The loo? Those windows weren't big enough to let her through. The stairs? Behind him. Oh god. Something must have happened. Something important.

'Sophia.'

What to do? Feign nonchalance? Pretend their meeting was normal? Why hadn't he simply phoned? And how come both he and Maria had found her here, in a place that usually offered escape?

'Hajo, what's happened?' she said

'I've the results for you.'

'Results?' She couldn't think straight, the room was vibrant with colour and sound.

'The result of blood tests from your friend.'

Skin tingled. She had to touch him. No. She had to get rid of him before he knew what she'd taken.

'Why didn't you just phone?'

Hajo grinned. 'I did. This morning.' He leaned towards her, eyeing her leggings and sheer black top. 'You look nice.'

'How did you find me?' She had to lean close, her mouth near his ear. He turned, eyes that deep shade of green.

'The hotel.'

She should have known. 'Well, tell me the results.' She had to lean into the circle of his arm, stare at the gentle dip between his shoulder and neck.

'You smell nice too.'

She tried to edge back. He pulled her closer. 'Listen. The blood tests came back positive. Steroids, lots of them. One of them, Mestanolone STS 646, is banned by the medical association.'

Lights. Noise. Too many people. Hajo's face was

swimming in and out of focus, as if she were very drunk, or very ill.

She'd left Hochberg training camp in '77, just as doping practice changed. Their doses were measured to the 6:1 ratio. If either counts, testosterone or epitestosterone, were over the 6:1 limit, you weren't permitted to travel, or compete. If you didn't compete, your trainer suffered and took it out on you.

'Käthe didn't train with me at sports camp.'

'How come she was still taking steroids? She wasn't still competing, was she?'

'Hajo, you're not listening. I've not seen Käthe since I left the GDR. I've got her parents' address, but haven't seen them to ask.' What a lame excuse. Two days and she'd done nothing. Did it count that she'd seen Maria that morning? No. She'd been wasting time, dithering because she was frightened of her own shadow. Wait. There was some other reason that he was here, something he wasn't saying. Someone had told him about her years of training inside the sports doping machine. That was it. Any moment now he'd tell her to pack up and go home. What to do? Perhaps she could say she was ill and make a hasty exit.

'Sophia?' He ran his hand lightly over her arm.

'Mm.' His shirt was warm; she could feel his heart beating: a small thunder.

'Are you aware everyone's watching?'

'Yes,' she nearly smiled, 'awful isn't it.' Why was he being so friendly just before he fired her? Maybe he felt bad? You couldn't have the past she'd had and not be suspected.

'The bouncer didn't want to let me in.' He sounded amused. He wouldn't be amused when he realised she'd taken drugs, and he would. Somehow Hajo saw things most people did not. 'Shall we dance?'

What?

'Come on, Sophi, dance with me.'

How did Hajo know her nickname? She had to do something, get away, right now. Perhaps faint? Or die? 'I can't dance. I feel ill.'

'Don't be such a coward,' he said and kissed her. He tasted of warm places, cigarette smoke and Hajo. She concentrated on the feel of him: solid, unyielding, so different from the others. His green eyes watched, waited, and she stopped thinking and went with him onto the dance floor.

Later, coat in hand, walking up the stairs, she was steadier in his arms, his hands gentle on her back. They made their way back towards the hotel, Hajo stopping once in the middle of the path and, like a ridiculous fool, kissing her. She'd linked hands around his neck, closed her eyes and held on tight.

They were in her room, on the bed, moving together: her body a long ache of wanting.

'Hajo.'

'Sshh.' His eyes had turned deep grey. His mouth serious. All of him focussed tightly on her. He smelled of tobacco and soap, stroking a hand across her skin, warming her. In the distance a door slammed as some other reveller retired for the night. The distant unfamiliar sounds were strangely reassuring. Sophia sighed. Thank god, she thought. Thank god. Hajo's hand, then mouth, was on her breast, hands slowly traced their way in between her legs. Heat burned from her feet to stomach. She arched her back and traced a line down his back. There were scars,

169

crisscrossing, as if he'd been cut. Her hands paused. Traced the lines from left to right.

'Sophi.' Hajo murmured in her ear and entered her. She cried out, a shocked half-gasp. She couldn't speak. Couldn't stop moving. The orgasm blew through her so she hid her face in his neck, sobbing and gasping.

'Look at me.' Hajo's face, dark, vivid, above hers Eyes fixed on her. She gasped as he moved inside her. He watched, the rhythm steady and slow. Building, until he cried out her name, and she his.

Her face was hidden in that gentle half-moon between his ear and shoulder, one hand tracing those vicious scars. They were a battered pair, she thought, not wanting to draw away because he felt so solid and deliciously safe.

'Next time, beautiful Sophi, we'll do this without you needing to take a drug.'

'Hajo.' Before she'd even begun to protest, he'd drawn himself up to lean on one elbow and began tracing the outline of her mouth, her neck, her breasts.

'It's okay, I understand.' He paused. Grinned. 'So, you want to know about the scars on my back?'

'Hmm.' There was nothing safe about him now. He was staring, as if he wanted to eat her up.

'Well, I guess you'll have to wait. I'm a long way from being finished with you.' She laughed, half-delight, half-surprise, as they began all over again.

It was only in the moments before she fell asleep, his warm shape spooned against her, that she realised that he'd still not told her. In the darkness she smiled at the notion that each of them had scars from lives before. She dreamed of diving into cool green water. There would be starfish and mermaids. She'd find Käthe's killers and lock them away and then she'd look for Diertha in between the rocks and caves; find her and pull her to the surface. Ask her why the hell she hadn't said a thing about a baby. But there wasn't a way through the seaweed that thickened and putrefied. Hajo was shouting, something about her being irresponsible, her behaviour unacceptable. She'd never been any of those things. Strange, he sounded more upset than truly irate.

'Wake up, Sophia.' Hajo was leaning over her, fully dressed, his hair still wet, smelling of her eucalyptus shampoo. 'I've got to get back to Berlin.'

What was he saying? Christ. They'd slept together. He'd be returning to report how she'd been found high on drugs in a seedy nightclub. How she'd been a GDR swimmer.

'Darling, stop it.' He leaned down and kissed her. Sophia wrapped her arms around his bearlike shape. Darling? Her heart ached, as if a part of it had somehow stretched.

'I haven't even asked you how your mother is.'

'I don't know.' She held on, remembering a runner's body, a cruel mouth, cold blue eyes, a boy, not a man. The boy she searched for in every nightclub. Someone she'd loved who'd not loved her. Hajo was here. Not the boy, Hajo, whose eyes were calm with waiting. 'She's not well at all. I don't know how to,' she paused, 'care for her. She wasn't there much when I needed her, and now she's got Mia. I don't know what I should do.' Petrus had preferred young women to Dagmar, but it hadn't made any difference. Her mother had just let him continue screwing around while she waited and prayed he'd return. If Sophia dared, she'd ask her why.

'We're a pair, aren't we?' Hajo waited until she'd moved sideways before sitting on the bed, holding her wrist, stroking the puckered line of old healed cuts. He wasn't laughing, or asking her questions, as he should be, rather he looked thoughtful, bringing his mouth to kiss where she had sliced so carefully. 'We had a call yesterday morning, someone with detailed information about something called "Theme 14.25". The caller said what I already knew, that you'd been an Olympic swimmer for the GDR.'

'That's why you came?' It had to have been Maria. Some bloody friend she'd turned out to be. Sophia sat up, willed him to say – so you must have Stasi connections – just get it over with.

'Partly. It would be better if you didn't talk to anyone about it,' he said. 'Do the inspection, but any whiff of your association to the Stasi, or 'Theme 14.25' gets out, and you're off the case.'

'Hajo, everyone here knows I was an Olympic swimmer.' There was some small satisfaction in seeing him surprised. 'I've spoken to Maria, so it's a little late.' He must know that this was the birthplace of whispers heard through walls, intimate knowledge collected and saved to catch those who dared to run.

'And this Maria kept in touch with Käthe?'

Here was the Hajo she knew. Details scrutinised, nothing missed.

'I've told you they hatched a plan to get me home, remember? Maria wrote. Käthe decided to come in person.'

There it was, clear as day. It was her fault Käthe had died. 'I found a scrap of paper in her pocket with my address.'

'You didn't report that.'

'No.'

'Why, Sophia? You know I'll have to.'

It was now or never. 'Here's the paperwork Maria sent.' Sophia took the letter from the drawer by the bed, grabbed the one mean blanket on the bed and wrapped it tightly around her. 'She says she has loads more like this. We had a tree, you know, a secret meeting place when we were children. Her mother was good to me, and she died in prison.' Why was she blabbering on about trivialities when he wanted information? 'Maria's a nurse. She worked at places similar to where I trained. So it's likely any papers are worth saving.'

'We'll get to that. You need to stop being a friend and start being a police officer. The fact that you withheld information about your friendship with someone who was murdered is bad enough.'

'Oh? What about you and your old buddy Martin?'

'Sophia, Martin isn't a murderer; neither is he dead.' He walked round the bed and put his hands on her shoulders. 'Why didn't you say?'

'I was frightened.'

'Of the dead woman?'

'No. Käthe had my address in her pocket and someone had killed her. Come on Hajo.'

'Do you have any ideas about who killed her?'

Sophia concentrated on the feel of Hajo's grey patterned jumper: slightly scratchy wool that smelled of smoke and aftershave.

'You think your father might have something to do with all this.' His voice was steady. No surprise, just careful deliberation.

'I have something to do with it, so he might too.'

'And?'

'I wanted a bit of time to find out.' She'd done nothing but shrink from the idea.

'You've had time.'

'Yes.' Sophia took out the scrap of paper so carefully folded into her notebook and handed it to him. Now he'd say pack up and return to Berlin with him, just as she was beginning to be brave enough to act.

'Sophi, I know what it's like to be in a situation where it's unclear what's right and wrong. You wanted to ask about my back. The scarring? I was working undercover. Someone in the police force slipped up, they said something they shouldn't and, well, my back was one of the ways the gang got their revenge.'

'Oh.' She ran a finger along his back; under the woollen jumper were those puckered scars. He was lucky to be alive. Was this his way of saying he understood and was concerned for her? How could he understand? Hajo couldn't know how complex the GDR system was. How the doping had been taken so far that some athletes couldn't find their way back to normal, but he had to believe that records were, most certainly, being shredded, burnt or doctored at Breden police station.

'On top of everything,' she said, 'I'm not convinced Mia is who she thinks she is.'

'Really, what reason would your mother have to lie?'

'Well, Diertha, my cousin, Mia's mother, was at training

camp with me. She was a bully who drank a lot and wasn't training as hard as she should. She was away for six weeks, during which she was supposed to have had Mia. She came back, and the next day they found her in the lake.'

'What?' Hajo was searching his coat pockets for his car keys. 'Look, I'm sure if there is confusion about who the girl is, we'll find out one way or the other. I'll need copies.' He held up the letter, photo and Käthe's handwritten note. 'They'll let you do that at the police precinct. Have you collected the mail from your mother's house? No? Right. Here's my copy of your instructions and a set of keys to the precinct. Yes, I did find it odd they have no file on Käthe Niedermann. As for your friend Maria's paperwork, I imagine she'll want something in return, right? Find out what and phone me when you've seen the victim's parents. I'll see you when you get back.' He hugged her, planted a perfunctory kiss on her forehead, and left.

Number one on Hajo's inspection list was to ensure that there had been a complete removal of barbed wire from around the station. Barbed wire? Why would a police station need barbed wire? Two: the reception area had to be professional and welcoming. And three: police vehicles, Trabant P50 and P60, must be replaced with the latest Mercedes. Lovely, she'd have to traipse around looking at cars. Four: computers installed in April should be in full use with past service records updated.

That complicated everything. If new computers had been installed, a long trawl through old records and police logs would be needed, hours of painstaking work to find any sort of paper trail. Records that were too easily available would almost certainly be doctored – incriminating

Stasi links deleted or re-written to appear as innocuous codes. It was a good thing she knew how to read GDR acronyms. Her life had been recorded in code, each letter or number hiding the real name of the steroid cocktail that made her invincible. She'd do what her mother asked; look to see if they had a file on her and Käthe, and finally she'd see what they had on Petrus.

The police had a habit of storing old paperwork for months, even years, before burning or shredding it, so she could look. It would do no harm to check if Diertha really was Mia's mother. She'd have to find the storage place before it was too late. Even then there were ways of finding things – you had to know where to look. How had Maria managed to collect paperwork the Stasi wanted destroyed? What if her friend was in danger? Stasi loyalists could be watching her, as they had Käthe?

Sophia picked up her notebook. The name 'Maria' had been written five times, each instance circled by daisies. She drew a thick line through each annoying daisy, and turned the page to write 'police station inspection' followed by 'professional and welcoming'. The flowers remained visible though the thin paper. '*Come on*,' they whispered, '*come back. Remember.*' Oh god, Maria had given her the painting from her mother. Her friend was operating within the old bartering system. Asking for help the only way she knew how. She had handed over an infinitely precious gift, and was waiting for something greater in return. Only then would Maria hand over whatever she'd collected.

CHAPTER TEN

~

Hedda Niedermann's mouth stretched left to right, rigid with distress. Hands gripped, loosened, gripped as she tried not to cry.

'He said she would be safe. He *said* nothing like this would happen.'

'Who said?' Sophia had made them coffee, extra sugar for Käthe's mother, a white-haired athletic woman she was trying hard to recognise. 'Your husband?'

'No. How would he know? We divorced when he decided that living in the West was better. I wanted to stay, for Käthe and my parents.'

'Hedda, who said she was going to be safe?'

'Käthe was a good girl. You know that, don't you? The three of you played together.'

'I remember.'

'She has medals.' Käthe's mother left the room, returning with silver and bronze. The design – Olympic champion on one side, Greek amphitheatre on the other – was well known. Sophia had the gold, hung by its ribbon, on the back of her door.

'Maria came to tell me.' Hedda re-wrapped the precious medals in tissue paper, placed them carefully in their boxes. 'I don't watch the Western programmes on the TV.' Tears kept so rigidly in check began to slide down her face. 'Dear Sophi, you will find out what happened, won't you?'

'Yes, of course I will, Hedda.' Her response was an echo of former promises the three of them had made as children: 'Now make sure you're back by seven.' 'Yes, Frau Niedermann,' they'd chorus, giggling the moment they reached the corner and were safely out of sight.

'Good.' The idea that someone would do something seemed to calm her.

'Please tell me who promised Käthe would be safe?'

'Petrus, of course. Your father. He promised.'

Her father? Petrus was involved, but how? Back at the hotel she was told that her father had rung. He'd arranged to meet with the consultant that morning. The problem was that Mia was insisting she accompany him to the hospital.

'Sophia.' He was waiting by the door, ready to greet her with a fleeting kiss on her left cheek. 'Just in time. I really can't take Mia.'

'Petrus, you know Käthe's dead, don't you. So why did you promise Hedda you'd look out for Käthe?' How she longed to demand that he tell her about his work for the Stasi. Ah, there it was: honest fury, or was that fear lurking under her father's careful veneer?

'I had heard, however, what I say is my business, not yours. And I must insist you don't poke your nose into local police matters. You know how careful we have to be.'

'Father, things have changed. The Wall is down.'

'Nothing has changed, Sophia. You'd do well to remember it.' The taxi pulled up. Petrus stepped past her and hurried down the path as a pyjama-clad child sloped down the stairs and into the kitchen.

'Why is Petrus cross with you?' Mia began folding Oma's clean laundry into a neat pile on the kitchen table.

'Because I don't always do what I'm told.'

'Oh. *Isn't* it dangerous to poke your nose into police business?' The child had been sitting on the top step, ears pinned.

'Not when you're a police officer. Mia, you need to get dressed.'

'But what about Oma's clothes?'

'I'll finish folding them.'

'I have to see her.' Mia looked horribly near tears. 'I need to tell her something.' She crumpled against the table and wept. What was Sophia supposed to do? She reached out a tentative hand and patted the girl's shoulder. Mia sobbed louder. The child was going to make herself sick. The thought had barely registered before Mia managed to turn and burrow her face against Sophia's stomach. Her arms wrapped themselves tightly around her like a baby octopus, squeezing. She felt the wetness of snot and tears seep through the uniform fabric. Any chance of Herr Rathmann's respect was spoiled before she even opened her mouth – there'd be no time to change.

'What do you need to tell her, sweet pea?'

'I don't know.' The girl hiccupped.

'What don't you know?'

'If she's being looked after properly,' Mia wailed. Sophia's right hand took on a life of its own, stroking Mia's soft clean hair. Her left arm pulled the child's slim frame closer.

'My father will make sure she is.'

'What if he doesn't? What if he doesn't want her to get better?' The child was beside herself. If Sophia hadn't snapped to she would have laid her head against Mia's head.

'Mia, listen to me.' She backed away as Mia sneezed, apologised and insisted on wiping Sophia's shirt with a grubby cloth from the sink. 'My father will do everything he can.'

'But what if he doesn't want her to get better?'

'Why on earth wouldn't he?'

'I don't know. Oma doesn't like him, she told me to come to you, not Petrus. It was like she was frightened of him.'

How could she not warm to this muddled, sad child? 'Petrus came to help you and Dagmar, so he'll do exactly that.'

'I found this.' Mia dug in her top pocket to produce a dented photograph. 'It's Petrus, isn't it?'

'Where on earth did you find that?'

'I looked in Oma's room last night. I wanted my birth certificate. I don't think I have one.' She looked up at Sophia. 'If I don't have one, does it mean no one really knows who I am?'

'Oh, Mia.'

'It was under loads of old pictures of you swimming or winning stuff. The other man is the chief of police, I re-membered 'cos he came to my primary school years ago.'

'Can I keep it?' Further evidence to link Petrus to the Stasi.

'Yes. Oma said Petrus wasn't a good grandfather. She wants me to stay with you.'

'Let's get you to school first. We'll talk about it later, okay?'

In between more tears, reasoning and sidelong apologies, Mia dressed, found her school bag and they reached an agreement. At twelve, Sophia would be at the school to take her to the hospital.

'You won't forget will you? Petrus says you aren't very reliable.'

'I won't forget.' Father was working his magic, like with his women he was turning people against each other so he had control. He'd made sure she was aware how grateful she should be for her life. So grateful she'd done all he asked and waited for a reward, a sign that he noticed her efforts. The harder she tried the more invisible she became. It was only now when she disobeyed him that he recognised her. In the week after the Montreal Olympics, unhinged by withdrawal symptoms from the steroids she so relied on, she'd had a moment of terrifying clarity: the steroids were going to kill her. That evening, passport and papers in a small bag, along with one change of clothes, she'd taken what money she could find from her parents' house and caught a train to Saafeld, changing to head for the tiny station of Eisfeld. Waiting on the platform, the sun sinking into night, she, as many others, watched carefully for escape guides: men (usually Russians) in coats large enough to hide a fugitive, would, for a fee, group together and take you through the woods and across the border. No one made eye contact. A middle-aged woman in a fur jacket waved her cigarette in the air. The end was attached to an ivory tip holder. A burly man with dirty hair offered her a light. The pair moved calmly towards the small lane leading towards the forest. They disappeared. Engine noises. One car? No. Two, three pulled up. Doors opened. Closed. Stamping feet. Someone yelled, 'Police'. Everyone scattered. Sophia ducked into the waiting room. Please let there be a back exit, please. Nothing but benches – and a stairway leading up to the stationmaster's room. Cramped under the stairway, Sophia shut her eyes. Boots. Coming nearer. Stopping. A familiar voice ordered her to 'come out now'. Her father was standing next to the police chief, whose back was carefully turned. In the safety of father's car, Sophia had begun to feel terribly ill. Petrus had taken her to the hospital. He'd been kind. Surprised when she told him she couldn't take more steroids, as if he really hadn't known what they were. Then, when she'd become so ill the doctors were prepared to let her die, he'd taken her to the West and saved her.

'I'm ready.' Mia was waiting by the door, bag in hand, trusting her.

Thirteen years ago they'd left Dagmar unprotected to answer to the Stasi for her and her father's abdication, a useful, awful ploy to give the Stasi someone to question and blame for allowing an athlete and a doctor to escape; a serious matter as both Sophia and Petrus had information the Stasi and Doping Committee wanted kept secret. That blame lay heavy in Sophia's belly. Had her mother chosen to stay? Or had Petrus left with clear instructions about what had to be done in order to secure Sophia's and Mia's lives? Some atonement was needed, a way of showing that Sophia loved her mother and that she was finally beginning to comprehend.

★★★

Police Precinct 66 loomed: a mountain of grey, wrapped in fog. Thick windows glinted from the walled expanse and electric, rather than barbed wire, encircled three-quarters of the station. Professional and welcoming?

It was ten o'clock. She was late, and about to rat on people she'd grown up with. People from her school, people who wore the same uniform as her. To get what she wanted, she'd need to be convincingly naive, polite and agreeable. Sophia practised a smile in the car mirror, remembering Hajo's warm kiss. Was it really only this morning she'd woken to the scent of him on her skin?

She'd ask Officer Rathmann about the lack of paperwork they'd volunteered for Käthe, to gauge the reaction. If she were to have any chance of finding anything, she'd have to be seen as incompetent enough to warrant being left unchaperoned in the records room. Once they did, she'd look. Never mind that father had told her not to ask anything. Never mind best buddy Martin would (no doubt) show only what he wanted her to see. She'd do her job and hope Hajo saw it as such. She'd look to see if there were files on Käthe and herself, and in doing so, perhaps learn how Petrus had planned to keep an eye on Käthe, as her mother had said.

Police cars were parked behind the building with a precision that defied normal. No mud, no chaos, no last-minute swearing before attempting to find some other miniscule space. Why was the reception window and buzzer fixed so stupidly low? A person had to lean down to press the button. Ah, of course – you became vulnerable when you had to bend.

The buzzer made no sound. Was it broken? Did they *really* have soundproofed walls? Eventually a disembodied voice asked for 'Name and the purpose of visit?' Sophia politely explained that she was here by appointment. Three long minutes later the door clicked open. The woman behind the desk, with bug eyes and a fleshy face, didn't even glance up. Dipping a dainty brush into a bottle of nail varnish, she continued to apply orange gloss to her left index nail.

Inside the reception area were two barred windows. One looked out onto the car park, the other onto the road. Nice to know they'd be safe under a sustained attack. Sophia took out her notebook and began to sketch a map of exit points, just in case. The silence was unnerving, not even a creak or door slam. The woman began painting the nails on her right hand. For want of anything better to do, Sophia drew the secretary sitting in the centre of the precinct as an electric generator, wires coming from her ears, eyes and fingernails. Sophia snorted and looked up. Her muse was glaring.

It was too quiet. Things were happening on the other side of that door. Things she needed to hear. In another ten minutes she'd explode, strangle Froggy-face and break the bloody door down. Breathing deeply she recalled a huge expanse of water, a girl swimming, her muscled form streaking though the whiteness. Athletes swarming through the pine forests, mating under the canopy of trees. Her blue-eyed stranger? Oh, how strange to truly remember. He was the boy from training camp. It had become a habit to find a copy of him in each nightclub. Berlin offering up a seemingly endless supply of slim-hipped, cruel-mouthed strangers, each one with the potential to make her remember the wildness and forget the police officer she'd become.

Mia had blue eyes and a sulky mouth. Dressed in her favourite pink/purple striped jumper, the girl resembled a bad-tempered bumble bee. She'd slotted inside Sophia's arms as if she belonged. If Petrus was implicated in Käthe's death, how could he care for the child? Would Mia somehow become her responsibility? There was guilt at the awfulness of Dagmar's file: the interrogations, medication, her mother's imminent death … but to look after a child?

The door opened and the secretary smiled at a trim, tired-looking man with a thin face and carefully back-combed brown hair. He returned her smile, revealing a row of browning teeth. She'd expected a bull-like, door-slamming imitation of Hajo, not this quiet man in a badly fitting police jacket.

'Officer Künstler?' Rathmann squeezed her hand as if he imagined it might leap up and slap him, letting go as quickly as he decently could. As they walked through the building, he apologised for keeping her waiting. They were short-staffed, he murmured. Most of the officers were re-training or had (he shrugged, refusing to meet her eye) been dismissed. The Commander General, a man named Günther Schenke, had recently been asked to resign after the discovery of documents linking him to the Stasi. Günther Schenke? The photo Mia had found. The name on the papers from Maria: Herr Schenke, code name Wolf. Günther would know who she was. The voice on the phone, that first night, had that been his?

She was walking into a hornets' nest.

Pause. Breathe. Don't give anything away. Smile at Martin before asking a suitably inane question about his speedy promotion.

'I've been given the job of managing the station until a suitable replacement can be found.' He looked embarrassed, even more so when she asked him to explain why electric wire surrounded the building.

'Ah, well you see, no one has the right qualifications to remove it.' He blushed as if somehow the fence was his personal failing, and she felt like a bully. They were walking down a long grey silent corridor. Through the window facing the car park two officers moved jauntily from police vehicle to building. One had overlong hair, the other looked familiar. Dark-haired, slim, shoulders held back, he strode across the car park – if he'd just turn, or pause? But Martin had opened his office door.

'Here we are. The furniture is from the commander's time,' he said, placing his jacket on the back of a chair, casting a dubious look around the sumptuous, beautifully furnished room. Perhaps he hoped the decor would fade into something more suitable: a plastic table and threadbare carpet?

'I hope I'm right in imagining coffee break would be the best time for you to meet the officers? We swap shifts at eleven, so I've asked that everyone attend,' he said. 'Shall I give you a tour of the rest of the building beforehand?'

If she said 'boo' loudly, he'd fall over, so she'd be reassuringly nice. His waning anxiety would make the job easier. This was a chance to prove herself to Hajo and stop being perceived by her colleagues as a version of her father.

Six new computers sat in the police writing-up room, glowing like a display in an art gallery. The old, now defunct monitors were piled up along the far wall. Frustratingly, every wire had been cut.

'This is where you can work,' Martin waved vaguely at the room. 'The specific records Hajo requested will be brought in when you've met the officers.'

Hajo had requested *all* working officers' records, not a select few. Sophia corrected him. Maybe he wasn't the frightened little mouse? Could he honestly think her that dense? It would be simple to get a master list from Berlin and check all officers' names against the files here. Hajo hadn't sent that list, and she hadn't thought to ask.

'And Käthe Niedermann's file?' She kept smiling. Martin's expression was deadpan. 'There's no one on record with that name,' he said, 'didn't Inspector Ewalder tell you?'

So they'd left Käthe's details in an unmarked file, or had it destroyed.

The tour lasted twenty minutes. Sophia noted the room, near the car park, where old records were kept; the place she really wanted access to, but couldn't ask. They'd know she was suspicious, but she didn't have the authority to insist. If she found discrepancies in the computer files today, Hajo would have to organise a search. The problem was, by the time he did so, the files would be gone.

They climbed the back stairs to emerge very near where they had begun. Muffled voices seeped out from the room at the end of the corridor. Sophia repeated her rehearsed reassurances. There was nothing to worry about, as far as she and Hajo were concerned – this was all routine, nothing more. Rathmann smiled, perhaps in relief, and opened the door. Sophia didn't at first notice the officers who sprawled on chairs, eating, talking, some staring – clearly hostile. All she saw was Maria's brother Jörg, his hair falling (absurdly long) across his face. That narrow jutting chin and those girly eyelashes, his sharp features blurring as he deliberately turned and slid out of Sophia's line of vision. Odious little Jörg. Stasi informer. Working for the police. This was why Maria had waited. Here was the deal. Her friend was going to ask Sophia to remain silent about her brother's former life as an informer and spy.

'Listen please. This is Police Detective Künstler.' Martin began his introduction, his gaze attempting to quell the sullen murmur, the overloud clunking of mugs. 'From Berlin,' he continued a little louder. 'At the express order of Detective Inspector Ewalder. She'll be reading person- nel files.'

'You'd think the fucking Westerners could put their minds to proper police work, not snoop on their own kind.'

Who'd said that? Wait. No point in reacting. Just try and spot him. Keep calm. Keep smiling. A squat muscle- bound man with a dark buzz cut appeared at her side. He introduced himself as Officer Gerd Neuman and asked how she wanted her coffee – and what about a biscuit?

There he was. It wasn't Jörg who had spoken so rudely but another guy, determinedly chewing on a sandwich, watching her through vicious blue eyes. Smiling an insidious, somehow all-too-familiar, smile.

'Sophia Künstler!' Neuman interrupted her train of thought. 'You're our Olympic swimmer. I saw you on the TV!'

Ignoring him, Sophia turned and scoured the room. Where was Jörg? The boy who'd scared her half to death as he watched her room at night. Standing under the bedroom window, on the corner where the road branched to the left. She'd told no one about his assault, nor his silent stalking – though her father would have known. Jörg with his Stasi connections could have caused trouble and she, golden future mapped, hadn't wanted to take any risks. Besides, she'd loved Maria too much to break their friendship. Now, just like before, Jörg had vanished.

As if on some pre-arranged signal, the officers scraped back their chairs and walked out slamming the door behind them.

'Officer Künstler?' Gerd, who'd stayed put, was joined by a tall angular policeman. They glanced at one another, at the floor. 'Uh, we're really sorry about their behaviour. With Officer Schenke leaving so suddenly and the West taking over … it's not been easy.'

She followed the pair out into the morning light. A distant plane burrowed through the thick air, casting a white trail. If only she were flying somewhere, anywhere. The Bahamas, Jamaica perhaps? Somewhere where there was warm sand and salty water, a place where no one knew her.

'This model has a table and chairs.' Lutz made a beeline for the shiny new van, enthusiastically polishing an imaginary mark from the bonnet. 'We're able to question suspects without having to bring them to the station.'

Over on the other side of the car park, two officers were heading out on patrol. The first, the man who'd spoken so rudely, had the most extraordinary blue eyes, the right eye slanting very slightly, towards his ear. She knew him, was so sure of it that when he turned away she sighed. His partner, Jörg, glared. Sophia held his stare. Bastard. Did he really think he could scare her? The minute she reported him he'd lose his job; receive no pay-out, no pension – nothing. And she'd make damn sure he knew it had been her.

★★★

Jörg's computer and paper records were squeaky clean. Years of spying washed away – and worse, there was no way of locating the originals today. Well, let him imagine he'd got away with it for the time being.

At first glance, Martin Rathmann's computer records looked solid. However, when she read the paper files Sophia saw years of service that were, at best, sketchy and incomplete. Rathmann had been working in Breden for ten years. In her book that automatically made him suspect. She found her proof in between the pages of a duty rota. Three years of service on the protocol stretch: East Berlin's airport at Schönefeld, to Niederschönhausen Castle, home to the GDR Head of Council. She knew the list of names. So, Martin had worked as 'officer on special assignment'. That meant working with the Stasi.

There was no trace of Günther Schenke's activities as a Stasi member. Those files, as with Käthe's, had almost certainly been shredded. Sophia knew how diligent the Stasi were. She also knew how they duplicated even the most mundane records. Such application might prove their downfall. Undaunted, she prowled through the files. Making notes, comparing each paper record with the computer transcription. Noting the differences, copying out information that had been carefully re-worded, or left out, she made a list of the officers she thought she knew. Clicked on the name Eberhard Borneman, and stared.

Heat tingled in her belly. Between her legs. Ebbe. Ebbe was the man who'd spoken so rudely as his ice-blue eyes stared and hated her. Her lovely cruel boy, the boy she looked for in the crowd, in the dance halls. Ebbe, the boy she'd lost herself to, was found.

CHAPTER ELEVEN

~

Hochberg 1976

Moonlight touched the base of the door, where, square to the mirror, Sophi twisted first right and left. Her stomach was flat and muscled, but her arms hulked on either side like cumbersome strangers. In the adjoining room, a sigh turned to a gasp, followed by a sharp slap. The rhythm began again, to shouts of encouragement and clamorous laughter. It was, she realised, the trainer's turn to perform.

She'd considered a dip in the nearby lake. No time for that. She'd showered, lathered on body lotion, pinched Diertha's nail varnish and painted each nail with a hideous coat of pink. The varnish felt thick and sticky as if her fingers were webbed. Diertha had been away for six whole weeks. Now she was back, and this small defiance was all Sophi had.

Next door, the man and girl reached climax; the bed heaved: one-two-three-four, against the wall.

A flake of paint dislodged from the ceiling and floated down to the carpet. Sophi didn't know any of them. The two girls had arrived that afternoon, grunted their way through training and refused to talk to anyone. The boys' voices were just as unfamiliar. Sophi slipped off her dressing gown as the second pair yelled. A gasp, silence and applause before the sound of running water and the door opening and slamming shut as the boys returned to their dormitory.

Even though she spent half her life in water, her hair was long, glossy and dark. It was the one thing that remained feminine.

I look like a man, Sophi decided, staring at her upper lip that hinted at a three o'clock shadow. Down *there* thick hair was already re-growing, strong and waxy, and she'd already shaved that day. Running her hand through the wet growth, she wished to god they'd hurry, wished they'd never come, wished she had some other way to appease the itching inside. I'm a giant mermaid she thought, imagining the lake closing over her, leading her down.

Outside the window she heard the warning shriek of a nightingale as Diertha's throaty laugh was followed by a giggle as someone pinched her. Four of them? The training session had run late and that meant they were high on steroids. Pulse racing, Sophi recited her weekly rule: never miss training, never ever miss training. Eric, her coach, a squat man with dry skin that flushed whenever he became annoyed, had laughed when, as a novice, she'd been foolish enough to ask him about the nightly orgies.

'You girls can't get enough can you? Sex is good. Work hard but play even harder.' Now he squeezed tight against her whenever he had the chance and, more often than not, he came with the rest; after the late training session – keeping an eye on her, he said, as he fucked her, his eyes the colour of dirty water, mouth panting to reveal a stained tongue and broken teeth.

They burst in through the door, jostling, laughing and stripping. Diertha caressed her first choice of mate and pulled him towards the second narrow bed.

'She'll do whatever you want,' she said, waving the others towards Sophi.

The three remaining boys stood watching the two moving on the bed. They giggled, looked sideways at one another. Two began to masturbate. The third turned to Sophi and lurched towards her as she lay down, legs spread. He propped himself above her, shut his eyes and brutally entered her; no doubt thinking of Diertha's coy teasing, her come-on laughter and explicit suggestion as he drove into Sophi again and again.

She lost herself in the sensation of movement, such bliss. Her body felt as if it were made for sex, skin and sensation, a push of life, a glorious wave of relief, and finally the silky explosion, groaning, gasping.

The next stood to take his turn, hollering out with an untimely ejaculation. At the sniggers of the third boy, the guy flinched, blushed crimson, slunk away.

Strong hands turned her over and opened her wide to bruise and caress.

Another joined another as the door opened and more athletes arrived. Beds were hastily created on the floor, sheets and blankets protecting skin as the seething, jerky, fluid motion escalated. Sophi opened her eyes. She could see the moonlight bend its light across moving naked flesh. Beauty, ugliness, what was the difference?

She sensed him standing, waiting in the shadows. Shoulders back, hips forward, blue eyes hooded – and knew he would be patient, his hand moving in practised rhythm. So she closed her eyes and lost herself once more.

They were leaving, some in pairs, some alone. The sound began to die, shouts turning to murmurs and laughter. Without warning he was next to her, pulling her close, rougher than all the others, hurting, making her bleed and cry out in pain and pleasure. Finally there was only cool air on her skin, and from out in the birch trees came the final keening of birdsong.

Sophi woke with a start. Ebbe was sleeping beside her. They were punished if they didn't report for training by six am, well rested, ready for work. Bad things would happen, not only to them but to their families. Food tokens might not arrive, the car might be taken away, travel permits to competitions abroad refused, and mama so wanted to have a holiday this year. Worse still: your parents could be taken to Stasi headquarters for questioning.

Each and every time, the boy looked younger than she'd remembered.

Dark hair, full lips and a determined chin. He held her even whilst asleep and she wondered for a moment why. He awoke and, with a seal-like turn, entered her. Kissing her into silence. They moved together before they lay spent and silent. Sophi stared into his strange bright eyes, noting the imperfect slant of his right eye, closer to his ear, the set of his mouth and thin cheekbones. He grinned, the smile not quite registering, kissed her mouth and slid out of the bed in one long flowing movement, pulling on his trousers and standing over her, strong and beautiful.

Sophi's legs shook as she stood under a hot jet of water in the shower room. There was blood between them and, right at that moment, she vowed: I'm not going to do this again. Ever.

She'd find another room today, or as soon as possible, another roommate. Sophi was only here for one more week, now even that felt too long. The last time, after three weeks of almost nightly orgies, she'd stopped bleeding altogether and had to have an operation. The translucent foetus removed before it grew. The weary doctor hadn't bothered to look up as he motioned a nurse to give the injection.

It wouldn't hurt, he'd said, but it had. A bruising pain in her belly, an ache behind her eyes, but Sophi hadn't cried. They were training for the games and, if she won a medal, she'd be eligible for a room of her own.

The hallway leading to the pool was silent; only the distant rasp of a scrubbing brush came from the pool area.

In the fourth cubicle, Sophi locked the door and checked every centimetre of space. Nothing had been moved or painted over. There were ways of knowing when or where a bug had been placed: newly painted walls, pictures that had been cleaned or re-hung. All was well. This cubicle was the same as yesterday: safe and wonderfully quiet. Her skin began to itch. Changing into the uniform swimsuit, she checked her legs and navel for new hair growth and saw her thighs were dotted with pinpricked circles. The last time that had happened she'd been given antibiotics but with the medicine her swimming time slowed. No way was that going to happen again.

Outside there was the usual patter as the other swimmers arrived. She'd learned how to judge distance at Hochberg. To know when someone was close enough to hear or when she was being listened to. The main doors opened and closed and from the far side of the pool Eric Röther shouted, 'Come on Künstler, hurry up.'

Her groin tightened, remembering last night's sex, counting how many times. I'm fifteen, she thought sliding her left hand between the seat and the wall, I'm fifteen. There it was. Her very own secret: the metal ridge of a new razor blade. As long as she could keep it safe everything else would be OK. As if he'd heard her, Eric began yelling at the other swimmers to change from their warm up to fast and slow laps.

'You're late.' He pointed to the nearest lane that had been kept clear for Sophi. She could smell his stale breath; recall his hands pinching her breasts, poking, squeezing until he'd done what he wanted. His daughters were the same age as her. Creamy fleshed, dimpled babies, she'd seen them sitting with their mother, applauding as his team came first.

The water was deliciously cool. The white and blue of the swimming-pool tiles magnified an underwater world, bringing her thoughts sharply into focus. If only she could talk to Ebbe as a normal girlfriend might. Maria had a boyfriend. She'd be doing the things normal kids did: walking around the town in a group, talking, laughing about things that were only funny to them. No one in this place could ever do things like that. With every vitamin, each injection or medication the athletes took, they slipped further away from the edge of normal.

After six lengths she paused and waited for the day's instruction – bursting to take on a challenge. That moment, the burning power in her muscles, the knowledge that she could fly through water and never really tire, made training worth every moment of pain.

After the hour's work, she was thinking about breakfast and dreading the excruciating hour of exercise theory. No need to join the queue for the vitamins they all knew to be steroids. No pills today. That afternoon she'd be in one of the hidden underground rooms, sitting in the submarine-like Barochamber, breathing in oxygen-reduced air. Following that the last series of painful steroid injections before the Olympic Games, then training in the wave pool with the hated mask over her face and a tube that fed in air.

A side-glance at Eric had her missing Maria again. Her friend would have made such fun of his fist of a face. Someone had upset the training schedule. Maybe she hadn't swum fast enough? Frightened, Sophi knew Eric could do terrible things. Her days could be turned into one long cycle of injections and 'exercise' alone with him.

In its hiding place the blade whispered a promise of escape. She dug her shaking hand between the seat and the wall, pinched the blunt end between her finger and thumb, running the blade lightly across her arm careful not to cut skin. They were swimming again straight after the theory class, and people were beginning to notice the scars on her arms and her breasts.

In the adjoining cubicle, pretty, snub-nosed Heike chatted away about the theatre trip that had been arranged. She waited so they could walk to the canteen together and talk about the latest method of hand roll to create smooth water flow.

'It's impossible,' Heike held her hands out, turning them

first one way then the other.

'Like this?' Sophi slowly cupped and tilted her hands as gracefully as she could, but out of water the movement looked clumsy and wrong. Heike laughed.

'How's your roommate?' she asked as Sophi looked away. Older athletes were primed to check on the younger ones. Reporting everything to the officials and getting rewarded for information with special favours. Heike didn't even know who Diertha was. She'd never asked anything like that before, only complaining, like they all did, about the gruelling schedule and the nearly impossible new swimming styles they were supposed to perfect.

'Everything's fine.'

Sophi turned left towards the sentry gate, slipping into the cramped reception office. Barely ten minutes left to make her weekly phone call. When Mama answered, Sophi asked for Papa and her heart sank when she heard him saying that he was late, in a hurry to leave for his surgery. Reciting the list of clothing down the phone, she longed to whisper 'Save me,' and tell him what happened every night, but she knew Papa wouldn't believe her. He'd told her that she was lucky to be chosen. He'd say she should do exactly what she'd been told to do; so she ended the call weeping silently into the arm of her sweatshirt.

After breakfast Eric was already ticking the last name on his list when Sophi astonished herself by stopping and asking him outright for a different room.

'Diertha stays up so late,' she said. 'I need rest if I'm going to win.' She amended her words to: 'I will win,' when he looked annoyed.

'Better than all the others now are you?'

'No Eric, I just need to sleep.'

Right there, at that moment, she nearly blurted out how she knew where his wife lived; she even had the phone number. If she did that she might as well cut her wrists properly. Eric would hardly miss her. There were new girls waiting to swim for him, girls that could be better than her, each one eager to give him whatever he wanted.

'Diertha Bernstock will be leaving soon enough,' he said. 'You'll have the room to yourself once she's gone.'

Paying scant attention to the theory lesson, her mind already imagining that promise of stillness, Sophi dreamed of sleep wrapped in clean white sheets, of winning the Olympics and escaping this place of nightmares into a world of colour.

CHAPTER TWELVE

~

Mia was already outside the school, kicking the wall as if she wanted an argument. Looking everywhere but over by the trees where Gerda made a great show of nudging her podgy dark-haired companion.

'You're late, just like Petrus said.' The girl hugged her backpack and scowled, revealing perfectly lined sharp teeth.

'I'm here aren't I?' The child's comment hurt more than it should. 'Your friends want a lift?'

'No.' Mia began biting her nails. The two other girls made an exaggerated show of giggling: hands covering mouths doubling over in fake mirth. The one who wasn't Gerda pretended to faint: arms spiralling, hand to chest. She leaned backwards about to fall. Gerda held onto her and they collapsed onto the ground shrieking.

Sophia wanted to knock their heads together.

'You have to deal with things,' she said, 'whether you want to or not.'

'Deal with what?' Mia's voice squeaked. 'Not having any friends?'

Oh, for goodness sake – was she the only one who saw how things were, that Mia's life was going to change and she'd just have to adapt. And how annoying to feel the echo of Mia's pain as if it were her own.

'You're going to have to deal with your Oma – my mother – Dagmar – being ill.' The word 'dying' lingered on her tongue. 'As for those two ninnies…' Sophia climbed out of the car and stood up straight in her uniform, smiling in vindication when the girls fell silent, turned tail and ran. 'If they can't be your friends now, they never really were.'

Beneath them the birch-tree roots she'd drawn as a child were growing, shifting in the earth. The underground places Sophia had imagined as secret and safe, a place for people to meet, to talk, were only make believe. The truth was that at training camp she'd been as isolated as Mia felt now, perhaps she should have said something kinder; found a phrase that might actually help the girl.

'Can we just go please?'

Lord. Ten to one Mia was going to cry again. What to do now? Tell Hajo she not only recognised two officers, but one had been her lover, the other a Stasi spy? What would he say? Martin was his friend; he might want to look the other way? Would Hajo, like her father, turn out to be something other? An evil she didn't want to see? No, he wouldn't. She had to act fast. Do something, or every scrap of evidence would disappear.

Father's voice whispered: just walk away. Maria would be grateful, Jörg would still have his job – no one would know any different and the world would continue to turn as it had always done.

Mia was unclipping the buckle on her school bag for the third time. She wasn't crying. Perhaps she was angry:

being angry was so much better than being sad.

'I don't want to stay with Petrus.' Mia stared fiercely ahead as they came to the hospital entrance. 'Oma said I should stay with you, and I can't stay with Gerda. She's not my friend anymore.'

Blindsided. Mia had planned her request so well. Even she wouldn't be that cruel to a child. Mia waited, eyes averted while Sophia silently prayed for Dagmar to get better.

'So,' Mia asked, 'can I?'

'Mia, I've got to go home. You're going to have to stay with him until Dagmar gets better.'

'Please.' Mia was crying now, quietly, as if she'd given up because no one cared enough to help. Sophia's heart ached, a sharp pain that came from those endless lonely days when she'd phoned her mother, begging to come home, only to have father say how ungrateful she was. That she should consider herself lucky to be given such an opportunity, to train and win for her country.

'Oh, Mia, don't cry. I'll ask my boss if I can take a few more days leave. But you'll have to stay with Petrus until I know. Now, let's go and see Dagmar.'

'Thank you.' As they parked, the child lunged, her wet face connecting with Sophia's neck, hugging as tightly as the space allowed.

The hospital was a hive of activity. Lunch was being served, no visitors allowed, and Petrus was waiting in the café with a sandwich for Mia.

'Go,' Sophia said. 'Have your lunch. I've got to make a phone call. Don't worry. I'll collect you in an hour.'

'I'll get a team there Monday at the latest,' Hajo said as

she tried to make him listen. 'Sophia, I must go. We've a lead on the man seen in the park with your friend the afternoon before she died.' He paused, took a breath. 'Sophi?' his voice softened to a murmur. 'Dearest, I really do have to go.'

'Hajo. The paperwork will be gone by the weekend.'

'Not if I call and say how pleased we are with your findings that no further action is required.'

She didn't bother to argue, she'd do what she had to do: go and find what she needed. Tonight. Before it was too late. Her mind was racing, joining the dots: they had a lead on the man who'd spoken with Käthe. That man could be Petrus. Petrus warning Käthe to stay away.

★★★

Wedged in between a hairdresser and vegetable shop, the provincial café was serving *Thüringer Klöße*, a long-forgotten favourite of potato dumplings with meat, cauliflower and a creamy cheese sauce. A moment of delicious escape; the dumplings revealing three crispy squares of buttered toast.

Stomach full, bill paid, she gazed across at the hospital entrance, duty lying heavy as lunch. She'd promised to collect Mia – when there were so many more important things to do. Ah. Good. There was Petrus, emerging from a side door near the hospital kitchens. Where was Mia? Maybe he'd left the child to spend time with her beloved Oma? Her father walked quickly across the car park and paused by the bus stop. Where was he going? She stood up, about to wave or call.

He was following someone. The gait was unmistakable.

He waited too long to cross the road, glanced over at the newspaper shop, stared at the window display as if the advertisements were captivating. While all the time he was watching his chosen prey in the glass reflection.

Age forty-two, Ilse Hammerman was still undeniably beautiful and as recognisable as a long-absent member of the family. A ghost of a memory floated into Sophia's mind: her father arriving home late, car lights picking out the profile of the driver. Her lovely young face turning to him for a kiss, Dagmar waiting inside the house, hidden in the shadows of the unlit sitting room.

Certain she wouldn't be seen, Sophia slipped out of the café and leaned against the wall, humiliated by the thrill of excitement and terror that ran from her toes to her fingers. A child again, snooping on her father.

Dressed in a beige trouser suit and a pea coat with deep- blue edging, Ilse captured the image of a successful doctor. Her bright blonde hair had been cut to a perfect bob that sashayed as she hurried through the car park, past the shops, crossing the road and making her way towards a new housing estate.

Sophia's father followed at a distance, his daughter trailing behind.

It wasn't easy to admit that, like everyone, Dagmar had wanted nothing more than to be loved. Sophia remembered a mother unbound from illness and saw her, as if from afar, gazing at Petrus with a fierce expression of love. Her mother's dark brown hair, formerly so abundant, had been carefully brushed back to show off two stud earrings in a deep blue stone. The blue matched her eyes. Perhaps the image came from an old photo?

Petrus turned a corner. Sophia hurried to catch up. She didn't want to lose this chance of seeing whether love or hate remained between them. Somehow during Petrus' quest for status and adoration, Dagmar had begun to fade. A flower with no water, she'd lived most of her life comparing herself with the women Petrus wanted. The belated realisation that Dagmar had blamed herself for not being good enough made Sophia even more determined to see what her father was up to. It would serve him right to be treated as he'd treated Dagmar, although, in her mother's place, Sophia would have found many ways to make Ilse's life difficult. Maybe he was going to warn her about the possibility of an investigation into sports doctors that drugged athletes. Maybe he *knew* it was all going to come out? There had been murmurings, but nothing concrete, because no one dared say, but now?

Sophia reached the corner. Ilse stopped, as if a string had been pulled tight, and turned around. Damn. Ducking behind the wall, Sophia couldn't hear a thing; all she could do was crane her neck and peer.

Oh god. Petrus had taken hold of her. Instead of avoiding him as she surely should, Ilse clung to him, her head brushing his shoulder, raising her face, kissing him. Sophia looked away. In her mind's eye she saw herself opening father's desk drawer. *That* letter; the monthly dates weren't conferences, they were meetings. Assignations. Her father had never left Ilse, he'd just pretended so that life just carried on. Stomach tight, hands clenched. She imagined walking up to them, killing them both by just looking at them, her childhood need for love grown into something new, something absolute and authoritative.

206

Why was Ilse weeping? Petrus guided her away from the possibility of prying eyes to the relative seclusion of a dark alleyway that ran opposite to where Sophia waited, squashed up against the damp wall. Their heads were inclined. They were talking. Touching the way lovers do when they've been apart for too long and their meetings have been kept a precious secret. They held one another in a tight yet furtive embrace. She read their need for reassurance, for a stability that would never materialise. Petrus began kissing Ilse's ear and neck as if he were starving.

Sophia looked away, seasick, the land an unsteady place. When she looked back, Ilse, playing the weepy-eyed tragedy queen, was walking away down the road one hand trailing as if she longed to stay. She turned right and Sophia followed, taking savage pleasure from the knowledge that her father must have seen her.

Ilse made her way along a short, narrow driveway. Sophia moved closer as Ilse put her key in the lock to open the front door. A miniature blonde child hurtled past, followed closely by a stocky red-faced boy squeezed into pale khaki shorts. Both were yelling. The boy held a fat black plastic spider in his hand which seemed magically to transform into an aeroplane flying through the air to land on his sister's head – provoking the girl to shriek. Ilse's daughter was a miniature image of her mother: white hair stuck to an indignant face and mouth that was stretched to its widest, maximizing the impact of her scream. Ilse caught both children in her arms. Plucked the offending spider from her son's hand and propelled the pair towards the doorway.

'The tickets arrived, the tickets arrived!' The girl threw

a furious look at her brother and stuck out her tongue, keeping a tight grip on her mother's hand.

'And a letter from our new school. Daddy opened it.' The boy was not going to be outdone; reaching behind his mother, he pinched his sister on her bottom. In between the girl's furious wails Ilse turned back to scold the boy, and saw Sophia watching from only yards away.

She seemed to quail; eyes darting left, right, as both children hauled at her arms.

What could be said to this woman who had floated so bright and unchanging in her mind for years? Nothing at all? Everything?

Did these children belong to Petrus? Her half-brother and half-sister?

Petrus and Ilse had been meeting for years; the two of them travelling across the barrier between East and West to continue a strange version of a love story. Dagmar must have known, and if so, Petrus would have known how ill she was. His surprise at Mia's arrival had been an act. Her mother had accepted that Petrus came to see his mistress, but never herself. Petrus would have seen glimpses of Mia growing from child to teenager. He could have helped in bringing her up. Far worse, he'd watched Dagmar's health steadily decline and had done absolutely nothing. How contemptible he was, with his easy deceit and smooth lies, his concentration on no one but himself.

Ilse was getting out before the medical profession caught on; before her file was discovered and her work with the Stasi made public. The family would be going far away, anywhere that was far enough from the prying eyes of West Germany.

The door shut. Sophia stayed where she was, staring at the house. Ilse needed to know that she wasn't a scared child any longer. The little girl's blotchy face appeared, peeping over the back of an armchair in the sitting room window, staring straight into Sophia's eyes. The child stuck her tongue out: a pink flag between reddened cheeks.

Ilse burst into the picture, scooping up the child, closing both curtains in two sharp sweeping motions.

Go on, you bitch, Sophia thought. Take your children and run. If I see any of you again, I'll break you. Those thoughts calmed her as she made her way back to the car, where Petrus was waiting, one hand on the passenger door. His eyes shifted when she glared. 'Ilse has a new post, a chance to start again,' he said, waiting for Sophia to unlock the passenger door.

Sophia opened the back door and placed the picture of the mermaid behind her seat. Perhaps it could be a talisman, a source of protection against all the lies that seemed to be layered over each other. Those traces were like the truth, a reality that Frau Schöller had tried to show her: that a person can become something better than the devastation all around. She traced a finger along the ridged wooden frame. She'd have to give the picture back to Maria. Make it clear that she would accept no form of bribery. No payment to keep Jörg's secrets safe.

'Sophia.' He was carefully peeling off his soft leather gloves, making sure he got his story right. 'Ilse helped us to get out.'

'Why? Why would she?'

'My dear – you know why. They refused to move you to a place where they could treat you.'

'I don't believe you.' Maria had said the same, yet Petrus always, always, lied.

'I'll explain, really I will. First, you need to know she saved your life, and now, I beg you, let her go.'

He was pleading for this woman but he'd done nothing to save Dagmar.

'You simply must listen.' Petrus had taken off his long soft coat. He folded it with care, climbed into the passenger seat and placed the coat across his knees. 'I knew Ilse was working with the Stasi, but I also knew that they wouldn't ever be truly interested in me.'

'What did you do for them?' she asked.

'This isn't about what I did,' he said. 'There was something they wanted, something very important.'

'Talking of important, I'd like to know if those children are yours. Perhaps I ought to go and say hello to my dear little brother and sister?'

'Don't be so absurd.' Petrus' mouth tightened, as it did each time he thought her behaviour juvenile. Now he'd work his magic. Make her feel like a bully, and he the innocent victim. 'Sophia.' His voice was gentle, the voice of a tiger purring before it pounced. 'Listen to me. The Stasi didn't want me. They wanted you. I was asked to keep an eye on you and because of you I began to work for them.'

She imagined him in that underground place, working to a tight schedule. The examination bed that served to make the athletes believe they were being cared for. Each perfect young body injected with enough steroids to make them mad for sex. She'd been in that secret place, but not with her father. She'd had injections and taken a pink then a blue pill after each Wednesday swim. Resting it on her tongue, waiting for the heat to begin in her belly then spread.

He'd been in Kreischa, the main hospital and treatment centre for any sports injury. Athletes came to him with strange injuries, torn muscles that wouldn't mend because their bones were unable to support such massive growth. He was told to fix the injuries quickly, to find new pills, stronger steroids to heal damaged tissue. Later his duties grew to include testing steroids packaged to look like vitamin tablets. Some came disguised as sweets. Sophia remembered the sticky, overly sweet chocolate with a chemical aftertaste.

'You weren't looking out for me, father. You were looking out for yourself. Don't you pretend,' she added, taking mean satisfaction from the way his mouth formed a shocked O. 'I really think the time for lies has gone. Don't you, father dear?' How she hated him at this moment, her father who'd only divulged the truth to save his lover, never to comfort his daughter. This burnished chameleon, shifting the moment you managed to pin blame.

'My dear.' He leaned back, eyes closed, planning. Shutting her out.

'So, what did you do to secure our safe escape?' She should have faced him with those letters found many years ago. Been braver, stronger, and now it was too late.

'I did what any father would do. The operation was a mess; the surgeon had no idea. I could see that something had to be done.'

He'd made a deal. She was to be sewn up while he contacted his old friend Günther, who, in return for on-going information from the West, gave them the necessary papers.

'What about my mother? What about Diertha and Mia?' She felt gratified, a child scoring a point when he flinched and turned away.

'Dagmar wouldn't come. She insisted that she stay and care for Mia.' Words poured from his mouth. 'My dear, you know how it was. No one had a choice, but I refused to treat you. I am your father after all, and the athletes were allowed to do things I simply couldn't face.'

Sophia saw the feral girl, pelting through the woods with a group of athletes whose feet streamed across the ground. It was her. There by the roots of an oak tree. Naked pock-marked flesh. Legs spread. Head back as a young blond man pumped in/out/in/out. Stop. Ebbe was here. He'd not want anyone to know about his past. That made him dangerous.

'What happened to Diertha?' She watched him arrange his features to appear thoughtful.

'Diertha was beyond all of us. She became pregnant and said nothing.'

Now was the time to ask. 'Father, did you ever see Käthe in Berlin?' If he denied it he was lying.

'Whatever makes you ask me such a question,' he said. 'Why would I?'

Mia appeared at the far end of the car park. She looked around, then began making her way towards them. Petrus opened his mouth, about to continue as Mia slammed the door and slumped: a silent miserable child, hiding in the back seat.

When they reached Dagmar's house Mia turned to Sophia. 'You haven't forgotten, have you?' she asked.

'You're staying longer? Promise?'

'Until Dagmar is home. Promise.' She made sure that Petrus heard as Mia leaned across to hug, then kiss her. 'I'll see you really, really, soon,' the child said. 'Don't you dare try and sneak away.'

★★★

'He's written his letter of resignation.' Maria said, pointing at Jörg who sat at the kitchen table, scowling into a frothing glass of beer. 'Go on. Show her.'

Jörg tossed the sheet of paper across the table. This was a silly game. Jörg had no intention of resigning while his sister had information to sell. Sophia placed the mermaid picture on the table, knowing how much she wanted to keep the small gift.

'I won't take bribes or payment, Maria,' she said, thinking of all the childhood secrets she and Maria had shared; of Mia, scared of her own grandfather, waiting for Sophia to come back. Of Petrus who was longing to be the one with Ilse, flying to a faraway country.

Maria put her hand in front of her mouth. A pantomime of shock.

'Oh don't be so stupid! You thought,' she pointed at the picture, '*that* was a bribe? How could you? That was from Mama, not me. It's your fault I didn't send it to you years ago. You disappeared, not me. Anyway, I told you I can give you something better, information that should have been burnt.' She waited, greedy and calculating, for Sophia to ask what she needed to do in order to secure this secret paperwork.

'Sophi, have you never wondered about your father?

What he was doing all those years in Kreischa? Why your mother looked after Mia?'

'I didn't know he worked there until today, and yes, he told me about Mia.'

Did Maria suspect him of hurting Käthe? No, she would have said so straight away. Maria knew what Petrus was; she'd made it her work to find out. As for Dagmar and Mia, Sophia would do what she could in reparation for her mother, and Mia would be cared for.

'Sophi, listen to me. I have records from places like Hochberg. Records that show they gave athletes drugs. Proof, so you see Käthe's death isn't wasted.' Maria smiled, triumphant in this, her moment of glory.

How she longed for Maria to turn back into the girl she'd once been. 'Kleine Jörg,' she said, turning to face him. 'You haven't really grown up at all, have you? Hiding behind your sister's skirts now, are you? Making sure she lies for you?'

Good. There it was. The fury she'd seen at the station. Jörg's narrow face tightening as he rose to do what he'd itched to do the moment he saw her.

'Watch your temper,' Maria hissed. 'Don't you go making things worse than you already have. And you,' she pointed at Sophia, 'you're not much better, coming back cleaner than snow to ruin people's chance at a future. We had nothing when Mother died. You could have helped Käthe, and you could have helped me. Now, if you have your way, we'll have nothing again.'

'Maria, I wasn't an informer like that little sneak.' It hurt so to be blamed for something she'd not known and never asked about.

'No, but you were part of it, all of it.' When Sophia began to argue she added, 'I'll show you.'

She signalled that Sophia should follow. An age-old journey up the stairs, one they'd done so often: running, shrieking, giggling their way into what was now a tidy but grey space. As they climbed, a sadness echoed between them, some bitter loss.

'You've been busy.' My god, she really needed to tell Hajo to come. Right now. Piles of paperwork had been neatly stacked on the table in the centre of the room. A treasure trove: secret files that the West German authorities would move mountains to get their hands on.

'Sophi.' Maria stood to one side. 'They're yours to take. But look here, look at this.' In Maria's palm lay a bracelet – *that* bracelet – one of three, made from cotton thread and beads. Blue and white fabric daisies had been attached to the chain at regular intervals.

'We made a promise, a promise you can't forget because you have the third.'

She dropped the friendship bracelet into her hand and held tight before Sophia could object. A promise to help. A pledge that couldn't be broken. Sophia's cold hand was trapped inside Maria's warm clasp. The plaited fabric was too short to circle her grown-up wrist. She wasn't going to tell Maria that her bracelet lived in her police jacket pocket: protection against bad luck. Sophia had imagined Käthe and Maria accompanying her through thick and thin, the old Käthe, razor sharp, funny and full of life, and Maria, soft and kind, not this strange, brittle woman, pleading for her understanding and help. 'You do remember it, don't you?' Maria said. 'Look. Käthe and I collected the files. There are loads of names we both know. I sent you the report that was linked to you.'

Sophia picked out a file labelled 'Rolf' and 'Meschke'. The list of steroids next to each athlete was terrifying. The names familiar as old friends: Käthe, Diertha, Sara.

Maria wasn't looking at her. 'I understand – I do understand – that after this we'll not be friends. You can have all the paperwork. Take it with you. I'll only ask for two things in return, nothing more. Please help Jörg to keep his job. If he loses it we lose this house and we don't have money to buy another. And second; please help me find out what really happened to Käthe and Diertha. I know Diertha was cruel to you when she should have been looking out for you, but she was your cousin. And Käthe was our friend. If you won't do this for me, do it for Mama? She loved you as much as she loved me.'

'Maria.' As they traipsed back to the kitchen, Sophia sought words that might reassure. 'I can ask that Jörg's case be given special consideration. But he won't be able to be an active police officer.'

'I told you.' Jörg was vibrating with anger, fists clenched. 'Stupid bitch has no intention of helping us.'

'I wonder, Jörg, if you remember?' Come on, she thought; let your anger out so Maria can see you for what you are. 'No? You don't remember? Up against that wall.' Ah, there it was again, lightning fury. Maria was staring at her brother as if she'd never seen him before.

'What did he do?' she asked.

'Yes, you tell your sister.' How electric it was not to fear him.

'Nothing. I did nothing, she's making it up. The little

slut always did lie.'

'He watched me at night from outside my bedroom, then one day you made me touch it, didn't you Jörg?'

'It wasn't like that.'

'No? Oh, I see – you thought I wanted to put my hand down there?'

'Shut your mouth.' He sat and put his head in his hands. No anger now, only humiliation and fear. Maria was staring, her face an unbearable expression of horror and grief. 'I didn't know,' she said.

'Maria. You were a child just as I was. I just want you to know that while I'll try and help, it's for your sake, not his.' Sophia put her arm around her friend's shoulder. 'Come on now. Make some tea for us, I'll tell him what he needs to write.'

Outside in the biting air, Sophia hoped her side of the deal would hold true. Jörg had been made to sign an honest declaration that included every detail of his work for the Stasi, the reason for his mother's imprisonment, her eventual death and the family's subsequent living situation. He wouldn't continue to work as an investigations officer. However, with the files Maria had collected, Hajo might be persuaded to agree that something of their lives could be salvaged, as a gesture, not payment in kind. In her hand she held the bracelet. She'd find out what happened to Käthe, and poor stupid Diertha. She hadn't needed Maria's gift to find resolution to look further.

CHAPTER THIRTEEN

~

Swapping her uniform for a sweatshirt and a warm fleece jacket, Sophia shoved the letters Maria had sent to her under the hotel mattress and jogged back down the stairs, keys in her pocket, driving through the evening light to the police station.

Before climbing out of the car, she clicked the interior reading light off: better safe than sorry. It would be just her luck if someone saw her. She had the keys to the station and could go in without alerting anyone. The neighbouring houses were clearly visible, their towering walls monumentally dark. Faint light profiled the alleyway. Now, from where she stood, Sophia could see both the public entrance and the car-port. The sky, which had been brooding all afternoon, promised sleet, maybe even snow. Parked up, the squad cars rested like slumbering beetles, their carapaces glimmering under the orange security lighting.

Hajo had been furious, insistent she stay put, wait for him. He'd sounded just like her father. Walk away. Look to the future. Forget. She'd asked, 'Did you find out who was with Käthe that afternoon?'

'Yes, we did. Sophi, it was your father.'

Mia's face slid into focus. The child's grief when she realised her Oma was so unwell. An unhappy child, as Sophia had been. Now, she was asleep in her room as Petrus made phone calls and plans. What to do? Who to warn, who to protect? Ebbe would be wondering. Jörg would be arguing with Maria, furious at what she'd learned: her brother assaulting her best friend. At the centre of it all stood Petrus.

Sophia made her way to the reception door. Thank god, the first key fitted and she slipped through into the reception area. Nothing stirred. There should have been a twenty-four hour operator at the call desk, plus two duty officers. Still, it was a rural station; perhaps the number would be switched through to the police rest room. The door to the offices, so firmly closed before, stood wide open. The incinerator would be out the back, in an area not far from the car-port. Passing silently by the door to the computer room, Sophia shivered. This was forbidden ground that had remained untouched for years. Whosoever foolishly stepped in the way of the Stasi, the People's Police, or anyone involved in Theme 14.25 would, in the past, have been silenced. Perhaps, now she thought of it, it would have been wiser to have brought her gun.

***

Mia thought she heard Petrus call, so she started down the stairs. She'd been crying again and was desperate for anything that might stop the panicky feeling.

He was talking to someone, quietly, urgently.

Something in his voice wasn't right. His strange whispery tone, like the one she used in class to tell Gerda the answers to stuff, made her certain he didn't want anyone to hear. It wasn't late, only around eight, so he couldn't think she was asleep. Mia didn't want to snoop. She hated it when people snooped, but she *had* to hear what he was saying.

'You will have to clear it all tonight. Yes, tomorrow will be too late. Sophia can't know.' He seemed reassured by the answer because he said, 'Good. I've done my part, so that will be the end of it,' and replaced the phone.

The end of what? He had to be doing something bad if he was whispering on the phone. Maybe *he'd* kill Oma? Stop giving her the right medication? Put something in that drip that had been inside her arm, something that would make her die? Maybe he'd do it so he could be with his girlfriend. The one Oma talked about, the one who lived on the new estate by the hospital.

Oma had been right to not trust him. He wasn't the person Mia had briefly thought he was. He was a doctor and knew about medicines, medicines that could kill people instead of making them well. He was a part of the thing that frightened her and everyone else who lived in East Germany. Even though it was all supposed to be over with the Wall and everything, it wasn't. The police, the Stasi, *those* people, could still hurt you for no reason at all.

Before the Wall came down those people would arrive in the early morning, acting normal, as if there was nothing wrong. They'd take you from your home because your sister or brother or niece or even your *friend* had tried to escape to the West. Sitting on the steps, Mia put her head between her knees. Please don't let Petrus come up, she prayed; remembering how frightened she'd been knowing Sophia was a police officer.

★★★

The rain finally arrived, thudding on to the precinct roof-top. Burning anything on such a wet night would be madness. A phone rang. Sophia could hear the voices of two officers in the rest room, grumbling.

'We've been told to carry on burning papers, not go out.'

'Well, one of us will have to go.'

'Who have they thumped this time?'

'Each other. Same as last week.'

The second voice made a decision. Sophia ran back to the reception area. A moment later, the headlights of the squad car flared, beaming through the pane as she flattened herself against the wall, listening for the sound of the security gates to roll back. The car pulled away. The building fell silent. Any relief at the departure gave way to dread. One officer would be as dangerous as two.

There was no need to worry. The stubby, pastry-faced officer had made himself a coffee and was taking a break with a portable TV, his feet resting on the table, arms linked behind a thick neck. Thank goodness, not Ebbe. His presence would have made the situation even more risky. If it had been Jörg? The prospect wasn't worth thinking about.

At the far end of the corridor a beam of light shone through the gap between carpet and door. Someone had been in there. Better still, they'd left the door open. Sophia waited. No sound. No movement.

The room was filled with paper. Towers of old reports teetered: a line of unsteady pensioners waiting to cross the road. Files were haphazardly stacked on grey metal cabinets

that lined the sides of two walls. On the table in the middle
of the room more papers were scattered, half in, half out
of loose, metal-edged containers. Three of the nine cabinets yawned open as if they were simply too tired to close.
Their innards, a mix of metal-edged files and brown cardboard, were exposed. The filing had been alphabetically
arranged. The cabinets labelled A–F were empty, everything gone. No trace of Diertha Bernstock, although she'd
not expected it, Sophia felt a pang of guilt and sadness for
her dead forgotten cousin. The name Eric Röther, left on
an empty file on the table, made her take a sharp in breath.
Why did her trainer have a file here? Cabinets S–Z were
empty. Damn. Günther Schenke and Jörg Schöller's reports
had been incinerated. Their past lives ceased to exist. They
thought they could still be anything they chose to be: except, of course, Sophia knew.

★★★

The grey feeling of loneliness stretched out its fingers and
whispered how useless Mia was, how selfish, how un-
wanted. Even her friends at school hadn't called to see if
she was okay, because no one cared enough to bother. Mia
shoved her favourite hand-knitted jumper and coat into
her bag. She needed Sophia. She'd find her and tell her
about Petrus talking about 'clearing things up' on the
phone. She'd warn her, and by warning her she'd be doing
something good.

Petrus was in the kitchen pouring a drink. She heard
the clink of the bottle against the glass and the sound of
the cupboard closing. The TV was blaring so he wouldn't
hear. She crept down the stairs, heart in mouth, with a

ready excuse should he see. Listened hard. He was watching a news programme about a sports doctor who'd talked to the papers, earning himself a load of money. She peeked round the open door frame. Petrus face was white, as if what he was hearing scared him.

Sophia had been an athlete! Petrus a doctor. The TV sports doctor said that many athletes didn't want to remember the experiences they'd had to endure. Sophia would tell me to shut up and stop being an idiot if I said I couldn't remember, she thought. The idea of being told off was comforting, it helped her to move quietly across the kitchen, unlock the back door and slip outside. Oh No. Petrus might be one of *those* doctors? It was better she was running away to Sophia. She'd tell her that as well, and then Sophia would say how well she'd done. Still, she locked the back door so that Petrus would be safe. Also, if he did try the door he'd not realise that she'd gone.

It was freezing. Just around the corner she put on her coat, zipping the hood right up. Last summer, she'd met up with Gerda in the evenings; they'd wanted to escape Gerda's annoying mother and Oma's loud TV. Gerda had decided to hang out with a group of older kids, kids Mia didn't like. They dressed in black and had chains around their necks and studs in their ears, mouths, even tongues. One of them boasted he had a piercing with a ring on his willy, gross as well as moronic. They also liked drinking. Gerda had thrown up because she hadn't drunk anything ever, but pretended she had. The group hadn't stayed to help as she vomited everywhere; they'd walked away laughing.

Now she realised that it had served Gerda right. She

and Tessa had laughed as they pretended to faint outside her school. Worse, Sophia had seen them. Gerda wasn't a friend. Sophia had been right all along. If your friends didn't help you when you needed them, they weren't your friends in the first place. So was that why Sophia didn't seem to have any friends herself?

The quickest route to the hotel was along this road. Cross at the junction and head into town. It wasn't that far, about forty minutes. Mia walked fast, keeping away from dark alleys, staying right in the middle of the road in areas where the streetlights were broken. The rain, a drizzle when she'd left, was now a steady sleety downpour. She tried to pull the hood of her coat even tighter, tugging at the straps, tying them in a bow, when she heard footsteps.

★★★

Käthe Niedermann's file was in the cabinet marked M–R. Inside was a report of an assault on a police officer and the use of illegal drugs, including steroids. A typed report stated that a ticket for Berlin, dated last Monday, had been bought. Surveillance had been requested. 'Romeo' (bloody hell, that was Petrus), was advised to intercept and report. Intervention would be requested if the suspect was delivering papers. *Intervention*? Oh god. Petrus had arrived before Käthe died? He wasn't strong enough to have hurt her. Maybe he'd warned her. Done what was requested and told Käthe to go home. Though why hadn't he said so when he'd already admitted so much?

Hang on. There was something else. The sheet of paper folded against the bottom of the file stated that: 'In accordance with Romeo's wishes, K. Niedermann is to be denied access to S. Künstler.'

Sophia shoved the note in her pocket. 'Get a grip,' she muttered, 'one step at a time.' Her hands were shaking, but not with fear. How could he? And how could she have allowed him such complete control over every aspect of her life?

Cabinet G–L hadn't been opened. She'd expected to find nothing more than a mention of her name, details of her rank prior to her visit, not her father's file mixed in with police records. In April 1962, Dr Künstler had been employed as doctor in charge of inmates' care and well-being. Everyone knew how badly prisoners suffered in the cells. Had Petrus tried to limit the brutality, or had he simply ignored it? 'October 1973' Ilse Hammerman was to instruct Romeo in the monthly delivery of anabolic steroids to Hochberg. You were promoted to be a *drugs courier*? Sophia thought. You, my father: a medical man who handed out poison to athletes.

'Please,' she prayed opening the second file, 'no more.'

★★★

A woman, not Petrus, came round the corner, hurrying along under a voluminous blue umbrella. She stopped, glanced up and opened her mouth to speak. Mia forced herself to turn, walk away and not glance back. If only she was still in Berlin. People minded their own business there. The alleyway she'd taken led in the right direction. The cobbled path was pitch black apart from one light right at the other end. God, how brainless she was. But the woman might have followed her to insist she go home.

Something ran through the darkness towards her, the rat-thing's feet scrabbling on the stones. Shrieking, Mia stumbled backward into the wall and bashed her shoulder. The rat-thing growled and bumped its runty furred body against her leg. She froze. Any moment it would bite.

A slice of bright yellow light fell across the path as a door directly opposite to her opened and a thickly set bald man wearing nothing but a vest and pants leaned out. He had a snake tattoo that went all round his neck

'Fipps,' he called 'Fippsi! Get in here.'

Mia tried to make herself invisible as the little sausage dog barked and jumped around her feet, before it scuttled towards the door, nails clipping on the cobbled stone.

'Daft dog.' The man slammed the door shut.

★★★

S. Künstler, Sophia read, international swimmer, daughter of P. Künstler. Competing for Hochberg Sports Club, supervised by the trainer Eric Röther, code-named 'Technik'.

She remembered a room painted white. *That* room with the examination bed, her body full of drugs. Outside there had been apple trees and birdsong. Inside she'd gradually changed from a girl into a monster. Wire brush hair, too long to be normal. Her voice had dropped to a growl; her legs muscled into tree trunks as her body grew engorged and ugly. Sophia remembered the wild power. The fury that made her want more than life could give. More than sex could offer. A fierce longing for something greater than the strength she'd had: to be able to swim forever.

The paper, dated February 1977, had nothing about her training, or the steroids she'd been given, nothing of the proof she now wanted. Her father's name, next to Günther Schenke, spoke of the agreement in which Petrus would continue his informant work in West Berlin. His payment: safe passage over the border for himself and his sick daughter, plus continuing ease of movement across the border if the information proved useful.

They'd worked together for years: Günther protecting her father; Petrus helping Günther. Then he'd left and continued to spy in West Berlin. It *had* been Günther on the phone that first night.

Someone was here. Move Sophi, *move now*.

★★★

Mia ran. Down the alley, across the street, round the corner onto Hinter Der Maur Strasse. She stopped under the archway that opened out into a square, directly opposite the hotel. Gasping for air, she looked behind. No one there. No one following. Dashing across the square, she climbed the few steps up to the hotel.

Mia had rehearsed a story that would get the lady at reception to phone through to Sophia's room, even though the visitor was wet and dirty. No one was there. Round the back of the desk were all the hooks with keys for the rooms. Sophia's key was right there. Number Seventeen, just as she'd said before she left Oma's house. That meant Sophia wasn't in her room – or perhaps the hotel had two keys? Mia couldn't go back to Petrus, so it really wasn't stealing. She'd unhooked the key just as the receptionist's heels clicked in the distance. By the time voices drew nearer, talking about night-shift rotas, Mia was already at the top of the first floor stair, hurrying along a carpeted hallway.

Room Seventeen was at the very end of the corridor. She knocked. Waited. Knocked a little louder and stuck her ear against the door. No sound, not even the drip of water running, which would have meant Sophia was in the shower. There were, however, voices behind her and rapid footsteps coming along the corridor. Mia shoved her key in the lock. Opened the door and closed it silently behind her.

Oh god. It was dark. If Sophia was asleep, she'd have her gun next to the bed.

Mia stood absolutely still. Nothing happened. No scream. No breathing noise. Nothing. She felt around the wall by the door for the light switch. Closed her eyes and braced herself for Sophia's yell of fury. Nothing. Outside, a car pulled into the car park. It reversed, stopped. The car door opened and shut. Mia opened her eyes and tiptoed to the window. Even though she wished hard that it was Sophia, it wasn't.

Shaking with cold and disappointment, she wondered what to do. Sophia's shirts were hung in the cupboard along with her police jacket. Her suitcase was half packed, which was weird because Sophia was seriously tidy. In the silence, Mia crept into the bathroom, taking great care not to get the carpet wet or dirty. Taking off her wet socks and shoes, she turned on the hot tap and kept her hands under the running water until they were warm; filled the sink and awkwardly washed one foot, followed by the other.

It was after nine. She'd wait until twelve. If Sophia

wasn't back? Well that wouldn't happen. Sophia didn't know anyone other than Petrus, so whoever she'd gone to see would be going to bed before midnight. Older people didn't stay up all night talking like her and Gerda, except they wouldn't talk now, nor ever again. Gerda would have to do her own homework; muddle through class on her own. Chat all night to Tessa if she wanted, because Mia would Never Ever speak to her again.

It was good to be annoyed. Sophia would be angry. In fact she'd be in a foul temper when she found Mia was in her room uninvited. She'd probably shout and tell her off for going outside on her own in the dark. She wouldn't ring Petrus. Mia knew that, just as she knew Sophia would listen to what Mia told her, and she wouldn't say how silly or how childish it all sounded.

Anyway, Sophia was probably at the police station, working her way through piles of boring paperwork. Mia pulled the blanket from the bed so as to wrap a bit of it round her. The corner of a brown envelope stuck out between the mattress and bed frame. Sophia wouldn't want her to open it. But what if Sophia was in danger and Petrus had been talking to someone he shouldn't have? Mia was the only one who knew both things. Anyway, what could be worse than what she'd already done?

★★★

Sharp, terrifying pain. Turn. Fight now, fight. A solid weight fractured against her head. Sophia kicked. The figure grunted. A pair of strong arms lifted her. She flew. Hit the wall. Crumpled. A door opened and shut: an icy breeze fingered her sore skin. Blackness.

Sophia woke to grey light edging in through a cracked window. Everything was wrong. Who'd broken into the apartment and broken the bedroom window? No water, no painkillers? Someone had moved them from where she kept them, always within easy reach. The bed felt hard. Every part of her was raw and aching.

She wasn't in a bed. She was curled up on the floor. When she moved, the room slid around like oil on water. Was this dying? Her head was sticky. *Blood*? Please, she prayed, let someone come. But then she was slipping away to a calm place, a place where nothing mattered, where she could rest and float under the sea.

Left for dead. She could lie on the whispering sea bed and remember Diertha.

Sophia eased her legs out straight. *Die*? Not bloody likely. Not at the hand of a fellow officer. The roaring in her ears was like the sea. *Concentrate.* The wall was just there, she could feel it with the sole of her foot. Right hand wedged against the floor, she pushed until her back felt its cold firm comforting strength. Hajo would be furious if she died in an anonymous storage room, unable to protect herself as she'd been taught.

There was a length of thick wire by her left hand. The wire trailed all the way up to the top of the cabinet. Mistakenly, Sophia tried to move her head. When she woke, the wavering outline of a telephone mocked her. *Come on.* She pulled. The phone rattled. If that bloody thing fell on her head, she'd be finished.

She pulled harder. *Fuck.* The phone hit her neck with a wet thud followed by a whine as the receiver disconnected. Her hands were shaking and turning a strange greeny blue.

The number? What was the bloody number? She couldn't remember.

God, she wanted her mother. 'Mama,' she sobbed, hating the weak, salty, useless emotion, closing her eyes. She cried for Dagmar who had let her go. Dagmar who hadn't kept her safe. Her mother who had given everything to a child called Mia.

A fierce small voice told Sophia to stop being so dumb. 'Come on,' the child voice insisted. 'Wake up. Stop being so pathetic. Of course you remember! Open your eyes and dial.'

Sophia remembered. She dialled her mother's number, waiting for what seemed like a lifetime before Petrus answered, and could only whimper when he asked with growing anger and anxiety: who was there?

'Papa,' she whispered in a voice that sounded more like a child's than her own, 'help me,' before the darkness came like a warm thick blanket and took her away.

★★★

Mia read the list of weird-sounding names. Pages of what looked like codes. Luckily Sophia had put all her thoughts onto one page, so all the rest of the paperwork went back in the envelope and she concentrated on that page.

'Theme 14.25'? She had no idea what that was but everyone knew that Hochberg Sports Centre was where the best swimmers went. Sophia would have gone there when she was a girl.

Eric's code name is 'Technik'. Schiemann is 'Meschke'? Code names? Mia read them again and felt scared. Maybe these were the files Petrus had been talking about? Sophia had them, so the person he'd been talking to wouldn't know where to look. But if Sophia was looking for more people who used code names, bad things would happen. The police would come. They'd take you away in a small van that said 'fruit and vegetable delivery' on the side, but everyone knew it delivered people. The Stasi would push you onto a chair with no proper seat so your bum slipped through. They would shove you in a wet room with dripping walls and floor that made your skin peel away from bone. They might sit you on a comfy sofa in a room filled with burning light bulbs. Every time you dozed off an alarm would fizz electricity into your arm. Oma had been interrogated. Like everything else no one ever talked about it, but Mia saw how her grandmother shook if anyone came to the door uninvited.

Those kinds of bad things were happening now, even though the Wall was down. OH NO. Petrus' name was next to Chief Schenke's name, halfway down the page, next to code names 'Romeo' and 'Wolf'. Maybe Petrus had been talking to him on the phone? Then she saw a name, and next to it: Did Petrus kill Käthe, or order the attack?

Mia pulled the bedclothes loose, put the paper and envelope back under the mattress, curled up as tight as she could and she shut her eyes.

'Sophia, please come,' she whispered. 'Come quickly.'

CHAPTER FOURTEEN

~

Sophia was deep inside the sea, floating under shoaling creatures. Scales glinted once, twice, as the sun hit the water. The shoal vanished and once more the silver weave of the ocean held her in its arms. She didn't know where she was, hardly cared. This place, unsettled, silent, safe, was the only home she knew.

Predators were circling closer. Her arms were ice cold. She pulled against tight muscle, water and terror. Concentrated on each stroke, aligning her head the way he'd told her to; moving her hands with the water, *being* water, never separating one element from the other. He'd said, 'You are liquid, so move like liquid.' Her muscles were burning, heat thawing ice. Stronger. A child made of water, powerful, never tiring. A being that could swim forever. So why was she frightened of the glittering whiteness? A dark shape squatted, leaning out over the surface. Darkness moved over the pool, stretching out, long and thin. A finger. Pointing straight to her.

Sophia screamed. She pulled at the needle that was inserted inside her arm and tried to strike the person standing by her bed.

'Oh no, you don't.' The nurse's thick brown glasses

magnified her eyes. What was she doing in hospital? Sophia moved her head. Christ that hurt. Fighting nausea, she made out the shape of curtains and a heart monitor by her side.

'Petrus?'

'Your father is just outside, Frau Künstler.'

When she moved, the shadow beside the pool reared up and formed into a thick set man with sullen eyes. Eric Röther, her trainer. The man who'd raped her.

'Frau Künstler, stop pulling at your arm.' The nurse turned to a gaunt doctor who stood watching and making tut-tutting sounds. He checked her pulse, and told her to stay still.

'You're lucky your father got to you as soon as he did.'

Her father? Sophia tried to focus on his doubleness: a father who'd lied about everything, a father who both attacked his child then came to her aid?

There he was. White-faced, taking her hand, checking to make sure she was all right. She tried to tell him about Käthe, about his work as an informer, about the dark man, the water and the mermaids.

'Sleep,' he said. And she was at once relieved and obedient.

★★★

Mia burrowed deeper under the covers. It was way too early for Oma to be banging on the door, and she was so tired.

'Go *away*,' she mumbled when the knocking came again.

'Mia? Are you in there?'

Petrus! Mia scrambled out of the bed and stared at the door. There were people talking on the other side. Someone inserted a key in the lock and tried to turn it. Thank god she'd left her key in there. Oh no! Sophia was on the other side. Sophia couldn't get in her own room so she'd gone to get Petrus and they were both here. Mia shrank back against the cushions. Sophia was going to kill her for taking her room and locking it from the inside. She'd never listen to her now. The room seemed tight, walls squishing in so she couldn't breathe.

They knocked again. A new voice. Not Petrus. Not Sophia. The hotel manager? Mia sat bolt upright, scuttled from the bed and unlocked the door. The hotel receptionist barrelled through first, thrusting her out of the way, followed by two police officers, Petrus and a big man who hardly fitted into the small space. Petrus stared at her, hugged her, peering into the room behind her as if he were willing someone else to be there.

'Where's Sophia?' Mia asked. She could see his hands were shaking and that made her scared. 'I want her. What's happened?'

The officers were looking through Sophia's things. That wasn't right. Sophia wouldn't like that. Mia told them to stop. They didn't have a warrant. She was an under-age female and no female officer was present as far as she could see. She had a right to ask them to leave. The big man's eyes widened, and she thought he smiled.

'It's all right, Mia,' he said. 'I'm Hajo, Sophia's boss. They're trying to help.'

They left and began talking in low tones while Petrus told her that Sophia had gone to the police station and had been attacked.

'No, don't worry. She's all right,' he said when Mia began to cry. Sophia had managed to phone him. Sophia was a survivor, he said. He'd gone to get her.

Mia remembered the phone call she'd heard. Petrus must have made that call before Sophia was hurt. He'd arranged to have her hurt!

No, that wasn't right. All he'd said was that Sophia shouldn't know. But maybe all that meant was Sophia shouldn't know who had hurt her? Mia was so scared that when she asked Petrus to wait outside so she could get dressed her voice came out as a frightened squeak. Pulling the envelope from under the mattress; she stuffed it in her bag. Took off her jumper and shoved it on top of the envelope so as to hide it, before pulling on one of Sophia's sweatshirts. It smelled of Sophia, who wouldn't let anyone mess her about. Mia would be like her.

People had secrets, secrets that sometimes made them do things that they would never normally do. But hurting your own daughter? Her skin felt prickly just thinking about it. She'd go and see Sophia straight away, tell her to be careful and not trust her father.

Hajo was waiting in the corridor. He looked at Mia as if he could see what was going on inside her head, as if he knew that she had his papers inside her bag. 'You've forgotten your shoes,' he said.

Mia blushed, heat spreading from her neck to the top of her head as she returned to the bathroom to get them. When she came out again, shoes tied, hair pulled back, Hajo smiled. His two officers and Petrus went inside the room as Hajo asked her questions. *Loads* of questions.

When had she arrived? Why had she run from her house? Didn't she realise it was dangerous? Had she seen Sophia?

Mia didn't know what to admit. It was scary not knowing who was who anymore. She needed someone who understood, someone who would take care of her. Someone she trusted completely. Mia pinched her nose hard and concentrated on Hajo's shoes. They were shiny black ankle boots, very clean and expensive. Tears leaked down her cheeks, and her nose ran. She dug in her pocket for a hanky and came up with nothing.

'There, there.' Hajo patted her absentmindedly on the shoulder and handed her a clean white hanky with a '1. FC Union Berlin' football team logo embroidered on one corner.

'So, tell me again Mia, why did you leave your house?' Hajo asked again, like they did in films and cop shows. Trying to see if she lied the first time, then couldn't remember the lie.

'I wanted to see Sophia, and I thought Dr Künstler would say no, that's all.' Mia blew her nose and felt sorry for Hajo. He couldn't help but look at his spoiled hanky. Through the door she could see the police unpacking Sophia's suitcase. They were searching through every single item, even her socks.

'I really need to see Sophia and Oma.' Mia slipped past Hajo, pelting along the corridor and down the stairs before he could say no or grab her. Everyone she passed stared and the receptionist called out: was she all right? Even though it was pretty obvious she wasn't. In the fresh cold air, Mia made a promise, whispering it fiercely so that it would have more chance of coming true. First she'd see

Sophia, give her the papers, and after that she'd insist she stay with her in Breden until Oma was better. If Sophia said no, well she was old enough to stay on her own.

She could smell her own panic. Like almonds or vinegar, it made her lightheaded. Hajo looked so angry when he burst out from the hotel, Petrus close behind. But she insisted that she had to go to the hospital now, and Hajo nodded. One of the officers opened the door of the smaller of the two police cars. Petrus got in the back seat and waited for her to follow. Patted the seat. She didn't want him to come, but there was nothing she could do.

Instead of looking at Petrus, Mia hugged the backpack to her chest. She could feel how much he wanted to talk to her, because he kept peering over and starting to say things, before stopping. She kept her head turned away and thought about what she'd tell Sophia and Oma. When they arrived at the hospital, instead of going to the ward, Petrus pointed to the huge hospital café by the shop.

'Breakfast?' he asked, trying to smile.

Mia couldn't run away again so she sat down. There were lots of people around making it safe, plus she was starving. The croissant tasted so good she asked for another and ate that before drinking a glass of orange juice.

'You heard. Didn't you Mia?' Petrus spoke quietly.

She jumped, spilling some of her drink on the table. 'What?' What if he *was* dangerous, what if he could arrange to hurt her, like he did Käthe and Sophia, what should she do?

'You heard me talking on the phone. Last night.' Petrus sounded sad. Mia had to be ready. She would throw the cup at him and run away screaming: whatever it took.

'Mia,' he said. 'I was speaking to the man who attacked Sophia, but I had no idea Sophia had gone to the station. No idea whatsoever until she rang. We'd agreed that he remove old records. Records of no use to anyone. In fact, they could do more damage than good.'

'But Sophia got hurt,' she said. 'She got hurt because you told that man to go there.'

'Mia, it's so much more complicated than you realise. Officer Ewalder knows. I phoned him as soon as Sophia was safe.'

A proper officer wouldn't let something like that just go. He would come here and make sure that Petrus and the man on the phone were punished. Except Petrus didn't look like someone who would hurt anyone, he looked sad and old and very tired. Just like Oma had when she'd been trying to pretend that she wasn't ill. Everything was changing and Mia wanted the changes to stop.

'Dear child. There's something else.'

Why did he look like that? Oh no. He was going to say something really awful, more awful than anything in the whole world.

'Mia, you're going to have to be really brave.'

The floor was a strange swirly brown pattern. She wanted to tell him to shut up because the floor kept moving. Round and round.

'Mia? Mia! Breathe, or you'll faint.' Petrus was kneeling in front of her. Everyone was staring.

'It's Oma, isn't it?' she whispered. Petrus looked down. 'You said she'd be all right. You said she was going to come home.' She was wailing, the sound echoing around the huge hospital café. Everything was white and huge and she was falling. Oma was dead and she was alone.

Petrus vanished, and then was back, holding a glass filled with white liquid. 'Drink,' he said, and she tried. It was bitter, like poison, burning in her throat, so that before she could say anything, or warn him, she threw up all over Petrus' nice clean pale-blue shirt and trousers.

Voices were calling. Some saying breathe, others saying 'over here', or 'over there', and 'watch out'. She was in a small room. Petrus had gone. A nurse was holding her hand, one finger on her wrist, taking her pulse.

'Now, you just sit still,' she said.

'I want to see Sophia.' Sophia would understand. She'd make things better.

'Yes, when you're feeling a little steadier.' The nurse sat next to her and took both of her hands. Mia was sobbing again. Her stomach really hurt. Her heart, thumping inside her, just ached. She'd not been there. The one time Oma needed her, she'd been running across town to see Sophia.

Petrus was at the door. He was wearing a white shirt that was too big, and dark blue uniform trousers. His hair was messy, as if he'd rushed back to see if she was all right. No, that wasn't right. He was the bad person. Mia knew that now, so why was he being so careful? Asking her if she he might come in, if he might sit down, if he might speak with her?

Mia took a deep breath. She had to be strong for Oma's sake. She had to make sure everything turned out as it should, so that Oma would know that Mia was doing as she was told.

'Let's go and see Sophia,' she said, using the same voice she'd used when Oma was unable to make even simple decisions. Petrus tried to smile, like he knew what she was doing.

'Yes, that's a good idea,' he said.

CHAPTER FIFTEEN

~

Mia straightened the bedspread before plucking Maria's hand-delivered card from the nearby cabinet and placing it centre stage on the windowsill. It was pretty: a profusion of cowslips against a bright blue sky.

'Dr Werner's not happy, Sophia,' she said. 'Apparently you need more medicine.'

'Really?

'Yep, that's what Dr Werner says. Petrus says it's two days since you sustained your injuries and you are most certainly strong enough to recover without additional medication.' Mia rendered a near-perfect impression of Sophia's father. Each word carefully enunciated. Thick eyelashes narrowed so only a mere glint of blue remained. 'They're in the kitchen arguing. No, sorry, having a *professional disagreement.*'

She gave the bedspread a last tug. Sophia heard her tread warily down the stairs, stop midway. No doubt craning her ears to hear further details. For the last two days, Mia had been utterly lost, unable to believe that Dagmar wasn't a short drive away, recovering in hospital. She'd been calm, acting as if the whole episode were a bad dream, then hysterical. Sobbing as if she'd never stop, telling Petrus he'd not done enough, until even Sophia felt a small pang of sympathy for her father. When Mia tried to accept that her Oma was no longer there, the nightmare wouldn't go. On the contrary her grief would wait for the shock to pass before working its way deep inside the child's mind, forming part of the person she would one day become. Don't be like me, Mia, she thought in surprise: don't live to rigid rules that are all you have to keep you safe.

When had those rules become too tight? The thought made her heart lurch from initial indifference to acute sensation.

The girl had stayed tightly glued to Sophia. Perhaps she believed Sophia's presence would keep the monsters at bay? Whatever the reason, Petrus watched their strange dance, lips tightening; his eyes focussed on some distant spot, not liking what he saw. Sophia had calmly explained to him what she'd found, her father watching, monitoring how much she knew. She couldn't feel anger, only sadness at her mother's death. She'd wanted a chance to know her better, to save Käthe, to have had the bravery to do all the things she had not done; and now she was off the case, finished before she'd even started. Worse, the bash on her head had jostled memories so that moments of her past kept popping up. Some arrived in colour, others remained monochrome. There was a dark bungalow hidden by apple and cherry trees. Near a wooden jetty, pale-blue boats wobbled on a lake surrounded by birch trees and the occasional towering oak. A narrow path wound its way to a conservatory and a stately house – where, via the open glass doors, she could see ornate tables, art deco lamps and a second door that led into the dining room where chandeliers hung.

Worst was a memory of injections that prickled and burned through her arms and legs and the tidal wave of energy that roared through her so she believed herself nothing without it. The birch trees at the water's edge opened into soft mossy woods that turned into a thick fir-tree forest. Such a vast silence. Her remembered footfall the only sound. The intense deep green of the trees, the smell of wood and pine, the soft floor layered in cones equalled unequivocal bliss.

Under water, in a cramped yet fathomless pool, wearing a purpose-built diving mask with black goggles that stretched over both nose and mouth, she'd pitted her strength against a wave machine, learning to control her breathing as she conquered her panic.

Maria's papers, and the contract between Günther and her father, were in Hajo's safe hands. But there were more questions she needed answers to. For instance: where were her training records? The steroids she'd taken? Her mother had said to look, as if she knew they'd been there. As if they were important.

Petrus denied any involvement in Käthe's death. 'I was trying to help,' he said when he came upstairs with Hajo, 'but she insisted that she see Sophia.'

'Why couldn't she see me?' Sophia's hands started to shake, making Hajo place his warm palm over hers. 'Leave this for now,' he said as Sophia tried to edge her hands loose, fed up with being told to wait, forget, sleep, recover; whatever they said to stop her getting answers. 'I want to know.'

'Yes.' Petrus cleared his throat. Mia was banging doors in the kitchen, preparing vegetables for a soup. The radio was on as the girl seemed to hate silence. 'I asked Käthe to be careful. She had a great deal of information on the Stasi, and Theme 14.25. Since the Wall came down, she'd been coming over to talk to reporters in West Berlin. They were paying her for information, and she was using the money to buy steroids. I had contacted her mother to warn her Käthe was being foolish. The police have a record of that call. I went to see Hedda and tried to help her understand, but I truly don't know what happened. I may be despicable in your eyes, Sophia. I simply didn't want her bringing that trouble to you.'

'So you were *protecting* me?' He really was brilliant, turning every angle to suit. 'So who killed her, if it wasn't you?'

'Sophia.' Hajo placed a warning hand on her arm.

'I don't believe you don't know,' she told her father, taking some satisfaction when he paled and looked away. 'I think you're protecting yourself and Ilse, no one else.' She turned away, wanting him gone. Hating the fact that she was trapped in bed in her dead mother's spare room, a bedridden patient who'd only been discharged if she promised to stay under a doctor's supervision.

Mia had saved all the papers from under Sophia's hotel mattress. Also in Hajo's hands, they were the high point of the girl's night of adventure.

'Putting stuff under there was really dumb,' she'd said at the hospital, as if Sophia's misjudgement ruled out her own stupidity in walking across the town alone at night to voice her misgivings about Petrus.

Mia had lost someone utterly dear to her, but she hadn't

pulled back or built a wall around her heart to avoid any further distress. Rather, she'd managed to burrow herself a safe place inside Sophia's heart and decided to trust her. Added to that, she spoke gently to Petrus. As if he, not Mia, was the one who was hurting. For Sophia no such conviction existed. Petrus had phoned Günther that Thursday night to warn him that, as far as he knew, his daughter would be returning to look at all the old paper files in the police archives. Far better, he'd said, to clear everything up before the weekend. In her mind, one idea spoke loud and clear. Her father had given Günther permission to stop her even if that meant assaulting her, just as he must have given others the permission to stop Käthe.

Now she slept, dreaming of mosquitoes biting her skin so a hundred pinpricks dotted her arms and legs. In her dream each sting was inflicted not by an insect but by a question. Whatever remained concealed behind the horror of needles and pain was waiting to be found. However, the more that memory was encouraged to emerge, the further back it crouched until she was unsure it had ever existed. Yet when she woke, the image that remained was of a child's pearly hand, doll-sized, curled and resting.

She had to go back to the house and lake: any chance of finding her records was there. Going back would show her mother she had really listened. The house wasn't far. In fact, the route seemed as clear in her mind as a line drawn by pen. She had to go and find out what had really happened to her.

Hajo was sitting by the bed, scribbling in a notebook. The back of his hair was sticking up as though to confirm he'd slept badly and not bothered with a comb.

'That fucking man thought he'd destroyed all the records,' he said as soon as he realised she was awake. He ran his fingers through the stubble and Sophia's hands ached to reach out and do the same.

'Yes. So he didn't burn all of them?'

'Not quite, thank goodness. I'm staying a few days. First – to sort out this mess and try to work out to what extent your father is involved, find a replacement for Martin and investigate Käthe Niedermann's murder. No, I hadn't forgotten.' He reached over and took her hand. 'Darling Sophi, I'm so sorry.'

Darling? No one had ever called her that.

He kissed her. Not on the cheek: both were bruised, sporting a livid range of purple and orange, but on her lips. His mouth warm against hers. He tasted of old tobacco and the musky scent of aftershave.

'Sorry for what?' She wanted to grasp hold of him and keep the heat between them.

'Neglecting to listen or believe you when you suggested there was more. Utter stupidity? Putting you in danger?' His finger traced its way along her bruised face.

'Never mind that, Hajo, I need to know what's happening.'

'Exactly. So get better, and then you can help.' He squeezed her hand and smiled. She squeezed back. 'So listen. It was Schenke who gave the order to harm Käthe. She fought them. We've got three. The fourth man is proving harder to find.'

Sophia saw it all. Käthe, fuelled by years of rage, fighting back. She'd have done the same in her shoes. Hajo was staring. Maybe he'd kiss her again?

'Even your lips are bruised,' he said and touched her bottom lip with the tip of his finger.

'Does it *still* hurt?' Mia peered round the door and glanced suspiciously from Sophia, to Hajo. When they both turned to face her, she came in and placed a bowl of soup on the table by the bed. 'D'you want some, Hajo?' she asked him.

'Hmm, what kind is it?'

'Broccoli and potato. I made it myself. Petrus can't cook and he's waiting for you downstairs.'

'Well, in that case, I'd love to try some.'

Sophia knew Mia wanted to ask a question, but each time an opportunity was there for the taking, the child backed away as if the answer were too important. If Sophia misunderstood, or said the wrong thing, the child would be troubled or hurt because she'd interfered in something Mia needed to do alone.

'Mia – I'll come to the funeral with you. If you'll let me,' she said and watched as first relief, followed by fresh upset, appeared on Mia's face.

'How did you know what I was going to ask?' The child sat on the bed trying valiantly not to cry and Sophia felt the pull in her heart that had become as familiar as seeing Mia each day. Any guilt that Dagmar had died without her was tinged with an honest regret that there had been no moment of opportunity. No time when they might have shared an understanding for this child who, even now, stood between them: a beacon of light in such a dark, unhappy place.

'Well, she was my mother.'

'I just didn't think you'd want to go.' Mia stared mutinously at the bedspread and plucked at a strand of blue cotton, working it loose from the floral pattern. 'Sophia, I'd like to know more about my own mother and father. And I can't stay with Petrus now that he's being questioned by the police, so it makes sense that I come and live with you.'

Unable to explain the complexity of her feelings, Sophia asked rather feebly, 'How's Gerda?'

'Okay. Can I, Sophia?'

'Are you friends again?' She'd have given anything for her own mother to have asked the same and yet it occurred to her that her mother had been there to listen, it had been Sophia who'd been desperate to escape her mother's sadness.

'You said that proper friends were there when you needed them.'

Goodness. The child had taken her advice to heart. Taken it in and believed her. So it was part astonishment that made her pick up the bowl of soup and say, 'Well, she does seem to be trying to help now.'

'Maybe. But you haven't said.'

'What?'

'You haven't said about me, coming to live with you.'

Oh god, the child's hands were shaking. 'We'll work it out.' What was she to say? She couldn't leave Mia with her father, could she? Someone had to take responsibility.

'I'll look after myself. I'll clean and cook.'

'Dearest, stop. I'll look after you. I promised.'

Mia crept to the door as Sophia put the bowl to one side and closed her eyes. When Maria had delivered her get-well card, she thanked her for sending Western police to gather up all her saved records and allowing Jörg to retrain, and apologised for Sophia's injury as if she were responsible for the attack.

She'd been crazy enough to invite her old friend to visit in Berlin. The idea had, at first, appeared as exciting as hidden chocolate. Here was a friend who knew her well enough not to be put off by sharp words and an antisocial need for solitude. As soon as she'd opened her mouth, she'd been plagued by doubt. A stranger sleeping in her apartment wasn't welcome, and she'd been adopted by a child! What on earth had she been thinking?

When she woke much later, it was evening and the decision had been made. She'd go to the house and lake. She'd find her records. This was the last chance to know whether her nightmares were real, or a warped fantasy of nightly orgies with Diertha always present, goading her to take another lover until Ebbe came. Those images of running through the forest, coupling under trees, could all be nonsense.

Wait. Cutting herself wasn't a dream; her arms were a crisscross of scars, but she'd dreamed of bleached water, a child's limb, red and floating.

Setting the alarm for six am, she climbed awkwardly out of bed, every part of her body conspiring to make even the window seem a long way away. That bastard Schenke had really hurt her. She'd pay him back by finding out who she was and in doing so shed light on what Theme 14.25 had created.

Snow, light as icing sugar, drifted from a dark sky, settling on the steely ground. On the landing, the downstairs TV murmured in the background and Mia's voice rose and fell as she chatted on the phone to Gerda.

There was no time to be to be squeamish. Sophia limped to the bathroom and co-ordinated her movements in the mirror to gently peel back the dressing and reveal a livid scar with blackened stitching that ran from ear to crown.

★★★

In the morning, when the alarm rang, the pain in her head was so corrosive she considered taking more pills and falling back to sleep, but the muffled drone from under the pillow insisted that it was time to wake. It hurt to stand, let alone bend down and pull on jeans, socks and finally, a fleece jumper. With six pills in her back pocket (god, let that be enough), Sophia tiptoed out to the hallway and down the stairs. How many times had she slipped out of her parents' old house as a young girl to run through the town into fields and up to the forest? Thank goodness the original wildness was in her now, a strong pulse keeping the weakness away.

The kitchen was dark. Only the wooden cupboards and old gas cooker could be seen in the orange glow of a streetlamp. There were no keys on the table but her shoes sat clean and polished by the kitchen door next to Mia's. Creeping along the hallway, Sophia hit her shoulder against the banister and mewled in pain. In the dim light, the outline of a coat rack promised a jacket, and in its pockets, hopefully, car keys. She had to sit down to get her shoes on. When she glanced up Mia was standing at the bottom of the stairs, fully dressed in coat, boots and hat, clutching her backpack.

'I ... I'm coming with you.'

They both heard Petrus cough, mutter and turn in his bed. Sophia put a finger to her lips and silently opened the door. Mia nodded and they slipped out into the dark where the shock of icy air made Sophia stagger. Each tender stitch was being stroked with an inquisitive icy finger.

'Put this on.' Mia pulled at her arm and handed her the striped woolly hat, but she couldn't raise her arms high enough.

'Come on now. Bend down.' The child stretched the hat gently across her head and the worst of the nausea seemed to pass. Sophia almost turned back. Nothing was worth such pain – but Mia had pulled on the handle of the car door until the driver's side opened, before scrambling over to the passenger seat.

'Quick. Get in,' she said.

Sophia eased gingerly onto the arctic seat. Using no headlights, she drove at a snail's pace around the corner, then stopped.

'Mia?'

'You were sneaking off home, weren't you?' Mia pulled a flask from her bag and poured hot chocolate into the cup. 'And you *promised.*'

'And how did you know?'

'Easy. You set the alarm.' Holding out the cup, Mia waited until Sophia drank.

Water had begun to puddle on the dashboard as ice melted on the inside of the windscreen. Outside, the yellow street lights began their dying flicker.

'I'm going to Hochberg,' Sophia said. 'To where I trained to be an athlete.'

'Oh. That's where my mother lived. It's not far from here.' The girl seemed to collect herself, as if the idea that Sophia might be going anywhere other than home was actually a good thing. 'But, you know that's crazy, don't you, Sophia? You shouldn't even be out of bed.'

Yes, she knew, and if she sent the child back, as any adult should, this final window of chance would disappear.

As she drove, part of her floated weightless above the car, watching it beetle through one sleeping village after another. Most of the houses were dark. One or two had a thin line of white smoke curling from the chimney, or a faint night light shining in the hallway: a flare in the pre-dawn grey. They crossed the train line and veered right through Grünwalde, driving over the line for a second time at Engelsberg, a hamlet on the forest's edge which offered little more than a shop and train platform.

Mia looked increasingly nervous as the trees thickened into a never-ending line of dirty green pines; an endless plantation that was too tall to harvest and too wide to imagine any edge. Sophia knew. She'd added the sum up many times. There were eighteen kilometres of trees, sentries and danger. Breathing fast, she remembered that behind the big house, in the meltingly damp bungalow, was Ebbe, her lovely cruel boy with his wet mouth and gentle probing hands. A second man waited, half-hidden behind Diertha, poor greedy Diertha who exercised her mastery of power with sex.

They were all there, waiting.

Mia shrieked and grabbed the steering wheel as the car veered from the road. Thickly covered branches groaned against metal, catching the wing mirror, ripping it with a snap; before they were back on the road, tyres slipping on the tarmac.

'OK, we're fine, we're fine.' Sophia stopped the car and opened her window to breathe. Outside, the air smelt of ice and pine cones. Inside the car smelled of fresh panic.

'You're not hurt?'

Mia shook her head and made an attempt to hide her tears by rummaging about in her bag. Sophia gave her arm a gentle squeeze. 'Look, sweet pea. Isn't that amazing?' She pointed to where the shadowy outline of an owl could be seen swooping through the trees. He dipped, silver feathered, beautiful against the miles of green and grey.

The final stretch was driven with particular care. Soon enough they'd see the narrow rooms with miles of steel grey wire that ran to and from monitors: eyes would scrutinise their every move, make notes on performance, speed, strength and condition.

Finally, around the corner came the familiar straggle of houses. Sophia pointed to the phone box, the nursery, the empty block of apartments for cooks and cleaners. Further on, near the training centre, she ignored the ghostly whispered warning to 'Turn around and run.' Drove on past the entrance barrier and deserted sentry box, following the left wall that ran all the way to the big house.

Most dwellings remained dark. One dim light, the slight twitch of a curtain in an upstairs bedroom, told her that a warm body was slipping from the bed, compelled to tiptoe to the curtain and note the car, the registration and time as they drove by. Everyone who lived here owed their livelihood to the training camp. They would have been watching from the moment her headlights were seen in the distance.

So let them think she *had* gone. Sophia carried on past the big house and the closed sentry box and turned off the car lights before veering left, rolling behind the towering wall as far across the grass as the car would go, until they were nearly on the lakeside verge.

'Best you stay here, Mia.' Sophia looked around, half expecting her old companions to emerge from the shadows as she took out two pills and swallowed them dry.

Mia was out the car before she'd finished speaking.

'I'll come back. I promise. Look, if I'm not here in twenty minutes, go to the phone box in the village and phone the police.' Would this child never do as she was told?

'No way.' Mia moved closer. 'I'm not staying on my own.'

Nothing stirred. The air, thick with a damp frost, hung heavy over the lake. In the distance, water rippled under the weak pre-dawn light. On the far side were the outlines of bungalows, and nearer them, to the left, the solid rising bulk of the main house. There was the jetty, exactly as remembered, stretching across the lake as if it were forever trying to reach the far side. The bobbing boats were nothing more than smudges of black against the dark water.

'Besides,' Mia continued, 'you can't even stand up!'

True, Sophia's arms were unbearably heavy and the ground kept weaving from grass to stone. Come on, she reminded herself: training at six, followed by breakfast. From seven to eight: school studies followed by laps and underwater breathing. If she could do all that then, surely she could just remember how to breathe now. She tripped on a patch of ice and nearly fell. Mia grabbed and held on.

'I'll be fine. Stop fretting. Honestly.' Sophia reached for the child's hand. Such warmth and strength derived from a simple gesture.

Many years ago, the house had been a holiday residence for Honecker, who had visited during the summer months. She'd occasionally imagined him, a broad-shouldered, fatherly figure, striding leisurely along the lake shore, sitting in the winter garden with coffee or beer, entertaining friends and associates.

'Watch your step.' Sophia led the way across the grass to the back of the house, down a narrow pathway that would take them to the cooks' entrance.

'Ow.' A wet branch sprang back, catching Mia's face. A brown residue trailed across her nose and cheek. 'Yuck.' She stumbled, swiping with the back of her hand.

'Sshh.' Sophia fumbled with the gate. Good, the morning light hadn't reached the narrow corridor that hugged the back of the house. People were still here, which meant the clearing of all damning evidence wasn't finished. Hopefully not many people, but enough to make it dangerous. This was the only way to bypass all main doors. Diertha and she had sneaked in through the window enough times to steal vodka and wine. Now the window with the broken latch had been replaced by a door.

'It's scary here.' Mia gripped her hand as Sophia tried to think of something reassuring to say. The lake re-emerged into partial view, waxy-blue, smooth in the grey light. Snow had encircled it and now, from where she stood, she could see that the jetty sagged, its centre completely submerged. She could lie. Say it was all a big adventure. Yet didn't Mia deserve the truth?

'We need to get inside.' Sophia leaned against the rotting wood, too dizzy to do more than stain both arms with green mould.

'I'll do it.' Mia gently edged her to one side and launched herself at the mouldy frame. It squelched and leaked water. She thrust again and this time the door gave way and they stumbled through the gap into pitch black.

'We could go to jail for this. Couldn't we?' The child sounded terrified and, at the same time, absurdly delighted.

'We could. But we're not going to.'

The kitchen was icy cold. Mia fumbled in her bag to produce a torch which threw a thin beam of light along the floor.

'Sophia?'

'Yes'

'Are you scared?'

There was nothing to say. Sophia put her arm carefully around the girl's shoulders guiding her forward. The door to the left opened out to a private bar and restaurant. The offices were upstairs: best to start looking there. Sophia could hear her child-self calling. Telling her that whatever she was looking for was somewhere close. The disused kitchen was stacked high with tables and chairs, leaving only a narrow space to move in between. Of course. She hadn't been thinking straight. Everything would be done in order of priority. Firstly the workers would clear away the most incriminating files in the hidden underground facility on the far side of the complex, burning all evidence of wrongdoing in the mammoth incinerator that was just across from where they were now. Then they'd clear the house, and finally the training facility and accommodation that lay dotted across the site.

From outside came a distant thud. A gate being opened?

'The torch!' Darkness. Sophia waited. What kind of fool would bring a child into such danger? No. Everything was all right. There was only silence. They crept up the stairs into a sizable room with windows that let in faint light. Nothing here, apart from five empty metal cabinets. The floorboards creaked as they tiptoed out and Sophia signalled Mia to edge her feet to either side of the landing. In the second room papers had been stuffed into boxes, ready for the incinerator. Sophia picked a sheet from the box nearest to her as downstairs a door opened. Mia would have screamed if Sophia hadn't dropped the paper and clamped her hand tightly over her mouth.

She pointed and they crept into the gap behind the door.

'You saw what? Lights?' A man's voice came from the hallway.

'From my bathroom window.' The woman's voice had the timbre of a perpetual whine.

'This time you're sure?' He sounded irritated.

'Well – not completely, no. But we were *told* to look.'

'So we'll look.'

The voices faded. The pair tramped to the back of the house, toward the conservatory. Grasping Mia's hand, Sophia pulled her out from behind the door, down the stairs and through the front door. They ran over the lawn, past the closed barrier, ducking behind the sentry box as the woman came round the back of the house.

'You go upstairs.' She hurried past them, important in a long dark coat that ballooned as she moved. 'I'll phone him.'

The man came into view. He was cavernous and dark. When he turned, Sophia saw a bulbous nose and prominent moustache.

Mia pulled her arm and they were walking silent and fast toward trees. Cherry and apple trees? Sophia stopped. She'd come home. The smell of apple blossom was everywhere. The air ripe with the drone of bees, honey and sex.

A man bent over her, another was waiting.

He was jamming himself hard inside her; she could feel him, there, right inside her belly. Sweat dripped, drop by drop, on to her still body.

'What are you doing? Move.' Mia dragged Sophia along the pathway towards the first bungalow with its front door facing the lake. Moss and algae grew along the roof and walls, making the building seem part of the wild landscape. The door opened with a wet shudder. Inside (oh, so familiar) were two further doors – one on either side of the box-shaped hallway.

She turned left. Forgot to breathe. Diertha was lying naked on the bed, a young man moved over her, another lay beside her.

'Come over here, Sophi,' Diertha's voice came from deep inside her head as she stepped through the door back into her nightmare. There were two beds, one on the right wall – one on the left. The fawn carpet held a brown stain that had been half-heartedly concealed by a formica table. The window facing the apple and cherry trees remained slightly open.

Mia crossed over to the cherry tree window.

'Phew, they've gone.'

But Diertha hadn't gone. She was opening the bathroom door, dancing, pink skinned from the shower. Muscular and powerful, moving in time to the pop music, playing on her cheap transportable radio.

CHAPTER SIXTEEN

~

She was lying on a filthy carpet. Everything was the same, yet utterly changed because Diertha and Mia didn't fit together. Diertha came from a lifetime ago, and Mia? Mia was Diertha's daughter! The girl was shining a torch in her eyes and muttering something about going home, but she *was* home and any minute now, the alarm would sound and she'd have to get ready for the morning's lap training.

'Sophia!'

Mia's face loomed close, her blue eyes wide with fright. 'Wake up. Wake Up Now!'

There were no sheets on the bed, no curtains covering the windows, nothing to explain why she was so afraid.

'You've got to get up!'

Mia pulled at her hands until Sophia gingerly sat up. Where was she? Ebbe had seemed so real; even now she could feel his slim body against hers with his particular musky scent, the gentle dip between his collarbone and neck, such a contrast to the cruelty of his face. This room should vanish like a bad dream. She ought to be in Breden, tucked up in bed. Though this was real because everything stayed the same: a dirty carpet, the two rusty metal-framed beds, that hideous formica table with a wobbly leg.

In the bathroom, cupping her hands under a stream of cold water that would help her to swallow two more pills: no dizziness, she wasn't going to faint again. For years she'd searched for Ebbe's blue gaze in every nightclub, in every dark place, but really, all that time she'd been looking to find a way back here, to her true self that had been here waiting to be found on a filthy bare mattress in Hochberg. There was a muzzy outline of the child watching her. Mia. Why was Mia here? How could she have brought this carefully loved girl to such a dangerous place? No doubt, like every child, Mia was blissfully unaware how such devotion would have cost her Oma. Sophia knew. Love had never come easily to Dagmar, yet once it found root, it was the strongest of bonds. So why was it that only now she understood just how much her mother must have loved her? Was Mia's gentle naivety a reminder of Sophia's lost childhood? Or was it simply that the child had been loved?

'We have to go,' Mia peered out the window, 'before you collapse *again*.'

'Mia, I'm okay.' She laid her hands on the child's shoulder, shook her gently. 'See?'

She'd look after this child. Make certain she returned to safety and watch over her, like a guardian, or an older sister, a well-meant gesture of accord towards Dagmar. You could pledge yourself in love to a person after her death, in a real, honest-to-god way: she saw that now.

They left the bungalow. Slipping quietly out of the door and along the pathway by the lake, Sophia veered left where a wider track wound through the trees, past a newly built overly varnished log cabin with a veranda that faced out to a jetty at the lakeside.

'This isn't the way back.' Mia studied her; the child's thin face was serious, inscrutable.

'I know sweetie, come on. This way.' Sophia continued along the path through the trees.

On the far side of the road that ran the length of the sports complex was another red and white barrier marked: No Entry. Behind the barrier, bricks and sand had been piled next to boxes the size and shape of fridges. Each box was wrapped in weathered cellophane. A short distance to the right of the barrier, fir trees covered a man-made hill with the contours of a burial mound. At its summit a white turret with deeply set windows protruded. Beyond that, as far as the eye could see, fir trees stretched into a forest that ran all the way to the main road, crossing it to begin again.

'We're not going up there, are we?' Mia pointed.

'The lookout point? No, don't worry.'

Not far from here the trees served as a perfect camouflage for the oval running track. At its furthest point a cross-country path vanished into the woods. In that other life Sophia had taken to following it all the way to the village, the train station and that longed-for escape. Yet every time, at the very last point, she'd turned and headed back.

'What were they looking for?' Mia snared Sophia's hand and held on.

'Russians, mostly.' She pointed out the area behind the turret that had been designed to appear as a loading bay. There was room for a lorry to turn and back-up against a broad storeroom door.

'What did the Russians want?'

'To know what was in the underground facility.' Keep up your chattering, Mia, she thought. If the child fell silent, she'd not find the strength to move. She'd be glued here, right next to the sentry barrier, until they came and found her.

'Are we going underground?'

'I am. You stay here where it's light.'

'No!'

'If someone came, you could get help.'

'I'm coming with you and that's that. What would happen to you if you fainted?'

Once, sometimes twice a week, a helicopter had circled overhead. 'Bloody nosy Russians', their trainers had muttered, looking up at the ceiling, closing doors and moving their schedules late into the night after the helicopter had pulsed away.

The entrance to the labyrinth looked just like any door to the back of a store. Sophia knew the column of windows played tricks with reality: the window-line remained horizontal whilst the passageway sloped steeply down to a hallway where stairs led you further into the ground. There was, she noted, the added option of a miniature, yet modern, lift.

They took the stairs, Sophia taking the torch from Mia to shine a circle of light on damp walls and icy steps. Somewhere in the darkness below, water dripped, a steady trickle whose lonely sound was reminiscent of her life in water. Now, even though they were walking into danger, Sophia began to feel vital and alive. Here at last were the answers she needed. Eleven months ago the athletes would have been told to leave. Was she too late? The underground rooms might have been destroyed. If they were, surely the staircase would have been removed, she reasoned. The government had spent a fortune on wave pools, bikes, treadmills, surveillance cameras, treatment rooms and, of course, the Barochamber. They'd want to get all the equipment out first. Either way, if they were caught, she and Mia could be killed down here. If they were, they would be entombed, buried forever, and no one would ever know.

'Come on – if we're going?' The girl prodded her forward.

I'll look after her, Sophia promised her mother. I won't let her get hurt. She sensed that Käthe, Diertha and all the fallen athletes were with her, floating in the musty air; all those young men and women who hadn't had a chance to escape.

'You always were a sentimental idiot,' Diertha's imagined voice mocked as Sophia tripped on the stairs, swearing as she bumped into Mia. She was going mad. Diertha was dead and gone. The voice was just her imagination; fear making the past slide into the present. The hallway was dark and narrow, the smell of damp overwhelming. Mia's torch picked out mushrooming orange algae at the top and bottom edges of the wall. At the end of the corridor, on their left, a narrow room had been split by a dirty mustard curtain. To their right, a thick white metal panel lined the far wall. Each section was covered with buttons, gauges and dials. Tracing her hand along the wall, Sophia found the light switch. Overhead the strip-lights flickered on one by one, throwing shadows across the floor.

'Yuck, that's weird.' Mia stayed very close.

'They're just pressure controls.' Though yuck and weird were a better description for the switches that controlled the Barochamber pressure. Crammed just below the ceiling, the 25cm square monitor screens displayed the athletes' heart rate as they cycled or ran on the treadmill, each reading open to scrutiny set only on improving performance.

She was seeing things again. A chorus of shadowy faces turned towards the mustard curtain. Was whatever lay behind that drapery better seen alone?

'What's behind there?' Mia made a beeline for the curtain.

'Nothing. Come on, this way.'

'Oh. Is this what we're looking for?' Mia picked up a flag inscribed with '*DTSB der DDR*.' 'What does DTSB mean?'

'German Gymnastics and Sports Federation.' Sophia leaned over to get a better look at the various triangular gold, green, yellow, red and blue flags pinned to the wall. On the floor a poster soaked up damp.

'Come on, nothing here.' With the flags and posters came the uncomfortable reminder of how much she had wanted to be the very best.

'Everything smells of mushrooms or dead things.' Mia dropped the flag and followed her into the rest room with its black faux leather sofas arranged in a circular design. From here doors led off into different treatment areas. The Barochamber hatch was the same cream colour, but there were more gauges, monitors and bolts surrounding the mean opening that led inside. Through a second portal on the far side was a larger recovery area with soft chairs. Sophia's nerves shimmered with panic. Enclosed inside the cramped room, the heavy sound of the bolt closing had made her believe each time that no one would ever open it. They were below twenty-three feet of earth. Above them worms and beetles slid through the wet ground. There could be a landslide, a burst pipe, poisonous gas.

'Can I go in there? It looks like a prison cell.'

'No.' But the girl had already climbed in, demanding that Sophia explain how the Barochamber worked. How it would decrease oxygen and encourage Mia's body to make more blood cells.

'But why?'

'To help you work even harder in the gym.' How could she not warm to this irrepressible child?

Mia shook her head. 'That's so pointless,' she said, climbing out to follow Sophia through the double doors into the gym. 'Didn't you hate it?'

'Sometimes I loved it.'

Now Mia sat astride one of the fifteen training bikes neatly lined up along the left wall. Each bright blue metal frame supported a crossbar and handles. On the crossbar a yellow box with black wires linked the bike to sockets built into the wall. Metal screeched as the girl pedalled furiously, eyes glued to see whether the gauge moved.

'Mia, stop!' The noise was unbearable. If someone had come in after them, they'd now know exactly where to look.

'Sorry.' Mia grinned and jogged across the dimly lit room to the first of the five running machines. Each tread-mill was enclosed by three-foot ply-board frames. Sheets of white plastic had been stapled over the cheap wood: above this peculiar design only Mia's head and shoulders appeared as she bobbed up and down inside the oblong box. Even stranger was the heavy television set that had been fixed to the front bar so the athlete could watch TV while exercising. The girl was laughing, moving on the spot in an exaggerated slow motion run, but Sophia didn't see Mia, she saw Ebbe, beautiful Ebbe, pitting his strength against the machine as a throng of athletes urged him on.

'Lovely Ebbe,' Diertha's voice slid around inside her mind, refusing to leave.

'Bugger off and leave me alone,' Sophia muttered.

'Sophia! Who is it?' The white plastic mirrored Mia's face. 'Have those people found us? Is it my fault?'

Some athletes had escaped to the West; others had simply disappeared. Diertha was the only one she knew to have boiled up from the deep lake, engorged, putrid.

'There's no one here, so why were you talking? You're not going to faint again, are you?' The child had followed her out from the gym; now she collapsed rather dramatically onto one of the black settees. 'Can we leave now, please?'

'Just as soon as I finish looking. Stay put, I'll be back in a minute.'

'OK, but one minute. Promise?' Mia dug out a bar of chocolate and wriggled. The sofa produced a squawky fart that had her laughing again. '*Gross*,' she said, and wriggled again.

★★★

The chocolate tasted better here than it did at home,

probably because, although she didn't want to admit it, Mia was frightened. What might happen if Sophia fell over again, or if someone bad came? Either way, she would be the one to have to go and get help. I'm only a child, she thought and took another bite of her chocolate. The people who'd been snooping didn't seem like people she could ask for help. Most likely they'd kill her and bury her body next to Sophia's, in an unnamed grave. Petrus would never know where they were, or where they'd gone. The knowledge that Gerda would miss her brought a delicious thrill of comfort. Good. Gerda deserved to miss her.

Oma was dead. Mia curled up in a tight ball. Oma was dead and lying somewhere on her own, cold and grey and lonely; no one watching over her like they should. Mia had got it wrong again. She should be there, making sure Oma wasn't alone, but really she couldn't bear it. Mia wanted to remember her as she was when she was well. They'd had fun together. Oma teaching her how to make dumplings so they puffed up, tasting delicious. They'd played cards through the dark evenings in the winter. Not needing anyone else.

Mia sat up and scanned the damp room. If her mother had been as mean as she looked, it might be better not to know more, and concentrate on finding a father? The carpet was a bright red. A plastic lime-green bin sat empty on the floor. She put the chocolate wrapper in it. Ah. Better not. Sophia wouldn't want them to leave anything down here as proof. Down here. The words were terrifying. She couldn't hear Sophia anywhere. Maybe she'd gone? Maybe she'd brought her here on purpose? So that Sophia could run back to Berlin without her? No. That made absolutely no sense. It was Mia who'd insisted on coming along. Sophia had wanted to visit this place alone. That was the truth so Mia forced herself to calm down. She curled up again and shut her eyes, thinking hard about being safe in her own lovely room with nothing to worry about apart from what she'd have for breakfast.

***

Sophia knew that whoever had been in the big house would have rung their boss. Soon they'd spot the car and come looking, and when that happened, she wanted to be long gone.

'The curtain, Sophi, move the mustard curtain.' Who was that? Diertha? Käthe? Was the voice in her head a side effect of painkillers? Oh god. She had to be strong enough to get Mia out to safety.

She drew back the clammy curtain and stepped into the nightmare room with its everyday medical equipment: a chair and examination bed, desk with a heart monitor, and the less usual: a strap-on electro pulse-belt, a tube of nasal spray able to raise testosterone 237 per cent in fifteen minutes – virtually undetectable.

Opening the bottom drawer labelled '1976-77', she felt again that first thrill of being chosen, the dizzy shock of potential and limitless possibility. Her world had expanded from the simple East German town to encompass places she'd never dreamed of: Russia, Columbia, Canada. None of that magic remained.

Her file, Diertha's and Käthe's file, were here: every win, every training schedule, and every steroid dose. They'd told Käthe to leave in '86, a torn muscle that wouldn't heal in her shoulder. Poor dear foolish Käthe who'd decided to continue taking steroids, perhaps in the hope she'd make it back.

'Don't read about her. Read about *me*.' Diertha's voice. Sophia spilled the papers onto the table and held her head. It hurt. A throbbing red heat. The desk was dissolving, the examination bed sliding out of focus.

'Come on Sophi,' she murmured to herself, 'get a grip.' She'd promised her mother to look after Mia, and to do that she had to get her to get out of this awful place.

Diertha's medical report surmised that due to the abnormal size and shape of her clitoris, an immediate reduction of medication had to be agreed, meaning she would no longer compete.

That was when Diertha had gone away the first time. Poor fat Diertha readying herself for another night out: pink nails, bleached hair, feet oozing from overly tight yellow stilettos. Sophia recalled how none of the elaborate costumes had ever managed to disguise her roommate's unnaturally muscled body, the shadow of a beard, or her low, hateful voice.

She'd come back more savage than ever. Constantly picking fights and staying out late, only to arrive at their shared room with a new assortment of men. Had a child really been born then? Diertha had been huge, any pregnancy could be missed. Though could it? They had so many tests for blood, oxygen intake and hormone levels. Besides, how could a child as normal as Mia be born from a body so riddled with steroids? The second listed internal testes and chronic liver damage and five abortions. There was no child. Not one infant born. The last abortion in

February '76 resulted in severe internal scarring. The final note on the page read: patient showing signs of unpredictable behaviour. High risk. Consider termination.

The report was signed by Dr Künstler.

Every way she turned, Petrus was there – deep in the mess the GDR had created.

'Your dear father just threw us away.' Now the Diertha voice was joined by a chorus of athletes wailing their agreement. During that final year at Hochberg, when Diertha returned from her six-week absence, she'd ballooned from a muscular girl into a giant, hair springing up so thick on her legs and navel that clumps congealed around the shower plug when she shaved each morning. One night, late into competitive training, Diertha hadn't come back.

Even now Sophia could recall the taste of that first wonderful night of sleep. Each morning had felt clearer than the last.

The air smelling sweeter, her sleep disturbed only by Ebbe. In the hope that Diertha might never return, Sophia had scrubbed all traces of her roommate's phlegm from the sink, pulled handfuls of pubic hair from the shower plug and folded Diertha's clothing into the bottom drawer of their shared cupboard. Diertha's razor, shampoo, towels and toiletries were unceremoniously shoved into the corner of the bathroom window ledge.

Every time footsteps came near the bungalow, she'd panicked. Dreading the moment her roommate would roll through the door and turn on Sophia because she'd touched her stuff, and you never ever touched Diertha's stuff. Not ever. After four nights of waiting, Sophia stood taller and breathed easier. Eric had said that people like Diertha didn't stay. Sophia thought she must have returned home. Diertha's mother, a bulky nervous blonde woman who'd flirted with Eric, had come looking. Her daughter was gifted, she said, a true athlete. Why wouldn't they tell her where she was? Why were they saying she wasn't good enough to stay?

The next morning, drinking in the scent of dew-soaked grass and conifers, Sophia had walked to the lake and along the jetty to watch the sun come up. She'd been happy, cocooned in a warm glow that came from escaping the constant threat of her roommate and Eric. At the end of the platform she'd sat gazing across the elbow-shaped lake towards the rising sun: a pale distant glow that drew misty circles on the water and sent the mosquitoes into a zigzagging frenzy. A lazy carp bobbed to the surface, blowing a circle of bubbles before flipping its brown and yellow-finned body out of the water and diving. To the left the thick pelt of green pondweed smelled over-ripe. She'd leaned over to get a better look.

There had been no suicide. Sophia knew that now. On her father's order, someone at Hochberg had killed Diertha and placed her weighted body in the lake. Even now she could smell that putrefying flesh and see her younger self, hands pressed over nose and mouth, staring at Diertha's bulging tapioca eyes as her bloated body floated, half-submerged, in the dark-green water.

★★★

Time to call Mia and leave. Sophia grabbed all three files. A page slipped out, drifted to the floor. She bent to retrieve it: February 1977. Patient: age sixteen. Name: S Künstler. Diagnosis: seven months into pregnancy with severely in-flamed ovaries. Foetus presents as fully developed. Patient suffering internal bleeding.

The report (it had to be a lie) was written in her father's neat hand.

None of it made sense. She'd been thirteen years old the first time they told her she was to have an abortion. She'd been ill whilst taking the pill she thought made her safe. The metal barb inside her belly had snagged: wet flesh, soft skin – a fish-hook. Pain, deep like no other, had transported her to a place where the world was red and aching. Following the first operation there had been three more such mistakes and, after each mistake, orders to terminate the pregnancy.

The night the August '76 Montreal Olympics ended, the weather had been blistering. Tarmac melted. The ground shimmered. She and Ebbe celebrated winning gold by meeting secretly in his empty room: the others had gone to toast success with their companions. On his bed, skin covered in a glaze of sweat, she'd drunk in his particular beauty; gazed up at the perfect curve of him leaning over her, his eyes hooded and brooding – somewhere between mockery and sated pleasure. And she'd told him how she loved him.

How could she have been pregnant and not known? Each former 'error' had made itself instantly recognisable: her swim time horribly slow; her skin clearing until almost translucent. In the late autumn of '76 she'd been distraught, outside her own body with withdrawal symptoms: dry itching skin, her breasts tight and sore so they ached, and a rage that took away all reason until crippling fatigue forced her to seek medical help.

Sophia laid a hand on her stomach. Perhaps there was an imprint of each baby's short life hidden inside her womb? She remembered her dream where the child's delicate, bloodied limb had bobbed through clear water. The later dream of an infant's curled hand, pink as the inside of a seashell. But *seven months*?

Dagmar couldn't have known about any of them. Her mother's Baptist beliefs would never have tolerated so ungodly an act. Yet something tugged at Sophia's memory. A younger version of her mother watching with all too knowing eyes as her daughter left for training camp. She'd placed a note in Sophia's hand with the telephone number of her minister, a well-meant gesture sure to make her daughter snap.

'You don't have to go,' Dagmar had said when there was absolutely nothing to stay for.

Now she read: Infant delivered by Dr Künstler and Dr Hammerman, 17th February 1977. No? Her heart twisted with reluctance to believe. Were they doctors who, as well as giving out steroids, had carried out abortions for the Sports Association?

Her father's meticulous notes reported that the premature infant, a girl, had been placed with Dagmar. Why? So she could bury it? Nurse it?

No. She looked again. The notes were lying. No baby had *ever* been born. No child would have survived the steroid doses she'd been given and actually live, would it? But of course there hadn't been any steroids after the games, only exhaustion and useless rage.

Sophia remembered returning home and listening to Maria's daft school stories. Petrus had made his deal with Günther Schenke and taken her across the border to West Germany where in a starched white-walled surgery a doctor had spoken kindly as the pain and memory faded.

Oh god. Quick. Pull the papers from the file, cram them inside her coat pocket, she could sense people were coming. She had to leave. Take the girl. Get out. Hurry *hurry* before the workers arrived to continue clearing.

A mad idea flew through the air, settled, and she knew. Mia.

★★★

The child lay coiled up on the seat, fast asleep. As if seeing her for the first time, Sophia acknowledged that this combination of herself and Ebbe had mixed the best, not the worst of them. Dagmar and Petrus had created a story to protect her and the child. Had Petrus orchestrated Diertha's death as a convenient way to protect his grandchild? She'd considered him capable of murdering Käthe, why not also believe he could give the order for Diertha's death and let someone else do the work? Mia had grown up believing her mother dead. She'd avoided being taken into institutional care, as every child was if they were left by fleeing parents. In the state-run orphanages, care was lacking, resulting in children leaving as soon as they were old enough. Dagmar had done everything she could to save and care for this child yet, in doing so, she'd lost Sophia.

'Wake up, Mia.' She didn't dare touch her. 'We need to get out.'

'Why.? What's happened?' Mia scrambled blearily to her feet.

'Noises.' Someone was coming down the stairs. Sophia turned and headed towards the door nearest to them, praying it was a rear exit.

'That's the wrong way again!'

'Never mind.' She heard the girl's sharp intake of breath, her own anxiety rising to match as they ran through a side door, along the cramped passageway, out into a cavernous, dark, green-tiled room.

'I'm really scared.'

'I'll look after you, dearest.' She put her hand out to turn on the lights, the other arm pulling the girl close.

Mia's skin touched hers, soft, so utterly familiar now. Would her mother have held Mia just so, spooned up against her side, one arm protecting her from the world and all its evil?

The pool should be at the far end, the double doors beyond leading out to the shot-put grounds where there'd be some safety before the long walk back to the car. She'd phone Hajo and tell him about Mia and they'd be safe.

'Are you going to ask him?' Diertha and Käthe's voices were simply her own thoughts. Why had she thought they were ghosts? Of course she was going to ask. No. She was going to demand Petrus tell her everything.

This room was as remembered but the pool, once a clear oblong of water, had been divided into five solid lanes. Fitted to two sections were perfectly spaced black plastic canoe seats, each allowing the rower enough space to simulate rowing. Half submerged in filthy water, red and green oars jutted like a child's collection of seesaws. The door to the next room was locked. Reaching high above the frame, Sophia found the key, a little rusty, lying exactly where it should.

Something hit the water. They both heard it. Mia yelped, grabbed tight to Sophia's coat.

'Mia, keep quiet.' Everything would be so much easier if she weren't so dizzy. Through the door she switched on the lights and saw a constricted yet deep pool nestling by a lean-to office. On the tiles near the water a mask and tube had been left on the ground. White from lack of use, the drying rubber was detailed with winding patterns. Sophia knew the tube connected to the mask's side to feed in oxygen, like she knew the tidal flow in the pool could be increased to make swimming against it almost impossible.

There, to the side of the lean-to, was the exit to the shot-put ground. She pointed and moved towards the lean-to as the lights went out and Mia screamed: the sound cut short by the walls and the water.

'Shh. Do you have the torch?' There were no voices, no footsteps – nothing other than a growing apprehension that was making her hands shake. 'Mia. No. *Don't* touch the switches.'

It was already too late. With a screech the wave machine started and a pungent smell rose up from the pool as stale water and chlorine churned.

'Sorry, *sorry*.' Mia backed out of the office, torchlight waving across the squalid cream walls as a huge shadow loomed and stretched towards them.

A fist hit the centre of Sophia's back. She thrust Mia towards the wall.

'Run, Mia.' She gripped the zip of a jacket with the other and held on tight. They waltzed by the poolside in slow motion, a two-step nearer and nearer the churning water. The man in police uniform looked down into her eyes and laughed.

'Sophi and little Mia!' Ebbe sneered. 'Ah! How sweet!'

'Ebbe?' Sophia stepped back and sideways, slowly, with glacial calm, closer and closer to the edge of the pool. Ebbe wasn't here by chance. The woman with the shrill voice had called him so he could come and kill them.

'You should have stayed away. Diertha and Käthe were easy, as easy as you'll be, Sophi dear. I wouldn't have hurt the child if you'd listened to your papa.'

Sophia stared into those piercing eyes that had followed her all her life. The warmth they had shared as children had never been love as she so foolishly believed, rather a spoiled version of physical need – nothing more. She hurled herself sideways, forcing him to fall with her into the churning icy water.

Mia's shape took flight, running towards the door.

Ebbe grabbed her shoulders and forced her under the water. Sophia closed her eyes. There she was, holding her mother's hand the day she joined the swimming club – her dreams nothing more than a child's desire to please. There was Mia curled up on the floor outside her apartment door, a cold and frightened child – *her* child.

She wasn't ready to die. Sophia reared up, a thing made in water. So strong, never tiring. No more fear – only rage: a mother saving her daughter. She seized a chunk of Ebbe's hair and pulled him under. He thrashed, catching her head with his fist so everything went white – but she held onto him spitting out blood and filth, shoving his head against the pool wall. Once. Twice. Breathe Sophi, breathe. When her mind cleared; there he was, floating beside her, a blurred shape in the murky water.

★★★

Mia flew through the door. Outside. She was outside. Dawn had arrived. The ground was flat and scuffed with the soles of many feet. The shot-put arena? Sophia had said there was one nearby: that must be the way out.

Where to go? She needed help now or Sophia would die and there would be two dead people. Mia pelted towards the trees. Sophia was drowning. Nothing. Just trees and darkness. She turned full circle, staring. Even those bad people would do. She'd make them come and help. There had to be something she could do. Terror rose hot in her throat and Mia screamed. Her voice echoed across the deserted pitch. Silence. She screamed again and began running back. If no one else came, that left only her.

A shape appeared, growing bigger as he ran towards her. Hajo. It was Hajo. Mia held her hands out like a prayer. Her knees shook but she wasn't crying. Not now.

'Sophia,' she said, and pointed to the door.

★★★

The wave machine was droning inside her head. A wet echoing sound. Strange lights flickered. On. Off. Torches. People had come. A small hand was firmly latched to hers.

'You were trying to *kill* him.'

Sophia squeezed Mia's hand. She supposed she had to make an effort to open her eyes, but in her shut-eyed state she replayed the moment Ebbe's eyes had met hers as she reached to pull him under once last time.

Why was Hajo standing there with a blanket? He leaned down so close heat radiated from him. His eyes were dark and furious.

'You nearly killed him, you complete idiot,' he said, his eyes making it clear he'd have said a lot more if Mia hadn't been present. He wrapped the blanket tightly round, so the coarse material rasped against her skin. Bloody hell, someone had taken all her clothes. Mortified she opened her mouth to tell Hajo to put them back on.

'It's okay. They left your underwear on.' Above her Mia's chin wobbled as she spoke. Hot tears dripped on Sophia's face. In the distance came the sounds of people shouting. Someone finally turned the damn tide machine off and, when they did, the stillness echoed and the lights came on.

'I'm going to carry you, my love. Hold tight if you can.'

Hajo strained to lift her from Mia's lap. Sophia hung on, her frozen arms draped round his shoulders, resting her sore head against the warmth of his neck.

'Hajo,' she murmured his name into the warmth, 'Hajo.'

He carried her out the door to his car, where he eased her into the back seat.

'My coat, Hajo, where's my coat? Can you look in the coat pocket?' Her words were slurred.

'Sophia, don't talk. My dear – you're safe, Mia's safe.'

'She wants you to look in her coat pocket.' Mia spoke as if Hajo were an incredibly stupid child, then edged in and took Sophia's hands, rubbing them between hers.

'Ow! Mia *stop*. Bloody hell that hurts.'

'Well you shouldn't have jumped into a freezing-cold swimming pool.'

Through the window, she could see Hajo walking away. He had to see the papers; they'd be wet but hopefully legible. He'd read how Mia belonged to her, and how Petrus had worked as a doctor here and given orders for Diertha and Käthe to be dealt with. Her father hadn't killed Mia at birth; the easiest and most logical solution. Sophia wasn't sure if he'd actually chosen not to. She sensed it was more that he'd not known how to make that decision, perhaps the action of terminating an infant grandchild was one step too far.

There was Ebbe, horribly alive, staring, hating her as she now hated him, being escorted to a second car by his colleagues.

Who had told Hajo that she was in danger? Her father or Jörg?

'Petrus phoned Hajo as soon as he realised we'd gone. He'll be here in a minute.' The girl was fiddling with the heating controls on the dashboard and Sophia wondered if she'd asked the question out loud, or if Mia could read her mind. 'What were you really doing, Sophia?' The child asked. 'He wouldn't really have hurt you, would he?'

'Yes, he would.' The warmer the car became the more the inner chill seemed to intensify. Rain was washing down the windscreen. If she didn't speak now she'd shut down piece by piece, eventually talking herself out of doing the bravest and most honest thing she'd ever done.

'Mia?'

'What?'

Dagmar had chosen silence when the baby had arrived,

creating a fairytale story to protect the child from un-wanted questions. When Petrus left and only returned to see Ilse, her mother's disappointment had developed into anger, hand in hand with nurturing the child.

'I found out something, something I need you to know.'

'Before you went mad and tried to kill a *police* officer?'

Your father, Sophia thought. I would have killed your father, but there was her father hurrying towards the car, gauntly beautiful as ever in his soft grey coat, red scarf wrapped around a regal neck. Now she could see that he was nothing more than a trick of the light, an adaptation, a chameleon that conformed to his surroundings. Dr Petrus Künstler, a functionary of the state. Her father who'd supplied drugs to athletes; a physician who'd injected death.

'Sophia, what on earth were you thinking?' He refused to meet her eyes.

'You said there was something I need to know?' Mia interrupted, staring first at her grandfather then Sophia. 'What is it?'

'Father,' she worked her mouth to form the words clearly, 'did you sign the authorisation papers for Diertha and Käthe?'

'What are you talking about? Look at you, Sophia, you're frozen, half drowned.'

'Did you?'

'What do you mean, did I? Did I what?'

'Authorise Ebbe to kill Diertha and Käthe.' Beside her Mia gasped, grabbed hold of Sophia's hand and held on tight.

'What utter nonsense. I signed papers that would give Diertha the support she needed. Her unfortunate death was her own doing. I told you how I warned Käthe to stop. How can you be so thoughtless to bring such terrible accusations in front of the child?'

Hajo called his name and he paused, irritation turning to apprehension when Hajo held out the sodden papers.

'What is this?' He turned the papers over and stared directly at his daughter, mouth slightly open, as if he were struggling to invent then foist a new lie on her, one in which he took on yet another persona. 'My dear,' he said. 'I can explain.'

'No, Father, you can't.' Sophia turned to the child. 'Mia,' she said simply, 'I'm your mother.'

CHAPTER SEVENTEEN

~

KaDeWe only opened at eleven on Sundays, so there were two hours before the day had to officially begin. Sophia dug out a clean pair of running trousers, and was pulling on a t-shirt and jacket before she realised Mia couldn't yet be left asleep and alone in the apartment for a whole hour. In what seemed a lifetime ago, Sophia would have happily shaken the girl awake. Not now. She showered, scrubbing away the delicious thoughts of Hajo and their return home last night, until her skin tingled. He'd stayed until late, put her to bed and somehow managed to end up in it. So careful with her sore face and bruised body, Sophia had simply melted. It had taken a week just to begin to sort everything out. Maria had stood on one side, Mia on the other, helping her see through the lies Petrus had woven. Apart from dark circles under her eyes, Sophia looked the same, but she *felt* different. Lighter, clearer, more like herself: the girl she'd once known.

Where was her face lotion? The girl must have swapped everything! Why? When? She wouldn't wake her and demand an answer. The past few days had taken a toll on all of them, the child needed time to recover and rest. It seemed best to seize the peaceful hours for painting.

In the quiet, a burdensome shape formed. Shades of blue and grey morphed into a monstrous fleshy outline that sank beneath black seaweed. The pregnant contour had one eye that turned and stared: a hollow whiteness where the pupil should be. The shape seemed horribly reminiscent of Diertha.

'That's scary.'

Sophia turned to see Mia pointing to the slash of white. As the child came nearer, there was a lingering scent of sleep and petrol fumes, as if yesterday's journey still clung to her.

'What on earth have you done with my face lotion, Mia?' Sophia added steel grey to the underside of the monster as Mia bumped into the trestle table that held palette and brushes. 'It's all right, I'm not cross.' She balanced the table with one hand, Mia with the other.

'I forgot! I'm sorry, really *really* sorry. That was when I met you. You *were* horrible and I was cross so I mixed the medicines and poured the lotion away.' She paused. 'I was going to buy you new ones so you wouldn't notice.'

Sophia hugged her and laughed. If she'd possessed half the anger and strength her daughter had, she might have questioned the people who were supposed to be caring for her.

When they finally made their way downstairs, Frau Weiner was waiting: hair shaped into a neat bun, dressed in her best Sunday jacket and skirt. How nice, she said, for Sophia to have such a pretty niece, someone to take care of her, keep her company when she grew older.

'I,' she added, sniffing through a rather angular nose, 'have no one.'

Sophia corrected her as they followed her into her neat apartment where she made a fuss of tucking foil-wrapped Lindt chocolates into Mia's willing hands.

'Your daughter? And you had no idea?'

'It's complicated.' Sophia held out her hand. 'Post?'

'Yes, of course. Telephone bill. Gas. Pay slip. You will tell me all about it, *nicht wahr*?' She looked up expectantly.

Mia glanced at Sophia, her mouth opened to answer but Sophia shook her head in warning and suggested another time. Once Frau Weiner got talking, they'd never get away.

By now it was raining, the steady deluge that usually settled in for days. Sophia stuffed the post inside her bag as they crossed the Landwehrkanal and walked the short stretch to Lützowstrasse. The market was already in full swing. Mia stopped by a collection of wrist-watches, and the stall owner's eyes lit up with Deutschmark signs. It was only Sophia's intervention that stopped her handing over an extensive chunk of pocket money. After that the girl stuck close as they headed for the bakery stall.

They ate hot sweet rolls, watching the crowds dodge past vendors who, despite the soaking conditions, were as upbeat as ever. Calling to passers-by, selling kitchen utensils, handbags, sausages with brown mustard, purple and red tulips brought in from Dutch greenhouses, sour-sweet gherkins, chocolates, seasonal vegetables – all at unbeatable prices.

When the clock above the Wittenbergplatz U-Bahn said ten to eleven, Sophia pointed out where they were going and, zigzagging past the stalls, they joined the queue waiting for the doors of KaDeWe to open. At precisely eleven, the metal security gates began to roll up, clanking like a giant roasting spit. The front row took a nervous step back as the metal grid wound its way out of sight, revealing two heavy glass doors that were opened by footmen in smart red and green livery.

★★★

Mia hugged Sophia's arm tight as they were pulled through the doors, crushed between loads of chattering people. Tourists huddled together by a towering information board. Mia could tell they were American because of the way they spoke – a kind of nasally sound. Plus she'd seen an American cowboy film at Gerda's house, one they weren't supposed to be watching, with guns and horses and women dressed in long skirts. This group wore pressed beige trousers with sneaker shoes and big, comfy-looking coats. One man tried to read the words on the board. He said *Erste Etage* like he had lollipops in his mouth. As Mia watched, a lady wearing high heels and carrying a clipboard came over and began to tick off people's names and, at the same time, translate. The group clapped and laughed.

The shop was amazing. Everything was wrapped in white and silver tissue. No. Not just everything, everyone. All the shop assistants were dressed up to look like *angels* in white sarong dresses with wings made out of paper feathers. They beckoned to shoppers to come and try out the latest Dior perfume. Mia had some sprayed on her wrist. Mmm. Expensive. Stars turned and twinkled, dangling from fine, almost see-through, string. The stars flashed, turning from silver to green. Manikins had been placed on podiums, dressed in nothing but jewels so you could see their breasts! Mia looked away. Far over on the other side were counters piled high with tons of lipstick and make-up.

She felt dizzy, a good, delicious, excited-dizzy, better than Christmas, better than her birthday, better than anything she could remember. Sophia was edging her towards the stairs.

'I don't like lifts,' she said, which was brainless because lifts were great. They took you up or down with no effort.

On the third floor: jeans! All kinds. Flared and drain-pipe. Straight jeans in different colours: grey and black and light blue. Mia wanted dark blue Levi flares so much her mouth felt dry like sandpaper; even though she had cleaned her teeth properly that morning. The dark-blue Levis were soft and *furry*. She'd wear them to her new school. Mia wasn't going to even bother looking at anything else yet; just take these off the rack and try them on. Sophia was saying something about meeting up in forty minutes and Mia nodded: good idea. Instead of one, she selected ten pairs of jeans and made her way across to the shop assistant. She'd try these on first and after that get some more.

Sophia found her usual choice of white work under-wear, no lace, no trim. No, that wouldn't do. She selected two packs of multicolours, with lace, before making her way back down to the third floor. The child could easily get lost, or spend too much before she really knew what she wanted, or what fitted.

'But I want to try them *all*.' Mia's voice reached Sophia from where she stood at the bottom of the stairs.

'Three. You are allowed three.' The sales assistant turned

to Sophia for help. 'The young lady won't let me measure her. How can she choose if she doesn't have the right measurement?'

Sophia laughed a strange joyous sound that had Mia glaring at her, before joining in – giggling as she was propelled into the changing rooms once more.

It wasn't long before the assistant and Mia returned. Following that it was only a matter of sorting through the mountain of jeans, to find that only four pairs were the right size.

Two pairs of pyjamas had been placed on the sales counter, fluffy, girly nightwear with a yellow and pink heart design – more suitable for a child of seven than for a teenager. Sophia took them back, selecting instead pyjamas in rose pink, finished with white ribbing and lace. Feminine, yet young. The kind of nightwear she would have chosen for her own childhood self. She paid and turned to see a slim and lovely girl dancing towards her, looking sideways at her bum, checking that the trousers really did fit and were not deceiving her.

'We're not going home yet are we?'

Sophia had formulated an answer, something along the lines of 'You've already spent your money', but Mia's eyes were blue and pleading, and really, what harm could another hour do?

'Make-up or underwear?' she asked and the girl threw her arms around Sophia and squeezed.

★★★

Sophia and Mother were two different things. One was strong, unbending as steel. The other – soft and confused, as if the actual person hadn't arrived yet.

First of all everything began with 'NO'. No new jeans. No cool new hats from the shop next door to KaDeWe, and definitely no more make-up. Sophia would get a faraway look on her face. As if she was hearing someone talking. Someone who was saying: 'No you can't, even more often than she had; then she'd change her mind, which was really good. Mia had bought the most amazing pair of cashmere gloves in orange and black stripes. They came all the way up to her elbow. They'd had a few mother/daughter talks. The first, she thought, of many. That thought was strangely comforting. Sophia had explained why Oma made up the story about her age. Diertha had been pregnant, but each time she'd had the baby taken out. Then she was killed. That was the worst bit of all, as Mia's grandfather had been involved. He had done it so that Sophia could be taken to a West German hospital because the eastern doctors were going to let her die. Everyone would think Mia was Diertha's child so that Sophia could escape, and Mia not be sent to an orphanage.

It was weird to be only thirteen, when she'd considered herself nearly grown up. What Mia didn't understand was why Petrus hadn't come back and taken Oma and her to West Berlin. He could have. Mia knew Sophia agreed, even though she didn't say. Petrus liked to keep everything separate. Sophia in Berlin, Oma and her in Breden. That doctor Ilse? Well, she didn't want to think about it. Old people weren't supposed to behave like that.

Petrus was going to have to go to court. Mia was going to be there – she just had to decide what to wear. Something smart and really grown up.

The dragonfly grips were stashed in her new jewellery box, kept for the most special of occasions. The bluest dragonfly was called Mia, the green, Sophia. As they were the very first present her mother had given her, they were doubly important. Mia had decided she would give them to her own daughter, if she had one. If it ever happened that someone looked at her like Hajo looked at Sophia. As if he wanted to eat her up. The thought made her skin fizz in an exciting way, like she was waiting for good things that really were going to happen.

They'd been sitting outside the school in the car having the same conversation they'd had a million times: how Mia *had* to go to school, how she'd met everyone in the class, even made friends with a girl called Britta, so there were no more excuses. Things were different, better, because she had the chance to start again, although perhaps not so different because, for the first time, Sophia was beginning to sound like Dagmar: frustrated and trying not to show it.

'Go on,' she said. 'Britta's waiting.'

They were *all* waiting, but that wasn't the point. The point was that her tummy hurt. It was all very well that Sophia was going drop her off. Sophia would just go back home and paint or whatever.

Maria had come to visit after Christmas. She'd brought a box of biscuits for Mia that tasted so much of home that Mia had slipped away to her room to cry. When Sophia found her, she hadn't made a fuss or said anything about behaving like a baby. She'd asked Mia to come and join them for a glass of wine. They'd sat talking together for ages about Berlin, Breden, and how things were so different now. For the first time Mia had felt like she belonged. As if they really wanted her there and weren't just pretending. So it was nice to know that Sophia had at least one friend. Hajo, Mia knew, was a whole lot more.

It was a good job she was wearing her new gloves today. Britta and her friends were dressed in really cool stuff. Patterned leggings – she only had her new jeans, the ones she'd thought so modern. They had ear muffs and hats with bobbles and string, and every single one of them had little wires leading to their ears. Headphones! Sophia would have to buy her a personal stereo for her birthday. She'd write 'personal stereo' first on her list that wasn't yet completed. Everything was different now, she felt like a little girl that really needed to grow up.

The tummy ache was getting worse. Mia worried that Sophia would go and do things on her own. Things Mia wouldn't know about. She might talk to Petrus and tell him she'd never forgive him. Sophia said Petrus was a criminal, and that his court hearing would be for spying – maybe even helping to hurt people. Mia knew that such things were possible, she'd seen how families spied on each other and knew what it was like to be frightened all the time. Because of that she knew what Petrus was: a lonely, frightened old man. She'd phoned him every day since they came home to make sure he was all right, he was her grandfather after all.

Most of all she was scared that Sophia might go back to work and discover even worse secrets. She'd drive away. Forget all about Mia waiting, just like that first time, outside her door.

The playground was full of giggling primary school

children who were dashing round and round playing kiss chase; the girls enjoying kissing more than the boys, who scowled and faked being disgusted, wiping their mouths on the backs of their coat sleeves. Over by the wall that separated primary from the middle school were Britta and the kids Mia was supposed to hang out with. They were another reason for her tummy ache.

She'd never been popular, never belonged to the cool group; the clique that was full of pretty girls like Britta with her tangled blonde hair and purple ankle boots. Mia had tried hard enough to keep Gerda – and now Gerda was in Breden and Mia was here.

The group were talking and laughing. One boy put his arm around Britta, pulling her close. Britta looked up, saw Mia and waved so energetically that her hair flew around in the cold air. Mia wished the ground would open up and swallow her and the whole car before the group had time to peel away from the wall, traipse across the playground and form a tight circle around the car.

'Hey, Mia.' Britta leaned in the window; her hands were wrapped in fluffy pink mittens. 'It's so cool you're finally, like, here.'

There was nothing else for it: she had to get out the car. As she grasped her bag, Mia ached for Dagmar and all the usual greyness of Before. The toast and sweet hot chocolate she'd had to make before school, getting up extra early so she could bring Oma coffee with biscuits. Knowing that she and Oma were together against the world had meant she'd known who she was and where she was. She'd been able to tell good from bad. All that had changed when Sophia arrived. Petrus had done terrible things. He'd taken babies out of girls' stomachs, girls the same age as Mia. But Petrus had saved Sophia, and her. Plus he'd made pancakes and been kind. How was she supposed to be friends with girls like Britta when she knew so many awful things?

'Go on, darling,' Sophia leaned over and tucked a stray hair behind Mia's ear. Outside in air that was freezing cold, Britta linked her arm through Mia's and said her gloves were amazing. Where had she got them? How much did they cost? The group stroked the cashmere and murmured their agreement, turning as one to flow up the steps into school. Mia looked back. It was okay: Sophia was still there waiting until she went into school.

The morning went so quickly. One minute she was in a maths class helping Britta through algebra. The next it was break and they were all talking and talking. She swapped beige nail varnish for pale lilac with a dark-eyed girl called Tanya who was going out with Christian, the most gorgeous boy in the group. They made arrangements to meet near KaDeWe that afternoon, while a heated discussion took place on who would wear what and whose parents could give them a lift, Mia longed for the simplicity of her room and the quiet that descended on the house whenever Sophia painted. Every half hour or so, paintbrush in hand, Sophia would ask if Mia wanted a glass of juice or a biscuit. Sometimes Mia would sit on her bed, waiting in her room, just so that she could hear Sophia's voice when she called.

At lunch time they poured out of the school gates to parked cars and buses and there, in the distance, was Sophia, looking fierce; running along the pavement dressed in black leggings and a black fleece top.

'Wow,' said Britta as the group turned and stared.

Sophia's police eyes moved across the group to settle on Mia and – just like that – Mia knew Sophia was never going to forget her. It's us against the world, she thought. You and me. You and me.

Acknowledgments

Eve Adams. Christiane Lauppe and Ingrid Öberföll, for their generous gift of memories of a German heritage. Susan Spiransa, for intricate translation and far reaching research, and Ulli Neumcke, Steven Ungerleider, Brigitte Berendonk, Marcus Welsch and Hajo Seppelt for help with historical research. The staff at Kienbaum who kindly let me stay and form what was the most vital portion of my writing and Libby Valdez, for her mermaid illustrations. Nigel Jenkins, Malcolm Macdonald, Pauline Bowerbank and Jennifer Cryer for their kind feedback, and Penny Thomas at Seren for believing the book was finally ready.

To all of you who simply put up with me during the writing of this novel, please accept my gratitude and sincere thanks.

About the Author

Anne Lauppe-Dunbar is a fiction writer and lecturer in Creative Writing at Swansea University. Her parents were born in Germany and both survived the War to meet in South Africa where they married and where Anne was born. The family left Africa during apartheid and went by boat to Germany, then Scotland, and finally the UK. Anne continued into Wales.

Anne is the the co-editor of *Swansea Review,* and her writing work includes short stories and poetry featured in collections with Seren, Cinnamon Press and Seventh Quarry. She counts herself truly lucky to live close to the sea, and swim as often as she can.